Summer hadn't seen it coming.

One minute, Zach was at the head of the class. The next, his big arms wrapped around her and saved her from hitting the mat, hard.

In the tangle of arms and legs, it took a few seconds to get her bearings. When she did, Summer gazed into his blue-green eyes and searched the oh-so-serious face that hovered inches from hers.

"If this was some sort of demonstration, you should have asked for volunteers. I don't appreciate being your guinea pig."

Zach's left eyebrow rose and his mouth slanted in a sly grin.

"Are you all right?" one of her classmates asked.

"I'll be fine," she bit out, "when this big gorilla lets me up."

She waited, but Zach didn't move.

"Let me up," she whispered.

"Make me," he whispered back.

Dear Reader,

According to the 10-year National Crime Victimization Survey (compiled by the Bureau of Justice Statistics), nearly one million violence-against-women cases are reported every year, and psychiatric professionals state that approximately 31 percent of their caseloads are made up of female patients traumatized by a violent attack.

These startling statistics made me wonder: What happens to women like my friend Brit (not her real name), who *don't* reach out for professional help? "The biggest regret of my life," she says, "is that I tried so hard to pretend I didn't need anyone or anything that I let the love of my life slip right through my fingers."

When *Once a Marine* begins, it seems our heroine might choose that same sad path. She has a lot to discover about herself before complete healing can take place. As for marine-turned-self-defense-instructor Zach Marshall, well, he's grappling with battle scars and ghosts from his own past, and when he meets Summer Lane, he isn't sure if he has the patience and selflessness required to be her man. (If you love change-and-grow stories as much as I do, I think you'll enjoy watching these two learn the meaning of unwavering love!)

I'd like to thank you for choosing to spend a few hours with Zach, Summer and me. Good health and happiness—and hopefully you'll return for the next books in Harlequin Heartwarming's Those Marshall Boys series, featuring Zach's handsome cowboy cousins, Nate and Sam Marshall, and the gorgeous gals who will change their lives...if they'll allow it!

All my best to you and yours,

Loree Lough

HEARTWARMING

Once a Marine

———

Loree Lough

HARLEQUIN®HEARTWARMING™

Recycling programs
for this product may
not exist in your area.

ISBN-13: 978-0-373-36713-9

Once a Marine

Printed in U.S.A.

HARLEQUIN®
www.Harlequin.com

Loree Lough once sang for her supper. Traveling by way of bus and train, she entertained folks in pubs and lounges across the US and Canada. Her favorite memories of "days on the road" are the hours spent singing to soldiers recovering from battle wounds in VA hospitals. Now and then she polishes up her Yamaha guitar to croon a tune or two, but mostly she writes. Her last Harlequin Heartwarming novel, *Saving Alyssa*, brought the total number of Loree's books-in-print to one hundred (fifteen bearing the Harlequin logo). Loree's work has earned numerous industry accolades, movie options and four- and five-star reviews, but what she treasures most are her Readers' Choice awards.

Loree and her real-life hero split their time between Baltimore's suburbs and a cabin in the Allegheny Mountains, where she continues to perfect her "identify the critter tracks" skills. A writer who believes in giving back, Loree donates a generous portion of her annual income to charity (see the Giving Back page of her website, loreelough.com, for details). She loves hearing from her readers and answers every letter personally. You can connect with her on Facebook, Twitter and Pinterest.

Books by Loree Lough

HARLEQUIN HEARTWARMING

Saving Alyssa
Devoted to Drew
Raising Connor

For more books by Loree Lough,
check out Harlequin.com.

Once a Marine is dedicated to survivors of violent crime and their families and friends, who so freely shared the personal experiences that allowed me to lend authenticity to this novel. Your strength, courage and forgiving hearts inspire those who know you to become better people.

Acknowledgments

I'd like to extend my thanks to my pal Jerry Espinoza for all his help with police procedural information in the story. Thanks, too, to the Denver and Vail Chambers of Commerce for helping me craft a "you are here" feel to the novel. A very special thank-you to Kevin O'Neill (actor/writer/director/producer with Olive Ranch Road Productions) for adding a realistic touch of Hollywood flair, and to Dan Schacter with Vail Resorts Management for providing a splash of local color in Tavern on the Square.

Last, but certainly not least, my heartfelt gratitude to Amy, Brit, Sue and Mary (real names withheld by request), whose willingness to share details about their own harrowing personal experiences allowed me to lend authenticity and poignant accuracy to this story.

CHAPTER ONE

ZACH'S DAD HADN'T said a word since ending the "Your daughter has been rushed to the hospital" call from the Vail Police Department.

Halfway into the nearly two-hour drive, his dad said, "Keep your eye on the speedometer, son. Last thing we need is to lose half an hour while some state trooper flexes his muscles."

Under normal circumstances, Zach might have shot back with a teasing, "Dad, you sound like a hippie." But there was nothing normal about the situation, and this was no time for jokes.

"You okay up there?" his mom asked.

No, he wasn't. But admitting it would only add to her stress.

"I'm fine." He glanced into the rearview mirror and met her gaze. "How 'bout you? Holding up?"

She sighed heavily. "I'll feel better when I *see* her."

Yeah, he could identify with that. Hopefully, his sister's condition wouldn't be anywhere near as bad as what his imagination had cooked up:

Libby, broken and battered. Libby, unconscious. Libby, connected to tubes and monitors...

Zach shook off the ugly images and focused on the dark highway and his dad's white-knuckled grip on the grab handle above the door. Who needed reminders of how much his dad hated driving the interstate with all the gasping and floor stomping going on in the passenger seat? Unfortunately, I-70 was the quickest route from their ranch outside Denver to Libby, all alone in the Vail hospital.

He was having a hard time wrapping his mind around the fact that violence had followed him home from Afghanistan, where bloodshed and battles were an almost daily occurrence. He thought he'd left the ugliness of war behind when he moved his gear back into his boyhood bedroom three weeks ago, but then, the phone call from the police.

Nothing would make his parents happier than if he decided to stay and help his cousin run the Double M. So why hadn't he unpacked?

Because he'd spent too many years taking orders from marines much younger than himself, and didn't want to test the strength of his and Nate's "just like brothers" relationship.

Zach had been a fair to middlin' skier back in the day. Maybe he'd take a job at one of the nearby resorts, teaching kids how to stand upright on the bunny slopes. At least then his baby sister would have family right there in town when she was released from the hospital.

Hospital. Would the Valley Medical Center have the equipment and staff to do more than set skiers' broken bones? The officer hadn't exactly sugarcoated things, so Zach knew it would take more than a clinic with an X-ray machine to handle Libby's injuries.

Half an hour later, when he and his folks walked into her ICU cubicle, his mom hid a tiny gasp behind one hand. The sight made his dad backpedal a few steps, too. "This must be the wrong room," he said, reading the numbers beside the door.

Libby was barely recognizable, thanks to bruised eye sockets, a bandage cap hiding her blond curls, casts on her left arm and right leg and a spaghetti-like tangle of tubes and wires connecting her to the monitors.

"Yeah, Dad," Zach whispered. "It's the right room." As evidence, he pointed to the big-as-a-suitcase black purse, monogrammed with the telltale sparkly *L*. Summoning all his self-control, he walked to the foot of her bed. "Man," he said, grinning, "the lengths some people will go to get some attention."

She opened one puffy eye and winced slightly

as the left corner of her mouth lifted in a smile. "'Bout time you guys got here."

Zach moved to the side of her bed, effectively blocking the monitor screens from his parents' view. Libby's fingers began to shake, and he gently wrapped his around them, as much to comfort her as to hide the tremors from his folks.

And for the next ten minutes, the three of them stood statue-still, listening to her sketchy version of what had happened to her, nearly twelve hours earlier. Zach didn't know whether to blame shock or painkillers for her halting speech, but he knew Libby. The rest of the story must have been truly horrible if his never-pulls-her-punches sister felt it necessary to protect the folks from the details. Not being able to talk about it was probably driving her crazy.

"I don't know about you two," he told his parents, "but I'm starving."

As if on cue, his mom's stomach growled, and his dad patted his back pocket. "Shoot. I left the house so fast, I forgot my wallet."

"It's three in the morning, son," his mother said. "I doubt anything is open."

Libby's nurse leaned into the room. "Sorry. Couldn't help but overhear," she said, smiling. "Remedies Café opens in a few hours. Until then, you'll find a bank of vending machines in the hall just outside the cafeteria."

"Thanks," Zach said. Following her back into the hall, he whispered, "What do you think? Is Libs gonna be all right?"

Bright blue reading glasses dangled from a matching ribbon around the nurse's neck. She put them on and glanced at a printout that he guessed was a summary of what the monitors registered. "Things look normal to me."

"What tests did the docs do?"

"The usual. X-rays, CT scan, MRI, some bloodwork—"

"And what were the results?"

"It's too soon for that," she said in a singsong voice that Zach translated to mean, "Don't you worry, silly man. We'll tell you what you need to know, when you need to know it."

Few things irked him more than being patronized. "I did three tours in Afghanistan. I know a serious condition when I see it, so there's no need to put a condescending spin on things."

Her jaw dropped slightly, but Zach didn't feel guilty for his brusque attitude. Hard experience had taught him that setting the right tone from the get-go would save everyone a lot of time.

The nurse's smile softened. "First of all, thank you for your service, Mr. Marshall. And my apologies if I came off as a pompous medical professional." She removed her glasses and stared him straight in the eye. "Your sister took quite a beating, but from everything I've seen, there's no permanent damage, and no signs of internal injury."

"In other words, despite how bad things look, Libs is already on the road to recovery?"

"The doctors hate it when nurses comment on questions like that. But I'll tell you this…" She glanced right and left then met his eyes. "She's doing really well, physically."

"Were you here when the cops interviewed her?"

"I was."

She hadn't elaborated. And she'd put extra emphasis on the word *physically*. Did it mean…

If he couldn't say it in the privacy of his mind, how did he expect to ask the question out loud?

Practice what you preach, Marshall.

"Do you know if she was, ah, sexually assaulted?"

"She wasn't."

That was a relief.

"A bystander screamed and interrupted your sister's attacker." The nurse glanced at Libby's cubicle, and when she looked back at Zach, an admiring smile lit her face. "Witnesses said she fought like a tiger."

But she hadn't fought *smart*. She hadn't known how. If he'd given her a couple of pointers last time he was home on leave, like she'd asked him to…

He cleared his throat. "I don't suppose the cops caught the son of a—"

"Not yet, but they have a pretty good description." She handed Zach a business card. "This officer spent a few minutes with her before the techs took her down to X-ray. He'll be back in the morning, but said if you have any questions, you should feel free to call, anytime."

Zach gave the card a quick once-over before tucking it into his shirt pocket. He followed the nurse's gaze, now fixed on his parents, who sat side by side watching their only daughter sleep. Zach looked at them, too…his mom's head resting on his dad's shoulder, their fingers linked as if drawing and giving strength to one another simultaneously. It warmed his heart, yet made him feel more lonely than he'd felt in a long, long time. Must be nice, he thought, to have someone to lean on at a time like this.

"I wish I could tell you more, Mr. Marshall, I really do."

Zach blinked away his self-pitying fog.

"The doctor will make his rounds in a couple of hours. By then, he'll have the test results, and I'm sure he can answer all your questions."

Zach nodded. He didn't have to like her "keep the details on the down-low" position to understand it.

"Thanks. And thanks for taking such good care of Libby."

She was asleep when he returned to her room. Zach resumed his sentry-like position in front of the monitors. Their blips and beeps kept time with his dad's agitated pacing while his mom stood, silently shaking her head. If he didn't get them out of here, they'd go crazy, waiting for Libby to wake up.

He peeled a couple twenties from his wallet, turning to his parents. "If I don't get something to eat soon, I'll go down like a felled tree."

His father pocketed the money. "What can we get you while we're downstairs?"

"Coffee. Sandwich. Chips. Maybe a candy bar. Doesn't matter what kind."

Nodding, he grasped his wife's elbow. "Come with me," he said, leading her toward the door. "I'm gonna need help carrying stuff."

Her eyes widened with disbelief. "John, you don't really expect me to leave her alone!"

"We'll only be gone a few minutes. And she won't be alone. Zach will stay with her. If her condition changes, even a little, he'll text us."

Her brows drew together as she considered it.

"He's right, Mom. Libs will be fine." Right hand forming the Scout's salute, he added, "I promise to call if her eyelids so much as flutter."

"Come on, Ellen," his dad called from the

doorway. "Who knows when we'll next have a chance to grab a bite to eat."

When she reached him, he leaned down to whisper something into her ear, something that inspired her to send Zach a sad smile.

So. They knew Libby had been holding back, and that he aimed to get more information from her. He couldn't predict what his sister might say when their folks left the room, but if it was bad news, he had no intention of adding to their worries.

He waited until they were out of sight then sat on the edge of her bed. "Okay, they're gone," he said, taking her hand. "Quit faking and let me have it. *All* of it this time."

"Faking? Who, me?"

"You've been awake for the past twenty minutes."

"Know-it-all."

"Can I help it if I'm a tell-it-like-it-is kinda guy?"

"Yeah. When it's convenient for *you*." She smirked then winced. "Ow. Stop making me smile, will ya?"

"Hey. It isn't my fault that you're so easily entertained."

Her face grew serious. "Okay, I'll talk. But first, you have to promise me something."

"What?"

"That you won't put on your private investigator hat and try to find the guy. Because the last thing Mom and Dad need is for you to get into trouble."

"Whoa. Does that mean you know the guy? Is that why you think he'll be so easy to find?"

"Of course not. He snuck up on me. Took me completely by surprise. I didn't see anything but the pavement, whooshing closer and closer to my face."

It wasn't likely the cops would share what they knew, but if he *could* get anything out of them…

"Promise you'll keep things to yourself, or I'm going back to sleep."

The heart monitor beeped a little faster. "All right. Okay. Settle down, will you?" He cleared his throat. "I promise not to get in trouble."

"Oh, you're a clever one, I'll give you that." She gave him a look that said, "I've got your number, pal."

"But not clever enough. I want to hear you say 'I promise not to tell Mom and Dad the rest of the story.'"

It wasn't likely he'd share any information with their folks, but just in case, he searched his mind for a way to appease her without making the promise.

"I'll be honest with you, partly because I need to talk about it as much as you need to hear what happened. But I can't. I *won't*. Not unless I have your word that you won't try to play the hero again."

Play the hero again? The comment took him back to when Libby was in college, and a couple of her roommates called him when they got tangled up with some unsavory characters.

"I just couldn't live with myself if you ended up in jail—or worse—because of me."

She looked so small and frail, so afraid and nervous, that the only thing keeping him from scooping her up into a huge hug was his fear of hurting her.

"Fine." He made no effort to sound pleased, because he wasn't. "I won't hunt him down like the animal he is and beat the stuffing outta him."

She relaxed slightly. "One more promise?"

"What now?"

"Stop looking so grim. If they come back and see you looking all serious and angry, they won't let up until I tell them, too. Or worse, walk around looking all 'poor Libby' for the rest of my life." She gave his hand a weak squeeze. "Thank goodness I don't have to worry *you'll* do that."

He feigned shock. "Hey. Just 'cause I'm a marine doesn't mean I'm devoid of feelings."

"It's *because* you're a big, tough marine that I can trust you to mask your feelings. You saw a lot of ugly stuff over there, but you learned how to compartmentalize it. If you feel sorry for me when I…once I've told you everything, well, at least you'll know how to pretend you don't."

Compartmentalize. Libby had chosen the right career, all right. Too bad she couldn't put her degree in psychology to use analyzing herself, figure out why she kept getting involved with losers, why she struggled in a one-woman practice when so many facilities wanted to hire her. Zach stifled a groan and sandwiched her hand between his. "You'll get no pity from me."

Libby returned his halfhearted smile and plunged into her story. Halfway through, the pace and volume of her words waned, and when she finished, Libby slipped into a fitful sleep.

Zach sat there, shaking his head and fighting tears. Part of him wished she *had* known the guy. At least he'd have a target for his fury. But her attacker was still out there somewhere. Was he aware that Libby couldn't identify him? If he thought otherwise, would he try to find her and make sure she couldn't testify against him? That possibility scared Zach almost as much as seeing the enemy churning through the Afghan dust.

His mind went into full marine mode, searching for proactive ways to help her, to make sure nothing like this ever happened to her again.

And then it hit him.

When the docs released her, he'd move into

Libby's town house and take care of her. While she recuperated, he'd start the wheels in motion to find a place of his own, preferably a shop of some kind with an upstairs apartment. He'd open a self-defense studio, right here in Vail. And when she was ready, Libby would be his first student.

"Let go of my hand, you goof. Your big meat hook is getting me all sweaty."

Snickering, he did as she asked, just as their folks returned, each carrying a cardboard food tray.

"Oh, good," his mom whispered, "she's still sleeping."

She was too busy doling out sandwiches and bags of chips to notice Libby's mouth curl into a tiny, sly grin.

It told him she'd be all right, and he had to put his back to the family to keep them from seeing his grateful tears.

CHAPTER TWO

September, two years later

ALEX PUT TWO grocery bags on the kitchen table and pointed to her answering machine. "Hey, Summer. Did you know you have a message?"

She followed the teen's gaze to the blinking red light. "Oh. That. I must have been upstairs when the phone rang, getting the guest room ready for my parents."

"When will they be here?"

"Day after tomorrow."

"Oh, yeah. I remember."

Something in his voice told her Alex didn't believe a word of her excuse.

He handed her the receipt. "Sorry, they didn't have hot fudge sauce."

"It's okay. I shouldn't be eating so many sweets, anyway." She pressed a twenty into his hand and smiled, grateful to Alex, grateful to her investment counselor for making recommendations that had kept her financially solvent all these months, grateful that she'd had the good sense to take his advice. "I'm sure they'll have some next time."

When he saw the amount of his tip, Alex's eyebrows disappeared behind dark, wavy bangs. "Whoa, this is way too much!"

"Nonsense." She would have paid twice the price to avoid leaving the town house to shop for herself. "You're getting your license in just a few months. I'm sure you can use a little extra cash."

"Well, if you say so." He tucked the bill into his back pocket. Brightening, he added, "Mom says I can drive her car if I pay my share of the insurance."

"See? There you go!"

Alex nodded, but it seemed there was something more on his mind than groceries and tip money. "Could I... Ah... Can I... Would you get mad if I asked you something?"

He'd never been one to pry—unlike his mother, who thought nothing of asking a person's weight, salary and far more personal information.

"I promise not to get mad," Summer assured him.

Alex slid a four-color, glossy flyer from the front pocket of his hooded sweatshirt. "Have you ever thought about taking some classes?" he began, tapping it on his thigh. "To help you deal with, ah, you know, what happened to you?"

Of course she'd considered it. What person in her shoes wouldn't have! If she'd heard "Stop living in the past" once, she'd heard it a hundred times, from her parents, her orthopedist, her best friend, Justin, and the therapist she'd left after only four sessions. Summer knew each of them had her best interests at heart, but that didn't make their advice more palatable.

"Maybe you could just talk to Zach," Alex continued, handing her the pamphlet. "I bet he could help you."

Help me what? she wondered, pretending to read the flyer.

"'Cause Mom's right. You're too young and too pretty to spend so much time in here, all alone."

Alex leaned both elbows on the kitchen's bar counter. "Did I ever tell you how I used to be scared of, well, just about everything?"

On more than one occasion, Rose had mentioned Alex's troubles with bullies. But Summer didn't want him to know that his mom couldn't be trusted with sensitive information. In the year since she'd moved next door to the Petersons, Summer had watched as one by one, his fears and inhibitions fell away, all thanks to this *Zach* person.

"I know how it feels to be scared. Not the same kind of scared as you were when..." His voice trailed off, but he quickly got back on track. "I just know Zach could help you. He's a cool dude. And amazing."

It had been a conscious decision to keep the details of the attack to herself. The only person who knew the whole sordid story was Richard O'Toole, and that was only because—

"If you're worried about being alone with Zach, I promise to stay with you. At least at first. If you decide to talk to him, that is, to find out how he can help you feel less, y'know, scared all the time."

More scared than she felt even *thinking* about calling Alex's friend? That didn't seem possible. Summer closed the flyer and slid it onto the counter, hoping Alex hadn't noticed her trembling hands.

He flexed both biceps. "I wasn't kidding when I said Zach is amazing. He taught me how building muscles helps build self-confidence. Did you see the *Karate Kid* movie? Mom made me watch it with her the other night. Thought I'd hate it, but I didn't. That old guy was right," he added, tapping a temple. "The bullies get you *here* long before they get you *here*." Smirking, he gave himself a fake punch to the jaw.

But...her bully had snuck up behind her, grabbed her ponytail and... Summer cringed inwardly.

"Well, I better go. Midterms are coming up, and I have a ton of studying to do. See you in a couple of days?"

"You bet. I'll email the list and credit card payment to the City Market." She walked with him to the door. "Thanks, kiddo. I honestly don't know what I'd do without you."

He shook his head. "Way better than you're doing now, I'll bet."

"What!" A nervous laugh escaped her lips. "That's just about the silliest thing I've heard all week!"

"Mom says I'm an enabler. That if I quit running your errands, you'd *have* to get out of this place."

Why couldn't Rose just mind her own business!

"Nothing could be further from the truth," Summer blurted, heart hammering with dread. "I'd only have to find someone else to pick up and deliver my groceries, so…"

"I don't mean any disrespect, but you *do* have a choice. It's like Zach told me when I first signed up for lessons—you don't have to live this way."

She was half tempted to arrange a meeting with the Amazing Zach, just so she could see what a perfect man looked like.

He paused in the doorway. "Will you do me a favor?"

"Sure. Of course." *Anything*, she thought, *if it means you won't quit.*

"Will you at least *think* about talking to Zach?"

"For the first time, I'm glad you aren't my kid," she joked. "I don't know how your mom says no to you!"

"Believe me, she says no. A *lot*." A relieved smile brightened his young face. "Does that mean you'll call him?"

"Yes, I'll call him."

"Cool. Later!" he said, closing the door behind him.

He'd been gone less than a minute when the phone rang.

Richard O'Toole's name flashed on the screen. How odd that he'd come to mind just moments ago. Summer hadn't talked to the detective since that day in court when, because she couldn't provide a positive identification and her attacker had left no DNA to link him to the rape and battery charges, prosecutors were forced to charge him with Class 5 Felony Theft. He'd served two years in the Denver County Jail, but only because the cops found Summer's wallet and three more in his jacket when they picked him up.

"Hello, Detective."

He chuckled. "All these years with caller ID, and I still feel like whoever I'm calling is a mind reader." A pause, and then, "So how are you, Miss Lane?"

"I'm fine. And please, call me Summer."

"Summer. Right." He cleared his throat. "I, ah, I promised to call you when Samuels was released."

Her pulse quickened. "I was afraid you might say that."

"He's due to hit the streets next week."

Next week!

O'Toole must have heard her gasp. "Now, now, there's no need to panic," he added quickly. "I did some checking, and the kid really cleaned up his act in there. Earned his GED, put in a lot of hours with the jail's headshrinker, did some serious rehab and got—"

"Wait. Don't tell me. He got Jesus. Isn't that what they all say?"

"Yeah. Pretty much. That, and 'I'm innocent!' or 'I've been framed!' Look, Summer, I don't blame you for being cynical. What happened to you was…"

Why the hesitation? Was he picturing her during their initial interview at the hospital? Or was he thinking about how she'd testified from a wheelchair, instead of on the witness stand, because even after two surgeries and months of physical therapy, she still couldn't walk unassisted? If she told him that she still limped slightly, and that it might require another operation to repair the deep gash Samuels had carved into her cheek, would it give him just cause to keep that maniac in jail, where he belonged?

"Do you have any idea where he'll go?" she said instead. "Does he have a job? An apartment?"

"He's moving in with his grandmother. According to my sources, she's on the Denver bus line, which will make it easy for him to get to and from work until he earns enough to buy a car and get a place of his own."

"Well, isn't that just peachy. I'm so happy for him. He's got his whole life all cleaned up, literally and figuratively."

While I'm a prisoner in my own home.

She glanced at the flyer Alex had left on the kitchen table. *A prisoner of my own making*, she admitted. How had her young friend put it? *You* do *have a choice. You don't have to live this way.*

"I doubt he'll bother you," O'Toole said. "But if he does…"

"I know, I know," came her sarcastic reply. "I should feel free to call, anytime. And you'll come running to my defense while I hit my knees and pray you arrive before he has a chance to finish what he started."

A pang of guilt shot through her. It wasn't O'Toole's fault that she'd become a self-pitying, scared-of-her-own-shadow hermit.

"That wasn't fair. I have no right to take things out on you. You're the man who caught Samuels and gathered enough evidence to help prosecutors put him away, even if it was only for a short time. And you kept your promise to warn me when…when he was released." And she was behaving like an ungrateful brat. "I'm sorry," she said, meaning it.

"No need to apologize. I get it."

Summer hadn't been his first victim of violent crime, so of course he got it.

"I'm the one who's sorry," he said. "I only wish I could do more."

Short of providing her with a rock-solid guarantee that Samuels wouldn't make the trip from Denver to Vail to exact revenge, *ever*, what more could he do?

She remembered that the last time they spoke, O'Toole had just found out his wife was pregnant. He'd been ecstatic, but tried hard to hide his enthusiasm because of all Summer had gone through.

"So is the new baby a boy or a girl?"

"Boy. Arrived December 23." He sounded surprised that she'd asked. And why wouldn't he be, considering the way she'd moped and sniffled all through the interview process, the way she was still feeling sorry for herself, even after all these months.

She pictured a chubby-cheeked baby boy with fat, dimpled fingers wrapped around O'Toole's beefy thumb, and thought of her doctor's gloomy prognosis. "It's too soon to know for sure," he'd said. "But you should prepare yourself for the possibility that you might never have children of your own."

Summer forced a smile and took a deep breath. "What a lovely Christmas present."

"You can say that again! And the little guy got here just in time to legitimize a nice tax deduction."

During a break on the day he'd testified against Samuels, she'd overheard O'Toole on the phone, assuring his wife that he'd give serious thought to a promotion that would take him off the streets and keep him safely behind a desk.

"Did you accept that promotion you were up for?"

"You bet I did. Took some getting used to, but the wife and I both sleep better."

After another moment of small talk and a final reminder for her to call him anytime she felt the need to, they wished each other well and hung up. It was nearly suppertime, and thanks to Alex, Summer had a pizza in the freezer. She set the oven to 400 degrees and, while waiting for it to heat up, flicked on the kitchen TV.

A news story filled the screen: a young woman had been brutally attacked and left for dead in Chicago. *Her* story, except that Summer had been attacked after recording a commercial for a Denver car dealership.

"It's a miracle she survived," the anchorman was saying. Had the woman's assailant subdued her by grabbing a handful of long hair, the way Samuels had?

In the chrome finish of the toaster, Summer caught sight of her chin-length hair. She'd badgered Justin into giving her a boy cut before she'd been released from the hospital, but had kept it a little longer since. Now when she took the time to style it—which was rare, since she never went anywhere—the side curls almost hid the scar on her cheek.

Her cell phone pinged, making her jump. She opened the text from her dad.

We missed our plane, so Mom and I are taking a flight out in two days. That gives you plenty of time to make reservations so the three of us can go skiing when we get there!

She typed back a response.

Can't wait. Love you guys!

Her message was only half-true. Summer tensed, thinking of the lectures they'd subject her to when they learned she wouldn't be joining them on the slopes. That she'd only been out of the house twice—both times to see her orthopedist—since they'd left to film a movie in Africa. Any day now, they'd stand face-to-face with the truth about who she'd allowed herself to become.

Oh, she'd kept up with physical therapy—what else was there to do, all alone in her house every day!—but she hadn't been outside, not even to pick up the mail or newspaper at the community box on the corner. She eased the guilt by telling herself that her parents were actors, accustomed to disappointment. But that frustration had come in the form of producer- and director-delivered rejections. Finding out that she'd deliberately misled them, no matter the reason, was a completely different kind of distress, and she knew it.

"I can't believe I'm saying this," her mom had said as she packed for the trip to Botswana, "but your dad and I miss the plucky risk-taker you were before the accident."

Accident, indeed. If they couldn't deal with the facts, how did they expect her to face them?

Again, Alex's words echoed in her head: *you don't have to live this way.*

The oven beeped, telling her it had finished preheating. She slid the pizza onto the top rack, set the timer and changed the channel. Not even watching a young man trying to coax his aging mother to give up years' worth of hoarded possessions could distract her from Alex's wise advice. The boy was right. She couldn't stay in this house forever.

Summer combed her fingers through her bangs. It had become a nervous habit, like feeling sorry for herself and hiding from the world. Things needed to change, and the sooner, the better.

She grabbed the flyer. What could it hurt, she thought, picking up the phone, to talk to the Amazing Zach?

CHAPTER THREE

ALEX PRESSED THE receiver to his chest and waved his boss closer to the reception counter. Zach draped a towel around his neck, using the corner to blot perspiration from his upper lip. "What's up, buddy?"

"Remember that lady I told you about? Well," he said, pointing at the phone's mouthpiece, "this is her!"

Like a one-man PR firm, Alex had brought clients of all genders, sizes and ages to Zach's studio. "You've told me about lots of ladies," he said, grinning. "Help me out here, kid."

"Summer Lane. You know, the one who lives next door to Mom and me? Who's afraid to come out of her house 'cause she was attacked couple years ago?"

Oh. That one. What kind of people named their daughter Summer? "Hippies!" his dad would say. Zach pictured a long-haired, cringing spinster, darting from window to window, checking locks and peeking at the world through dusty Venetian blinds.

"She wants to ask you a couple questions. About signing up for classes, I hope." He put the phone back up to his ear. "Hey, Summer, Zach is—"

Based on the sudden disappointment on the boy's face, Zach could only assume the poor old thing had changed her mind.

"No, wait! Please don't hang up, Summer, he's standing right here!"

Alex thrust the phone into Zach's hand. "Go easy on her, will ya? Mom says she's kinda fragile."

Fragile. The very word Zach's mom had used to describe Libby right after her ordeal. But unlike the woman on the phone, Libby bounced back quickly, due in part to the unwavering support of friends and family…and her own stubborn determination to put the nightmare behind her. He knew next to nothing about this Summer person, but from what little Alex had told him, Zach guessed she wasn't made of the same sturdy stuff.

"Miss Lane? Zach Marshall here." He caught a distant glimpse of himself in the floor-to-ceiling mirror at the back of the room. *What are you smiling about, you big idiot. She can't see you.* "What can I do for you?" he said, putting his back to his reflection.

"You'll probably think I'm being ridiculous,"

she began, "but I don't know enough about your studio—or self-defense, for that matter—to even voice an intelligent question. What I *do* know is that Alex speaks very highly of you. And that he swears that what you've taught him has improved every area of his life."

That smooth, sultry voice sure didn't go with his image of a cringing spinster. She'd roused his curiosity, for sure.

"Just so happens Wednesday is our slow day," he said. "If you're not busy now, c'mon down. I'll give you the nickel tour, and do my best to answer whatever ques—"

Alex heaved a frustrated sigh and slapped a palm over his eyes. "She never leaves her house," he whispered through clenched teeth. "Not ever. Remember?"

"Trust me," Zach mouthed.

"On second thought," he said into the phone, "I have a better idea. Alex needs some behind-the-wheel time before his big driver's test. How about we drive over, pick you up and bring you back here. There's a small class starting in about an hour. You could watch, and maybe that'll answer some of your questions."

"I, well, but…"

Alex leaned closer and said into the mouthpiece, "Say yes, Summer. Please? I could use the driving practice. You'll be doing me a really, really big favor."

Her sigh filtered into Zach's ear. Frustration? Angst? Uncertainty? Not that it mattered. Patience had been the main ingredient in Libby's recovery. That, and an ample supply of tenacity. Maybe Miss Lane had both, and just didn't know it. Yet.

Alex, palm extended and fingers wiggling, asked for the phone, and Zach gladly handed it over. He had no patience and very little pity for people who didn't at least try.

"If we leave right now," the boy told her, "we can be there in ten minutes." He hung up and grabbed his parka from the hook beside the door. "Let's make tracks, before she changes her mind."

"She said yes?"

Alex shrugged. "She didn't say *no*..."

Zach told his assistant, Emma, that he'd be back within the hour then tossed Alex his keys to his pickup. As the teen unlocked the doors, Zach shrugged into his jacket. "Don't make me regret this, okay?"

"Don't worry, I'll be careful. My entire driving future is riding on it." Alex laughed and climbed in behind the wheel. "Hey. That's a pun." He stuck the key into the ignition. "My entire driving future is riding on it. Get it?"

"Yeah, I get it. And my good-driver insurance policy is riding on it, too, so keep that in mind."

Zach buckled his seat belt. "To be honest, I'm not half as worried about what you'll do behind the wheel as I am about what *she'll* do when we get there."

"Do? What could she do?"

"Oh, I dunno. She could meet us at the door, brandishing a shotgun, for starters."

"Summer?" Alex laughed. "No way. She won't even squish a spider."

Probably afraid to, Zach thought as Alex backed out of the parking space.

A car horn blared, and the boy slammed on the brakes.

"Crazy kid!" an elderly man bellowed, shaking his fist. "Where'd you get your license, in a bubble gum machine?"

Alex's shoulders slumped, and Zach raised his eyebrows. "You know what you did wrong, right?"

"Didn't check the mirrors." Smiling sheepishly, he added, "Sorry. Won't happen again. Promise."

"Let's hope not. Your entire driving future is riding on it, remember."

For the duration of the short trip, Alex kept his word, even while chattering about the attack that turned Summer Lane into a recluse. The kid didn't have many details, though, so Zach decided that tonight he'd fire up the laptop, see what he could find out about her online. *Wouldn't it be faster and easier to* ask *her?*

Alex took the corner a little sharply, distracting Zach from the question.

"Sorry. I'll be more careful at the next corner," Alex said. "You think we'll get that snow they're calling for?"

Zach held tight to the grab handle. "Probably, but I hope not."

As Alex pulled into her driveway, Zach saw the blinds beside her front door snap shut. Had she been standing there, watching, since the kid hung up the phone?

Alex got out of the truck first, and waved as he approached the town house. "Hey, Summer," he called. "It's us. Zach and me."

He whispered to Zach, "She'll never leave here, but this is a start."

The door opened slowly, and there it was again, that lovely, amazing voice.

"Please," she said from somewhere in the shadows. "Come in."

"You've been baking again, haven't you," Alex said, heading straight for the kitchen.

Baking *again*? Libby made things from fabric and yarn. Sweaters. Mittens. Curtains and throw pillows, and called her craft projects "coping mechanisms." Did the oven serve the same purpose for Summer?

"Man, oh man," Alex said around a mouthful of cookie. "I think these are your best ever!"

"Thanks," she said. "Have as many as you like. I can't eat them all by myself."

For half a second, silence. Then all three laughed, because Alex had stuffed one cookie into his mouth, and held one in each hand.

"Name's Marshall. Zach Marshall," he said, offering his hand. "But I'm guessing you already knew that."

For a minute there, it didn't look like she'd reciprocate. He felt awkward, his hand dangling in midair. When at last she accepted his greeting, he noticed a slight tremor in her cool-to-the-touch fingertips. Cold hands, warm heart? If the warmth glowing in her eyes and smile was any indicator, the answer was yes.

"Summer Lane," she said, and quickly folded both arms over her chest. "But I expect you already knew that, too."

At the moment, Zach didn't know much, except that he liked her. Or was pity the more accurate word? "Aw, Zach," Alex mumbled. "You really gotta try one of these. They're excellent, man. *Excellent.*"

Every thread of common sense in him said,

look at Alex. Look at the cookies. You've seen gorgeous women before, so stop gawking at her!

She must have thought he was staring at the slightly raised pink scar that ran the length of her left cheek, because she cupped her chin in her palm and hid it behind her fingers. What other reminders—physical and emotional—had her attacker left her with?

"There are soft drinks in the fridge," she said. "Or I could fix you a cup of coffee. Or tea. Or hot chocolate?" Summer pointed at the coffee-maker on the counter and the carousel that held a colorful variety of pods.

He didn't need a degree in psychology to know Alex was right. She wouldn't leave the town house today. Maybe not tomorrow, either. Asking her to consider checking out the studio would only add to her unease. Maybe she'd let her guard down enough that he could show her a few basic moves right here in her living room. Zach made note of her stiff-backed stance and nervous smile. *Or maybe not.*

"I told my assistant we wouldn't be gone long," he said, "but coffee sounds great."

As she made her way to the other side of the bar counter, Zach noticed her limp. Alex had mentioned multiple surgeries to repair a shattered femur. Not an easy injury to recover from;

he'd learned that while visiting guys he'd served with who'd been shot or who'd stepped on IEDs.

While she added water to the machine, he remembered that Libby's attacker had been high on PCP, and the slick defense attorney blamed the drug, not his client, for the crime. The judge gave her attacker a choice: rehab facility or prison. Naturally, he chose treatment. The punishment didn't fit the crime, in Zach's opinion. If asked to explain his harsh judgment, he would have said "The guy hurt my kid sister! Hang him by his heels!" As it turned out, the guy punished himself. Months after being released, he died of a heroin overdose.

When Summer turned to face him, her smile faded, like the smoke from a spent match. Evidently, the memory of what had happened to Libby was still very fresh, and his anguish was written all over his face. He half expected her to shrink back in fear, but to her credit, Summer held her ground and, mug in hand, asked how he liked his coffee.

"Black. High-test if you've got it."

"Cool," Alex said, looking from Zach to Summer and back again. "Something else you two have in common."

Summer's left brow quirked upward.

"Something else?" Zach said.

"Black coffee and…and…" The teen blinked

then helped himself to another cookie as a red flush crept up his neck. "Well, you guys are about the same age."

Nice recovery. He could almost read the kid's mind: *black coffee and a close connection to violent crime.* Had Summer picked up on it, too?

"Much as I hate to quote my mom," Alex said, "I have to eat and run. Midterms. Argh." Alex stood beside Summer and whispered, "Will you, uh, are you okay being alone with you-know-who?" He aimed a thumb at Zach, trying to hide it behind a cupped hand.

Goofy kid, he thought. If God ever blessed him with a son, Zach wouldn't mind a bit if he was just like Alex.

"I sent a short grocery list to your email," she said. "Specialty items for my parents' visit. Bean sprouts, oatmeal, tofu..."

"Gross!" He wrinkled his nose. "I almost forgot they're vegetarians."

"Vegans."

Alex groaned, whimpered and opened the door. "Guess we won't be grilling any steaks while they're in town, then, huh?"

Smiling, Summer said, "If we do, we won't have to worry about sharing them with Mom and Dad."

He stepped outside, but turned back. "Do me a favor, will ya, and tell them boiling cabbage is against community association rules. My grandmother had an apartment in a seniors' high-rise. Every time we visited, the whole building reeked of the stuff." He pointed left. "There's just a wall between your house and mine, and you remember the time I burned popcorn in the microwave."

It was Summer's turn to groan. "I didn't think I'd ever get that awful smell out of here!"

Alex was still snickering as the door clicked shut.

The room fell silent, save for the trickle of coffee filling a big white mug, the ticking clock and the hum of the fridge.

"That's one great kid," Zach said.

"Yes, he is." She clasped her hands at her waist. "So tell me, how many of your other clients are like me?"

Like her? If she meant beautiful, barely bigger than a minute, with a voice even more lovely than her face, he'd have to say none. But he knew what she meant. "Just one. My sister, Libby."

She handed him his coffee. "I'm sorry to hear she had to go through that."

"Happened a little over two years ago. The whole Marshall clan is proud of the way she pulled through it."

And to ensure Summer wouldn't think he was comparing her recovery to Libby's, Zach quickly added, "But she's a shrink, so she knows all the tricks. Too bad she can't nail down the reason she's the clumsiest person for miles around."

She gave him a look that said "What does that have to do with anything?" then slid a red mug under the coffeemaker's spout. North Pole, Alaska, was printed on one side.

Zach pointed. "Gift, or souvenir?"

"Both. I bought it for myself. Alaska had been at the top of my bucket list for years, and I crossed it off with a cruise along the Inside Passage, then went overland by train…"

Alone?

"…with a friend," she said, answering his unasked question.

Ah. Ex-boyfriend, probably. And based on her tone of voice, the breakup hadn't been easy.

"Have you been there? To Alaska, I mean?"

"Yeah. College pal and I backpacked and camped in Denali after graduation, before we enlisted with the marines. Alaska was our last hoorah, in case…" *In case we didn't make it home, like some of my guys.*

Her slow nod told him she understood. "Where did they send you?"

"One tour in Kuwait, three in Afghanistan." He hated talking about this stuff. Too many regrets. Too many hard memories. "Mind if I ask you a personal question?"

"It's a free country, thanks to men like you."

He never knew how to react when people said things like that. He'd enlisted because, after earning a business degree from Colorado State, he couldn't picture himself at a desk, balancing the Double M's books, or taking orders from his younger cousin, Nate. How heroic was that?

He set both forearms on the counter, putting his face a foot closer to hers. "How did you know it was safe to let Alex leave?"

"I didn't." She sat back, running her fingers through her bangs. "But as you pointed out, he's a great kid. If he says you're okay, that's good enough for me." Summer branded him with those big dark eyes, then frowned slightly. "That's a big fat lie. Letting him leave was a test."

He was mildly surprised. "Is that so? And did I pass?"

A quiet, melodic laugh passed her lips. "Oh, I wasn't testing *you*." Her brows drew together, and he read it as a sign that the subject was closed. "Besides, I've never met a marine who couldn't be trusted."

Oh, he could name a few. Zach knew one guy who'd survived hand-to-hand combat, only to return home so mentally scarred that he'd turned to whiskey for comfort. Another, plagued by nightmares of the things he'd seen, chose drugs to help him forget…and chose crime to help fund his addiction. There were a few skeletons in Zach's own closet, too, but what would be gained by admitting it?

Summer picked up a cookie, held it out to him. "They really are good, if I do say so myself."

He understood this gesture as another signal to change the subject. When he reached for it, his fingertips brushed hers. She inhaled sharply, a quick little gasp, and snapped back her hand so fast, the cookie broke. A succession of emotions skittered across her pretty face, from shock to dread to embarrassment.

"Guess your sister isn't the only clumsy one." Summer brushed crumbs into an upturned palm and ate them, then grabbed another cookie. "Let's try this again."

This time, Zach was careful not to touch her. He took a small bite and decided that if she signed up for a self-defense class, he'd pass her off to Emma. Somehow, he'd summoned the patience to help his sister cope with her male-induced skittishness, but Summer was a stranger. Besides, what worked for Libby might backfire with Summer.

"Wow," she said. "Just look at that frown. Don't you like chocolate chips?"

"Of course I do. Sorry. They're good. Really good." He met her eyes again. Those enormous, long-lashed, brown eyes. Zach swallowed. Hard. If he admitted his part in Libby's attack, Summer might never give the classes a chance. And he couldn't think of a person who needed them more.

Zach sipped his coffee. "Your recipe beats my mom's all to pieces, but if you tell her I said that, I'll deny it."

Either she didn't get the joke, or saw it as proof of his blatant dishonesty, because Summer got up and riffled through a drawer.

"I really *am* kind of clumsy sometimes," she said, patting her thigh, "thanks to this bum leg."

They hadn't been talking about the leg, or clumsiness, so he didn't understand why she'd mentioned either.

She plucked a sandwich bag from its box and added, "Do you think it'll be a problem? If I enroll in classes, that is?"

He still didn't get the connection. "The leg? No, it won't matter at all." Dave Reece was the only other person he knew who favored one leg the way Summer did. He'd earned his limp stepping on a land mine, and now he wore a prosthesis. Jeans hid her legs, so he had no way of knowing if she'd been fitted for one, too. If so, she'd earned it in a battle of an entirely different kind.

"One of my students is in her mideighties. And Emma, my assistant, teaches two kids who wear leg braces."

"Emma?" She began filling a second bag. "I thought Alex was your assistant."

"Well, he helps out. A lot. But until he earns his certificate, I can't let him work one-on-one with students. Insurance regs, you know?"

"I didn't realize credentials were a requirement for self-defense instructors."

"They are in *my* studio."

"Once a marine," she said, smiling, "always a marine, eh?"

"I wouldn't say that." He shrugged one shoulder and returned her grin. "Well, that might be part of it."

Zach wrapped his hands around the mug. "It's just that I won't take a chance that my students could get hurt in class—or afterward—because an instructor lacks experience or maturity. It's my responsibility to figure out what each person needs to learn. Some instinctively know how to spot danger before it happens. Some need to be taught what to look for. Because self-defense is as much psychological as it is physical, and involves a whole lot more than stance and protective maneuvers."

He hadn't said anything funny. At least, he didn't think he had. So why were her eyes glittering with amusement?

He cleared his throat. "What?"

"So Alex was right."

"About?"

"You really *are* the Amazing Zach."

"The Amazing… He called me that?"

"No, but that's the impression I get whenever he talks about you."

He felt the heat of a blush creep into his face. And how must *that* look? Big, tough, battle-scarred marine, sitting here all pink-cheeked, like a starry-eyed teenage girl. If he hadn't already finished his coffee, he'd take a sip now, just so he could hide behind the mug.

"I call him my one-man PR firm," Zach admitted. "But from the sound of things, he goes overboard from time to time."

"We'll see about that."

He raised an eyebrow.

"We'll see if your teaching skills are as amazing as Alex says they are."

So, she'd decided to enroll in classes and begin accepting help? Good!

Summer zipped both plastic bags, slid them near Zach's elbow then stood at the end of the counter and faced the front door.

Well, no one would accuse her of being overly subtle. But he hadn't planned to stay this long, anyway. Zach got to his feet and helped himself to one of the bags. "Thanks. These will make a great breakfast, dunked in coffee in the morning."

"Not the healthiest breakfast, but it's your stomach," she said, picking up the second bag. "Would you do me a favor and bring these to Alex on your way out?"

He was tempted to do it, but thought better of it. "Lesson number one—there are some things that, no matter how difficult, you need to do for yourself."

Her jaw dropped.

"Alex only lives next door," he said quickly.

Blinking, she snapped her mouth shut and took a half step back. He'd only told her what she needed to hear. So why did he feel like such a heel?

"Tell you what," he said. "I'll stand at the end of the sidewalk and keep a close eye on you while you deliver the cookies. Will that make it easier to go outside?"

For a second there, it looked like she might take him up on the offer. But pride must have gotten the better of her because she pulled back her shoulders and said, "No, you're right. I should do it myself." Her chin lifted a notch. "Don't worry. You needn't babysit me."

When you're right, you're right, he thought. But he didn't have time for moodiness. Zach grabbed the door handle, but a wood-framed photo on the foyer table stopped him. "Your folks?" he asked, pointing at it.

Summer nodded.

"I recognize them from a couple movies." He nodded. "Must be cool, having parents who are big stars. Ever been on the set when they're filming?"

"A few times. Mostly when I was a kid, and they couldn't line up a sitter."

"What are their names again?"

"Susannah and Harrison Lane."

She crossed her arms over her chest again, and Zach decided it was her shut-out-the-world stance.

He held up the baggy. "Well, thanks for these. And for the coffee, too."

"No problem."

He'd read the phrase, *her smile never made it to her eyes*, in a couple of novels, but it had never made sense to him...until this moment.

"There's a beginners class starting up on Monday evening. If you get there at five-thirty or so, you'll have plenty of time to fill out the enrollment forms before we get going at six."

"I'll be there."

He almost believed her.

But if she hadn't left the house in who knew how long, how would she get to the studio?

"Do you need a ride?"

"No," she said resignedly, "I have a car. I open the garage door once a week and start it, to keep the engine from getting all gummed up. And when my parents are in town, they drive it."

Something about her posture and sad eyes reminded him of the war-orphaned kids he'd met while deployed. She'd taken a beating. Maybe even more than a beating. But if those youngsters could pick their way through rubble and find ways to survive, so could a full-grown woman who lived in a luxurious town house in one of the nation's most prestigious ski resorts. He might be tempted to feel a little sorry for her...if she wasn't doing such a great job feeling sorry for *herself.*

"Guess I'd better head out."

"See you Monday," she said, closing the door.

Fractions of a second later, he heard the bolt slide into place. "Can't deliver cookies through a steel entry door..." he said to himself.

Would he see her on Monday? Or had she only made the promise to get rid of him? For her sake, he hoped she'd been serious. Hoped, too, that if she showed up, she'd stick with the program. Because if anybody needed some confidence-building lessons, it was Summer Lane.

"Strange woman," he muttered, taking out his keys. "Gorgeous, but strange."

He turned the key in the ignition, and as the pickup's motor came to life, he pictured her unenthusiastic reaction to stepping outside, even long enough to deliver a zipper bag of treats to her next-door neighbor.

If she met him halfway, he could show her how to strengthen muscle, help build her self-confidence; teach her how to feel in control of her surroundings. But dealing with her scary brew of emotional issues? That was Libby's field, not his.

He had three choices: call Libby and ask for tips on dealing with a woman like Summer, or get online, as he'd thought of earlier, to find out what he could about her past. Easiest of all, he could avoid her altogether. It wasn't likely she'd show up on Monday, anyway. He knew better than most that she couldn't hide from the evil in the world, but if she wanted to spend the rest of her days trying, he couldn't talk her out of it. Didn't *want* to talk her out of it.

At the stop sign half a block from her town house, Zach peered into the rearview mirror, and almost didn't believe his eyes.

There stood Summer, sandwich bag of cookies in one hand, the other raised to ring Alex's doorbell.

"Well, good for you, Summer. Good for you."

It wasn't much, but it was a start. He was happy for her, and strangely proud, too. What was it the sages said about every journey beginning with a single step? She'd finally taken it, and—

A car horn blared behind him. Startled, Zach waved a quick apology to the driver and took his foot off the brake. He was halfway home before reality dawned: going to Summer's house had been a stupid idea. Because now, like it or not—and he did *not*—he was committed to helping her.

From kindergarten on, teachers and parents alike praised him for coming to the aid of others: the new kid, too timid to play kick ball at recess; the boy in the wheelchair who couldn't reach a book from a high shelf; the girl with thick glasses and an overbite he'd invited to junior prom because no one else would. In marine boot camp, that same tendency earned him the nickname Champ, aka Champion of the Underdog. He'd used his precious few off-duty hours to coach the smaller, weaker guys who often got stuck with kitchen patrol or latrine duty when they fell seconds short of passing muster during drills.

If his mom hadn't done such a good job drilling the "do unto others" rule into his head, he wouldn't be in this fix. "Thanks, Mom," he said, grinning despite himself.

Helping others made him feel good, even when he hadn't been around to see the positive aftereffects. But getting involved had gotten him into serious trouble, too. He pictured Martha, and instantly shut down the memory. It wouldn't be like that with Summer. Zach accepted his fate, much as he'd accepted every awful assignment from his superiors.

But he didn't have to like it.

CHAPTER FOUR

ROSE HELPED HERSELF to a chocolate chip cookie then perched on a kitchen stool. "I should hang out here more often. Maybe your homemaker skills will rub off on me."

The place did look good, if Summer said so herself. But then, why wouldn't it, when she had little else to do but decorate and keep things tidy?

"Once I've done my exercises, I have nothing but time on my hands. And a person can only read and watch TV so many hours a day."

Her friend stared at her long and hard, and Summer braced herself for another lecture about getting out of the house.

Instead, Rose polished off the cookie. "How many of these fattening, addictive things did you make this time?"

"Oh, I don't know. Six, maybe eight dozen."

"Keep that up, and this—" Rose crossed her long legs "—will be impossible."

Summer laughed, hoping she'd escaped the spiel.

"So what's this I hear about you signing up for self-defense classes with Zach Marshall?"

Summer had thought the blabbermouth gene had skipped a generation, but clearly, Alex had inherited it. Summer ran a hand through her hair. "I probably will, but I'm not sure yet."

"I hope you're joking, because Alex is feeling pretty good about himself for talking you into it."

If she signed up, it would be because of Zach, not Alex. But if she admitted that to Rose, she'd tell Alex and hurt his feelings.

Summer flipped through her recipe file and plucked out the card for veggie lasagna. "My parents' plane will land soon, and I'm sure they'll be hungry when they get here."

"Where are they flying in from this time?"

"Malta."

"*Malta?* I don't even know where that is!"

When Summer entered high school, her folks thought it best that she stay in one place to attend school and live a more stable life than their own, and she'd kept track of their whereabouts on the big world map that now hung above her living room sofa. Knowing Rose would cry tears of boredom if she recited the precise location at 35.9°N and 14.5°E, she said, "It's in the Mediterranean, near Italy and Libya."

Rose nodded, squinting as if trying to picture the region. "Hmm. And where to next?"

"Who knows? They're nomads."

"It sounds like such a fascinating life." Rose sighed wistfully.

Summer knew better than to agree. "Would you and Alex like to join us for supper?" she said instead. "I'm sure they'd love to see you guys and share pictures and stories about the island and the movie, with all its pirates and scallywags and doubloons."

Rose glanced at the ingredients on the recipe card and wrinkled her nose. "Tofu?"

"'Fraid so."

She shoved the card closer to Summer. "Thanks, but I think I'd rather see that annoying superheroes movie Alex has been raving about."

Summer put a pot of water on to boil. "Tofu isn't all that horrible."

"Not all that horrible? Gee, there's a convincing argument." Rose laughed. "And speaking of arguments, help me understand why you're on the fence about these self-defense lessons."

Rose held her gaze then said, "I know you. In for a penny, in for a pound. Or in your case, it's all-in, or 100 percent *out*."

Much as Summer hated to admit it, Rose was right.

"How much do you know about the instructor?" she asked.

"Zach? Well, he's single, if that's what you mean."

No, it wasn't, but for a reason Summer couldn't explain, that came as good news.

"He's also a man of his word. Honest to a fault. If anything ever happened to me, I'd like nothing better than for him to finish raising Alex." She sighed. "Only reason I can't name him as legal guardian is because it would break my brother's heart. He thinks the world of my kid."

"A whole lot of people think the world of Alex."

Rose waved away the compliment. "I have an uncle who was a marine. Never shuts up about his time in 'Nam. But Zach? He won't talk about his years in the military. I'm guessing that means he saw some pretty ugly stuff over there."

Summer added wide, whole wheat noodles to the boiling water and recalled the strange expression that had come over Zach's face when she'd said, "Once a marine, always a marine." Something between distress and dissatisfaction. Maybe what he'd survived explained the sadness that tinged his green eyes.

"If I'd been over there, they'd have to outfit me with a straitjacket and lock me in a padded room. I don't have the backbone to face danger and hardship, especially not all at the same time."

Rose's husband had been a logger, and died on the job when Alex was just a few months old. His insurance helped get her through those first rough months. Teaching third grade at Red Sandstone Elementary kept the wolf from the door during the school year. Only recently, after inheriting her unmarried aunt's estate, had she been able to give up her second job, waitressing weekends and summers. But as far as Summer knew, no one had helped Rose through the emotional hardships of widowhood and raising a kid alone.

"You're tougher than you let on," Summer said. "I wish I could be more like you."

"Whatever," Rose said, glossing over the comment. "So? What did you think of him?"

"The Amazing Zach, you mean?"

"You say that like you think he *isn't amazing*. Are you dippy, girl? The man is positively *dreamy*!"

"Oh, yeah? Well, if he's so great, then why is he still single at his age?"

"Listen to you." Rose chuckled. "Talking about him as if he's some doddering old man. I happen to know he'll turn thirty-five on his next birthday."

Summer glanced at the clock. Unless her parents' plane got in late, they'd arrive in an hour or so. She turned on the oven and opened a jar of pasta sauce as Rose counted off Zach's qualities on her fingers.

"He loves his family. He served his country. He moved into his sister, Libby's, condo after her attack and nursed her back to health. He owns his own business. He's great with kids. He's strong and handsome and decent and—"

"Why aren't *you* dating him?"

Rose's blue eyes widened. "Zach? And *me*? Oh, you're a regular comedian, aren't you? For one thing, he's too young for me."

"You talk about yourself as if you're a doddering old woman. You're only forty."

"Oh, like I needed the reminder." Rose grabbed another cookie. "Truth is, I couldn't date Zach. It would be like…like dating my brother!"

"Yeah, I guess I understand that. You and Zach have been friends a long time. I'd feel the same way if someone suggested I start dating Justin." Summer began assembling the pasta dish. "You're sure you won't join us for supper? I'm serving minestrone, salad and garlic bread, too—and chocolate mousse for dessert—so I guarantee you and Alex won't go home hungry, even if you don't want the lasagna."

"You haven't seen your folks in months. I

think you need some family time. How long will they be in town?"

"Hard to say. A week, maybe two?"

"Plenty of time, then, for Alex and me to interrogate them before they hit the road again." Rose hopped down from the stool and put on her jacket. "Can you believe the weather guy is calling for snow?"

"He also said this cold snap should end soon, and we'll go back to temps in the sixties during the day and thirties at night."

"I hope he's right. I'm not ready for full-fledged winter weather just yet." She opened the door then drew Summer into a sisterly hug. "Listen," she said, holding her at arm's length, "any time you want some real food while your mom and dad are here, just text me. I'll send Alex over with a plate of hot dogs or pizza. You can eat it after they've gone to bed."

"You're a sweetheart to offer, but honestly, I'll be okay. It's just for a few days, and let's not forget that I grew up on tofu and bean curd."

Rose hugged her again. "Oh, you poor little thing!" she said, and left laughing.

As Summer finished making supper, the things Rose had said about Zach hovered in her mind. She put yesterday's soup on the stove to warm and pictured his broad jaw and slow smile, blaming Rose's list of his finer qualities for the flutter-

ing of her heart. Was this silly, schoolgirl crush
the byproduct of avoiding men since the attack?
Or had her loneliness finally reached its peak?

CHAPTER FIVE

ZACH STARED AT the computer and shook his head. He'd looked up six variations of her name on Google and came up with summer menus, summer getaways, summer party ideas and summer bug repellents. He finally found some links with her name, and curious, he clicked a few, learning that she'd narrated hundreds of TV and radio ads. They helped him understand why her easy-on-the-ears voice sounded so familiar, but did nothing to answer questions about her attack or the court proceedings that might have followed. Could Alex have misunderstood or exaggerated what happened to her two years ago? If he hoped to teach her how to prevent future attacks, he needed to learn as much as possible about the one that changed her life—changed her.

He dialed Dave's cell phone, and his former marine buddy picked up on the first ring.

"Well, as I live and breathe, if it isn't the one and only Champ Marshall."

"How goes it, Reece?"

"It goes. You still teaching old ladies how to do half nelsons and Argentine leg locks?"

For some odd reason, Dave got a kick out of comparing self-defense tactics to wrestling holds, and Zach had learned the hard way that correcting him was an exercise in futility. He didn't expect that a dose of his own medicine would cure Dave, but Zach couldn't help himself. "And are you still the glorified secretary at Precinct Six?"

"Hey. This place couldn't run without a good desk sergeant."

"A *good* desk sergeant, eh? Sorry to hear they replaced you."

"Ha ha ha. Still a comedian, I see. If you ever get tired of coaching gymnastics, say the word. I know a guy who can get you a spot on open mic night at the Laugh Lounge." Dave snickered. "But I'm guessing you didn't call solely to cast aspersions on my career…"

"You're as perceptive as usual," Zach countered. And then he shared what little he knew about Summer's history. "I'm hoping you can use your powers of persuasion to get me a little more information."

"Why? You interested in her?"

Zach pictured her, pretty and petite, with a smile so warm it could thaw ice, and eyes that put Bambi's to shame.

"Only as a potential student," he fibbed. "She came out of that mess with some permanent injuries. I don't want to put her in any situations that could do more damage or trigger flashbacks to the attack."

"I hear ya. Hold on a sec. Got another call."

While Zach waited, he paced from kitchen to living room and back again. The 750-square-foot apartment above the studio served him well, with a steep staircase leading to the loft bedroom, a closet-sized bathroom and a built-in storage unit that ran the entire length of the living room. He'd furnished it simply, with an overstuffed leather love seat and matching recliner, a narrow coffee table where he ate most of his meals, and a wrought-iron floor lamp. He stopped momentarily to take stock. With no knickknacks, no valances atop the wood blinds and no pictures on the white walls, the place looked bleak and boring, especially when compared with Summer's inviting town house.

Zach slapped a hand to the back of his neck and resumed pacing. He'd spent all of thirty minutes in her presence, and here he was, wondering what his place might look like if she had a chance to decorate it?

"Bad idea," he grumbled. Bad on so many levels, he didn't know where to begin. Soon after returning home from Afghanistan, he'd made a promise to himself, thanks in no small part to Libby's unsolicited advice: "No more knight-in-shining-armor behavior."

It made him more determined than ever to hand Summer off to Emma…if she decided to enroll at the studio. His assistant's teaching methods, though vastly different from his own, produced positive results. And in Summer's still-fragile physical and emotional state, working woman-to-woman would probably be best for her.

In that case, why bother digging into her past? If she ever found out about it, he'd look like some crazy stalker, not someone bent on doing what was best for her.

He was about to hang up when Dave came back on the line.

"Sorry that took so long. Had to process a perp. Now, where were we?"

"Y'know, I should have given this look-into-her-background thing a lot more thought. Let's just forget it, okay?"

"Too late, Champ. The wheels of investigation are already rolling."

When had he had time? Zach didn't know what went into processing a perp, but surely it required some concentration. And more than five minutes.

"I did a cursory search," Dave said, answering Zach's unasked question. "But it came up empty. So I shot an email to Adam. If he can't dig up some good dirt, it'll mean there isn't any."

Dave's twin had earned a reputation for being one of the most hard-nosed assistant district attorneys in the Denver prosecutor's office. Chances that he'd get involved in something as trivial as this were about as good as Summer showing up at the studio on Monday. That put Zach at ease. He thanked Dave, exchanged a few more good-natured barbs and ended the call.

He'd no sooner returned the handset back to its cradle when the phone rang.

"Uh oh," Libby said, "what's wrong?"

"Nothing's wrong, you nut. What a crazy question."

"Watch your language, big brother. People in my line of work are sensitive to words like nut and crazy. And you of all people should know I'm not that easily distracted. You sound…off. So how about you save us both a lot of time and tell me why your voice is all tight and gravelly, because I won't let up until you do."

And she wouldn't. Zach saw no harm in bringing her up-to-date on what he laughingly referred to as the Summer Chronicles.

"You better hope your DA friend doesn't decide to bend the rules just because his brother asked him to," she warned.

He had his own reasons for wanting the same thing, but curiosity compelled him to ask why she shared his concerns.

"Need I remind you about that night during my senior year at the University of Denver?"

He'd been home for a rare, month-long leave when Libby opted to spend time with him rather than join her dorm-mates for a downtown pub crawl. Both girls were from out of state, so when homesickness or trouble erupted, they turned to the Marshalls. That night, Zach answered the phone. Annie, on the verge of hysteria, explained how they'd met a guy who must have spiked Taylor's drink. "She was only out of my sight for half an hour, and now she can't walk or talk or keep her eyes open!" He'd ordered Annie to get Taylor to the hospital, promised to meet them at the ER, and called the police. It didn't take long to confirm that Taylor had been drugged, and the cops and medical staff agreed she was lucky to have survived the double dose of Rohypnol.

"Good thing no one would tell you the guy's name," Libby was saying.

In hindsight, he had to agree. But that night, when he saw Taylor lying limp as a rag doll on the exam table, he'd seen red. "Where's the guy who did that to her?" he'd demanded. Not "How is she?" or "Will she be okay?" but "I'm gonna murder him."

"You would have gone to jail," Libby added.

"It was a natural, knee-jerk reaction. Any decent person would have felt the same way."

"That might be true…if it was the only time you put yourself in a bad situation, defending a woman."

Zack knew what was coming, and he braced himself. Sure enough, Libby reminded him that moments before his best friend died, Buddy made Zach promise to watch over his wife. Martha didn't handle widowhood well at all, and repeatedly tried to deaden the pain of her loss with risky behavior, booze and pills. When Martha overdosed for the third time, it was Zach to the rescue, yet again. He insisted on therapy, and to make sure she got the help she needed, he drove her to every appointment. When the psychiatrist recommended outings, Zach bought tickets and sat through operas, the ballet and stage plays. Whatever it took, he told himself, to fulfill that promise to Buddy. In time, she got better, and he told himself Buddy would rest easier knowing that Zach and Martha had fallen in love. Well, Zach thought grimly, *he* had fallen in love, anyway.

"You remember what she did," Libby was saying, "after you stood by her through all that misery?"

Like it was yesterday.

"And what about those months you worked as a bouncer to pay your way through college, when all those flirty girls came running to you for protection?"

Yeah, he remembered that, too. For the most part, their fears had been legitimate, so he'd felt no remorse, escorting drunken brutes out of the bar. He'd kept a lid on his temper and got the job done without physical confrontations. He hadn't even considered roughing up those guys.

That wasn't the case, though, on the night Libby's roommate was drugged. Wasn't the case when Libby herself was attacked, either. He'd wanted to choke the life out of the animals who'd abused them, because the way he saw it—the way he *still* saw it—no man should get away with mistreating a woman. Ever. Period.

"So your quest to help this latest damsel in distress," she continued, "just proves one thing to me."

If she thought he intended to ask what it was, Libby had another think coming.

"You're still suffering from KISAS."

Knight in Shining Armor Syndrome. Zach harrumphed. He hadn't liked the title when she first labeled him with it, and he didn't like it now.

"Don't psychoanalyze me, Libs. I'm not one of your patients."

"No, you're my brother, and I don't want to

see you hurt again. If I could wish just one thing for you, it'd be that you'd hang up your super-hero cape, once and for all. This Summer person probably isn't anywhere near as vulnerable as you think she is. But even if you're right, and she's a big tangled mess of trouble and baggage, you can't save her. Only she can do that."

He sighed, and Libby did, too. *She only has your best interests at heart*, he reminded himself. Unfortunately, she was right. Again.

"Have dinner with me tomorrow," she said. "I'll make all your favorites…stuffed shells, garlic bread, meatballs. If you bring a bottle of my favorite wine, I'll even bake my famous cheesecake. *And* you have my word—no lectures."

"Sounds good," he said. "What time should I be there?"

"Seven?"

He decided to arrive at six so that if anything needed slicing or dicing, or involved a hot oven, he'd volunteer to do it for her.

He was about to sign off when he heard her say, "You know I love you, right? And that I only nag you because I want you to be happy?"

"Yeah, I know. Love you, too, kiddo."

Happy. What a peculiar word, he thought, hanging up. For some people, happiness was found in life's simple things, like music or travel, or tending a garden. For others, it could only be achieved by satisfying their every whim.

It wouldn't take much to make him happy. A humble house with a fenced-in yard, so he could get that golden retriever pup he'd always wanted. Two or three healthy kids. A strong, loving woman to share it all with. And no way Summer was that woman.

Getting a little ahead of yourself, aren't you, Marshall? What he knew about her would fit in one eye. She was a looker, no one could deny that. Smart, too. And not one to squander what she'd earned as a voice-over actress. Instead of spending her money on frivolous trinkets, she'd invested in the town house and filled it with things that turned it into a warm and welcoming home.

Don't think about that stuff, you idiot. Instead, focus on the way she recoiled when you touched her.

He felt bad about what she'd gone through. But Libby was right. He needed to hang up his superhero cape. Put away his armor. Admit that he couldn't rescue every damsel in distress.

In truth, he no longer wanted to rescue all of them.

Just the one with a smile as warm as her name.

CHAPTER SIX

"SO WHERE ARE your folks?"

"Having lunch in town with friends."

Rose laughed. "I didn't know Vail had any vegan restaurants."

"Oh, they always manage to find something organic on the menu," Summer said.

Rose tapped the folded edge of Zach's flyer on the counter, nodding as she munched a cookie. "You know what I think? If you're dead-set against ever going out of the house, you could make a handsome living, selling these cookies. I've never had any quite like them. What's your secret?"

Summer chose to ignore the "never going out" part of the observation. "If I told you," she said, topping off her neighbor's coffee, "it wouldn't be a secret anymore, now would it?"

"No, I'm serious. You could sell them to restaurants. I'll bet a few local bakeries would even buy them. They're that good!"

"I can see it now." Both hands forming the corners of an imaginary sign, she pretended to read,

"Summer Lane, founder of Chips Off the Old Block." Grinning, she shook her head. "Thanks, but no, thanks, because then I'd be obliged to fill orders. And fight off the reporters clamoring for an interview with the next Mrs. Meadows, Cookie Queen."

Rose threw her head back and laughed, a little too long and way too loud to sound sincere. But Summer overlooked that, too, because she wouldn't have offended her for the world.

"You're a hoot, girl." Then she got really serious, really fast. "I can't tell you how glad I am that your parents are here. It drives me crazy, thinking of you over here alone all the time, wasting that delightful sense of humor and all that gorgeousness. But if I said something like that in front of them, only God knows what sort of Pandora's box I'd open for you."

"I appreciate your discretion." Summer had heard it all before. She glanced at the clock.

"I'd better get supper started. They'll be back in time to eat."

"Oh. That's right. And you can count on them to be punctual." Sarcasm rang loud in her voice. "Like they were punctual last night, when you went to all that trouble to fix them a full vegan meal—which they didn't eat because they stopped at a restaurant on the way here, without bothering to call and let you know they were running late."

"Oh, it's all right," Summer said. "They fell all over themselves, apologizing when they got here." She wiggled her eyebrows. "But won't they be surprised when I reheat the entire meal tonight."

She saw no point in telling Rose that her parents' guilt had provided the perfect way to sidestep another In Your Own Best Interests speech about the dangers of skipping orthopedist appointments, or yet another lecture about why she should find a therapist who'd force her to get out of the house.

But how she'd avoid all that tonight was anybody's guess.

"Well, I don't envy you."

Rose was still holding Zach's flyer. She had that look in her eye, and Summer had a sinking suspicion it was behind all this chitchat.

"So how long did Zach stay this time?"

Summer should have known Rose would have seen his truck out front. Was it her imagination, or had her friend put extra emphasis on *this time*?

"He stayed just long enough for me to fill two more sandwich bags with cookies." Not the whole truth, but not a lie, either. "He dropped off his friend's flyer," she said, nodding at it.

He'd met Harry Wilson at a seminar, years

earlier. And since Harry was vacationing in town, he'd asked Zach's permission to lead a few classes. Monday's class, to be precise, and Zach thought it only fair to warn her that he and Emma wouldn't be the only instructors on site.

Rose dismissed the flyer. "So? Have you made up your mind yet?"

"About what?"

"Good grief, girl. Now I know what it feels like to be a dentist. Sometimes talking to you is like pulling teeth without the benefit of Novocain! What do you think of *him*?"

"I think you were absolutely right. He seems like a good guy. It was nice of him to give Alex some behind-the-wheel time." *And nice of him to give me a heads-up about Harry Wilson.*

Rose huffed. "That isn't what I meant."

"Well, he's still raving about my cookies, so I guess you could say he has good taste, too."

Rose clucked her tongue. "All right, I'll quit beating around the bush."

"I'm glad to hear it. It's unnecessarily hard on the shrubbery, and a waste of time, to boot."

She laughed, swatting playfully at Summer. "Be honest, now—just between you and me— isn't he *the* hunkiest hunk of man on two feet?"

Rose had a good heart, but she had absolutely no control over her tongue. There was no such thing as *between you and me* where Rose was concerned. Summer knew that anything she said in the moments that followed would be repeated, probably before morning.

She grabbed the teakettle, a perfect excuse to put her back to Rose. As she filled it with water, she thought of Zach, tall and blond and broad-shouldered, with a voice so deep and smooth, he could work as a voice-over actor if he wanted to. She'd had plenty of time to think about it, and still hadn't come up with a color to describe the blue-green shade of his eyes. Hadn't been able to rationalize the way she'd reacted when his warm fingertips grazed hers, either.

She felt the heat of a blush creeping from her neck to her cheeks and continued facing the stove, because the ever-perceptive Rose was sure to figure out why…and would never let Summer hear the end of it.

When at last she turned around, Rose was reading Zach's flyer. A not-so-subtle hint for Summer?

"What kind of tea can I get you?" she asked, riffling through her collection.

"Oh, sweetie. I'm sorry, but I can't stay. But thanks."

So Rose had stopped by for no reason other than to see if her opinion of Zach had changed between yesterday and today?

"Besides, if I stayed, I'd want to help you get

the food reheated for your folks, and that is a one-woman kitchen if ever I've seen one." She narrowed one eye. "Now, if you're smart, you'll invite Zach over for a meal sometime. I happen to know that meat-stuffed shells are his favorite main dish. You could ask him to rinse lettuce leaves or chop something while you do… whatever." Rose smirked. "Squeezing into that tiny space is sure to cure your aversion to being near him."

It wasn't just Zach, Summer thought. It was every man, with the exception of her dad and her best friend, Justin.

The teakettle started to whistle, and it dawned on her that the only way Rose could have known how she had reacted to Zach's touch was if he'd told Alex, and Alex told his mom. The heat in her cheeks intensified. How dare he drag an innocent teenager into…into whatever this was! Oh, she'd go to class on Monday, all right, if only to give him a piece of her mind. What she wanted to tell him couldn't be said on the phone!

The doorbell rang as she turned off the gas. *Saved by the bell*, she thought. "It's probably Justin," Summer said, heading for the front door.

"I'm sure you already know that you're doubly blessed," Rose said as he entered. "Who else has a best friend who's the most sought-after stylist in all of Vail…and he makes house calls!"

"Flattery will get you anywhere, Rose," Justin said. "But you still have to make an appointment like everybody else." Winking, he pressed a kiss to Summer's cheek. "I'm early, I know, but a client canceled, and I thought we could fill the extra time with a visit." He looked at Rose. "Sorry if I interrupted your girl talk."

"Girl talk indeed," Rose said, waving the comment away. "This one's lips are buttoned up tighter than Fort Knox." Grabbing her jacket, she shook a finger under Summer's nose. "You're surrounded by enablers, this guy and me, included. Is it any wonder that you've been stuck in this same old rut for so long?"

She hugged Summer and smiled at Justin, and with that, she was gone.

Summer couldn't meet Justin's eyes. She had a feeling that her friend of many years agreed with Rose.

She shook off her suspicions. "My folks are in town, but they'll be back in a couple of hours. I'm warming up some vegetable lasagna for supper," she told him, taking refuge in the kitchen. "Why don't you stay? I'm sure they'd love to see you."

"Wish I could, but I have plans."

If not for Justin and his family, she would have spent countless major holidays alone while her parents were on location. They'd been in Europe when she was attacked, and it had been Justin who'd spent the long hours with her at the hospital and rehab center. She couldn't help but wonder if he really had plans, or if he'd made up the story to avoid spending time with the couple who, in his words, had been absent every time their only child needed them.

"Then what can I get you to drink while we set up for the haircut?"

He sat down at the counter. "Coffee, if you've got it."

The friends launched into familiar, comfortable conversation that continued even as they moved the dining room table and covered the colorful rug with a white sheet, and while he cut and styled her hair. After he helped her put things back into place, he grabbed her hand.

"Sit down, Sums," he said, leading her to the living room sofa. "I have something to tell you. Something really important."

He plopped down beside her, looking more serious than she'd ever seen him look.

"Let me say this before I lose my nerve. Again."

Again? How long had he been planning this little speech?

"Do you like wearing your hair short?"

"Sure. You do a great job. I don't even miss the long 'do' anymore."

His expression grew even more serious. "You are the *only* client I make house calls for. You know that, right?"

Yes, she did. Just like she knew what an inconvenience it was for him to haul scissors and combs, dryer and styling tools from his shop on East Meadow to her place. She'd always done everything possible to show her appreciation, and sent him home with generous tips, his favorite desserts and healthy casseroles that he could freeze then bake when work left him no time to cook.

"I realize it's a hassle," she said. "Coming over here every month for nearly two years…if you need to charge more, or change the schedule so that—"

He grabbed her hands. "Summer. Shhh. Please?"

She didn't like his tone. Didn't like feeling like a misbehaving child, either. It made her remember what her dad had said during his last visit: "If you keep acting like a helpless child, you can't complain when people treat you like one." It hadn't been easy to hear then, and it wouldn't be easy, hearing it from her much-trusted friend.

"You know I love you like a sister, right?"

She nodded. "And I feel the same way about you."

Justin looked sad, and pained, and frustrated all at once. Her heart ached for the friend who'd always been there for her. If she loved him half as much as she claimed to, she'd spare him the ordeal of telling her the house calls had to stop.

She sat up straighter and forced a smile. "You know how much I appreciate all you do for me, right?"

One brow rose high on his forehead. "Uh, yeah…"

"So please don't take what I'm about to say the wrong way."

Eyes narrowed, he studied her face.

"I've let you baby me for far too long. It's time I stood on my own two feet, inside *and* outside of this house. So next time I need a trim, I'll come to your shop, just like any other client." As he'd done earlier, Summer raised a hand to silence his retort. "I've made up my mind, and there isn't a thing you can do to change it."

He pulled her into a brotherly hug then held her at arm's length. "I'm proud of you, Sums. Really proud!"

Summer did her best to match his happy smile…while hoping that someday, she'd share his feelings.

CHAPTER SEVEN

SINCE HER PARENTS' ARRIVAL, Summer had spent half of her daylight hours picking up things her dad left strewn about, and the other half looking for things her mom had put away. She glanced at the calendar, where her dad had used a fat red marker—it had bled through to the next page—to circle the twenty-first, the date they'd fly to Baltimore then drive to the annual Chesapeake Film Festival in historic Easton, Maryland. Summer loved them like crazy, and because she knew they meant well, she employed an assortment of coping strategies.

When the basket for her dad's keys, reading glasses and sunglasses, neatly folded handkerchiefs and breath mints overflowed, she added another one. As she rediscovered everyday items hidden by her mom, Summer simply returned them to their proper places. Her best idea yet had been the dartboard on the back of her bedroom door, the one and only room her parents never entered. After printing each irksome peculiarity on Post-it notes, she stuck them to the board. Then, after getting ready for bed each night, Summer would fire a feathered missile at the pastel squares.

Tonight, the dart zeroed in on *pancake griddle on top of fridge*. Since it had chosen that same note two days earlier, Summer lobbed it again. This time, it landed on *wet tea bag in dishwasher*, inspiring a burst of quiet laughter.

"Are you okay in there?"

"Yes, Mom."

"Are you sure? I thought I heard thumping, and thought maybe you'd fallen."

It was all she could do to stifle more giggles. "No, I'm fine. Must have been my dresser drawers. Sorry. I'll close them more quietly from now on."

Silence, and then a dubious, "All right, then. Good night, honey."

"Sweet dreams," she called back, "and thanks for checking on me."

"Oh. Speaking of dreams, I met your dreamy friend in town today."

"Who, Justin?"

"No, of course not. I've known Justin for years! It was that nice young man who owns Marshall Law. You know, the self-defense studio that's right next door to the Cascade Café?"

Summer leaped out of bed and threw open her bedroom door.

"I've been saving some citrus-lavender tea," she said, taking her mother's hand. Leading her down the hall, she whispered, "Let's have a cup while you tell me all about it. No sense waking Dad."

After filling the kettle and turning the burner on high, she sat beside her mom at the bar counter. "Now, then. Start at the beginning," Summer said, "and don't leave out a single detail."

"Well, Dad and I were sitting there at the café, looking at the itinerary for our trip, when this handsome man walks up and says 'Excuse me, I hate to intrude, but aren't you Mr. and Mrs. Lane?'" Susannah laughed. "Your father thought he wanted an autograph, so he grabbed a napkin and his pen and said, 'How would you like me to make it out?'"

Summer grinned, picturing the scene.

"So the man gets all tongue-tied and he says, 'Oh, no. Thank you, but I recognized you from a picture in your daughter's foyer, and I just wanted to introduce myself.' You should have seen the disappointed look on Dad's face! I asked him to join us, and after he sat down, I said to him, 'So, how do you know our girl?' And he says to me, 'I don't really *know* her. We only just met, through the boy who lives next door to her.'

And I said, 'Alex? He's just *the* sweetest boy!' And he says—"

Maybe it had been a mistake to ask her not to leave out any of the details. At this rate, they'd be here till dawn. What Summer really wanted to know was if Zach had sweet-talked her parents into revealing details about her past. And if so, how many secrets had they shared?

"I hope he didn't make you guys too uncomfortable, prying into my past."

"Oh, he didn't pry, honey. In fact, the only question he asked the whole time we talked was whether or not you're our daughter."

The whole time? How long had they talked?

The teakettle rattled, and Summer jumped up to turn it off before the whistle woke her dad. She filled two mugs with water then plopped a special-brew tea bag into each.

"You'll love this stuff," she said, pushing the sugar bowl closer to her mother's cup. "So tell me, how long did you guys visit with Zach?"

Susannah added a spoonful of sugar to her mug. "Fifteen, twenty minutes, maybe," she said, stirring.

Summer tensed. *Good grief. As fast as Mom talks, that was more than enough time to tell him my whole life story!* Though why he'd want to listen was anybody's guess.

"He said you're considering one of his self-defense classes?"

"I've given it a little thought."

"I hope you'll do more than think about it. Seems like a two-birds-with-one-stone solution for your problems."

Problems, plural? Summer resisted the urge to sigh.

"I mean, think about it, honey. You'd get some good exercise for your poor leg, a reason to get out of the house a couple times a week and you'd learn a few moves that will give you back some of your old confidence."

A couple times a week? Summer needed to re-read the brochure because she would have sworn the classes were weekly. No. She wasn't ready to commit to *two* days out of the house.

"And what a treat it'll be, taking lessons from that gorgeous man." Susannah held up a hand. "But lest you think I'm being shallow, all hung up on outward appearances, you should know that Dad and I talked about him all the way home from town. Zach is quite the impressive guy."

As Rose had done earlier, her mom began counting on her fingers.

"He's patriotic—you don't spend that many years in a marine uniform if you aren't—and hardworking. He's thoughtful, and he keeps in close touch with his family. And from the way he talks about Alex, it's clear that he adores children. Really, what's not to like!" Winking, she nudged Summer's shoulder. "Who knows? If you meet him halfway, he could be 'the one.'"

Why did everything her mom said have to sound like a movie plot? Didn't she realize that not every ending was a happy one?

Susannah took a sip of her tea. "Oh, my. You were right, honey. This stuff is delicious!" She put down her mug. "Do you know what else Zach is? He's considerate, that's what. When he heard how difficult it is for us to spend so much time away from you, he offered to keep an eye on you for us. You know, while we're in Maryland. He's a doll. A real sweetheart, I tell you!"

Yes, she'd hesitated about going outside to deliver Alex's cookies. But surely he hadn't seen that as reason enough to babysit her. If things kept up this way, she'd need note cards to deliver the speech she intended to make next time she saw him.

"Yeah. A real sweetheart, all right," she said under her breath.

"What's that, honey?"

Summer didn't reply. Instead, she feigned a yawn and put her mug in the sink. "Well, I'm beat. Think I'll turn in." She gave her mother a hug. "See you in the morning."

"Sweet dreams, honey."

Something told Summer that her dreams would be anything but sweet tonight.

And she was right. After hours of tossing and turning, she got up and wandered from window to window, peering out at the silent street. Light poured from the house directly across the way. To its left, a dim glow lit an upstairs room. In the next house, the colorful strobes of a TV flickered from downstairs. It was strangely comforting to know she wasn't the only one up at this ungodly hour.

A glance at the clock made her spine stiffen. Fifteen hours from now, she'd drive into Vail for the first time in months, and sign up for a lesson at Marshall Law.

Either that, or she'd make the difficult phone call to apologize for not showing up.

CHAPTER EIGHT

ZACH HAD EXPECTED Summer to bail tonight, but there she sat in a black jogging suit, filling out an enrollment form.

"She doesn't look very happy," Alex whispered. "I hope that doesn't mean she's thinking about changing her mind."

Zach had to agree, and wondered which question caused the worry lines to form on her forehead. Then it hit him: question six. The one that asked potential students to explain how a self-defense course might benefit them.

She crossed her ankles and sighed.

"You think she bought those sneakers just for class?"

Alex shook his head. "Nah. I told her socks or bare feet to protect the mats. Those just look new 'cause she hardly ever wears them."

As if on cue, she planted those bright pink shoes on the floor and limped toward them.

"Do you have a schedule?" she asked, putting the clipboard on the reception counter. "So I can choose classes?"

Alex piped up with, "Not much to choose from, Summer. We only do beginners classes on Monday evenings. Wednesdays are for intermediates, experts on Fridays. All the other slots are for private lessons, or people who want to come in and practice moves in front of the big mirrors." He looked up at Zach. "Right, boss?"

Zach winked. "Right."

Summer sighed again. "That's too bad. I'm only free on Thursdays."

Alex got the joke right away and burst out laughing. "You had me going there for a minute."

Zach figured it out, too. It was good to see that the brute who'd attacked her hadn't taken her sense of humor, too.

He nodded toward her outfit. "I hope you didn't go to a lot of expense, because tonight is mostly orientation. Workout clothes won't be necessary."

"Oh." She looked down at her track suit then exhaled. "You mean to say I got all decked out like a ninja wannabe for nothing?"

Grinning, Zach picked up the clipboard and scanned her enrollment form. "I see you haven't filled in the box for number of lessons."

"That's right," she said, meeting his steady gaze blink for blink.

After learning her history, Zach thought he understood what it had taken for her to get here.

He also believed that if he pushed too hard, she might leave tonight and never come back.

"The first night is free, so you'll have time to make up your mind."

He faced Alex again. "Is everybody signed up?"

Alex removed Summer's form from the clipboard and added it to those on the counter. "They are now."

"Then why don't you corral them into the meeting room and get the PowerPoint presentation ready."

"I'm on it, boss."

Once he was out of earshot, Zach focused on Summer. "I want you to know how much I admire you. I know it wasn't easy, coming here tonight."

"Oh, it was easier than you think." She laughed softly. "My folks are in town—as you well know—and although I love them to pieces, they're driving me a little crazy. It was almost a relief, having a valid excuse to get out of the house."

Almost? "Well, whatever the reason, I'm glad you're here, and I know Alex is, too."

"You can add my parents to the list because they've been after me to do something like this for ages. But then, you already know that, since you three—"

Summer stopped talking when a young woman joined them.

"Hi," she said, extending her hand. "I'm Emma."

Zach watched as the women exchanged friendly introductions. Was he imagining things, or did Summer seem disappointed when Emma announced that *she'd* be her instructor?

"So how long have you been in Vail?" Emma wanted to know.

"Two years, give or take a week."

Emma looked surprised. "Wow, really? You'd think I would have run into you sometime. I need to get out more!" She chuckled then added, "You're okay with this being an all-girl class?"

Summer nodded, and Emma turned to Zach. "Does she have a locker and everything?"

"Not yet. But if you have a few minutes, you could help her get squared away."

Instantly, Summer tensed.

"What's wrong?" Emma asked. "Did Alex forget to tell you to bring a padlock? Don't give it another thought. I always keep a few extras on hand. You're welcome to borrow one until you get your own."

Summer glanced at the exit, and Zach sensed that Summer hadn't gotten all fidgety and stiff because she was worried about her gear. Rather, faced with the reality of self-defense classes—

and the event that had inspired her to take them—it was more likely that Summer was calculating the time it would take to escape.

Emma took a step away from the counter. "I'll grab one, and when you've finished up here, bring your stuff and meet me in the locker room."

Summer tore her gaze from the exit to smile at Emma. She nodded, too, but something told Zach she hadn't heard half of what the other instructor said.

"Once we get you settled," Emma continued, "we'll head into the meeting room for Zach's, ah, *lecture*." Grinning, she started walking backward. "You don't fall asleep easily, do you, Summer?"

"No."

"That's good. 'Cause once this guy starts talking about the principles of women's self-defense, it's tough to stop him."

Summer draped her jacket over one arm, slung her purse strap over the opposite shoulder and let out a shaky breath.

"Your lessons with Emma will be a lot of things," Zach said as she passed by, "but boring won't be one of them."

She responded with a tiny smile and fell into step beside Emma. Zach had a feeling that Emma wouldn't be bored teaching her, either.

Had he ever felt more conflicted about a person? Not that he could recall. What she'd gone through had been awful, he wouldn't deny that. But she'd already wasted two years babying herself. He had no intention of encouraging her to keep traveling down Poor Summer Lane.

Amused by his little pun, Zach opened a drawer and removed his presentation notes. He thought of his younger sister. How could two women of the same age have such vastly different reactions to a similar, horrible event? After her attack, Libby put in long, grueling hours at work. When he asked why she pushed herself so hard, she'd said, "So that when I finally climb into bed, I'm too dog-tired to have nightmares." And Zach had always coped with tragedy in exactly the same way.

The old "walk a mile in my shoes" adage surfaced in his mind, followed by "different strokes for different folks." He had no idea what it was like to be in Summer's shoes, so what business did he have hypothesizing how she should react to her trauma?

"All set," Alex announced. "Laptop's ready, and I gave everybody a notepad and a pen."

"Good job, kiddo." He gave the boy's shoulder a fatherly squeeze. "Don't know what I'd do without you."

Emma breezed into the room with Summer close on her heels.

Zach did a quick head count. Eleven—if his star pupil didn't quit. It wasn't likely that any of them shared Summer's background. He hoped not. They ranged in age from thirty to sixty-five, and all appeared to be in reasonable physical condition.

Taking his place front and center, he raised a hand and got things started by asking the students to introduce themselves. Two nurses, four teachers, a lawyer, a housewife, a few office staffers...and Summer. When they finished, he signaled Alex, who lowered the lights and stood beside the laptop.

"We don't stand on ceremony here," Zach began, "so if you have questions, ask them."

A list appeared on the screen.

The Basics:

Wear comfortable clothes.

Wear thick socks (unless you prefer bare feet).

Arrive 5-10 minutes early to stow personal items.

No perfume. Some students are allergic.

Sessions Will Begin Promptly.

"If you don't already have one, we'll rent you a padlock for your locker, where you *will* leave your cell phones and jewelry. Absolutely no exceptions. We'll also provide towels and bottled water, but you might want to bring some throat lozenges, because we do a lot of yelling in here."

"No kidding," Alex said, snickering.

Grinning at his sidekick, Zach continued. "But no gum or lozenges while we're working out. Not only are they a choking hazard, we don't need things sticking to the mats."

He pointed at the screen. "Pay particular attention to the *no perfume* rule, because it impacts proper breathing." He looked at each student in turn. "Any questions so far?"

Zach didn't let his gaze linger on Summer, even though he wanted to; she was the prettiest woman in the group. But he couldn't take the chance that the others might mistake his attention for favoritism.

"Emma here will be your instructor. But I'll make frequent visits to every class." He stood at attention. "For those of you who don't already know, I'm a former marine lieutenant. Which means I will not waste your time—or mine— candy-coating things. If you're not working to potential, believe me. You. Will. Know."

He gave them a moment to let that sink in, more than long enough to notice that Summer was the only student who wasn't fidgeting. Zach didn't know what to make of that. He also noticed that she'd moved to the back of the room... and closer to the door.

"We'll start every session with drills. Strength training designed to build your endurance. Squats, deadlifts, crunches, sit-ups, weight exercises for your arms. Three sets of fifteen reps to begin, with short rest periods in between. I expect you to do these workouts at home, too, at least three times a week, because we're shooting for fifty before the last class." Zach met every woman's eyes again. "You're probably thinking, 'I didn't sign up for an aerobics class, so what's with all the exercises?'"

He signaled at Alex, whose deft fingers flew over the keyboard. Now, in place of the basics list, a dark, menacing image appeared: a masked man stalking an average-looking woman, who wore her hair in a ponytail. In his peripheral vision, Zach noticed that Summer had shaded her eyes.

Alex hit play, and the video began, proving just how little time it could take an attacker to subdue an unsuspecting woman. The clip lasted less than fifteen seconds, and in that short window, the masked man grabbed the woman's ponytail and jerked her to the ground. Alex paused on the guy's raised fist...and the terrified woman's face.

"*This* is why I will insist that you exercise, hard. You just saw for yourself that it only takes seconds for someone to take full control of you.

An attack can be fast and explosive, meaning your reactions have to be fast and explosive, too. If your legs won't hold you up, the opponent can take you down in a heartbeat. If your arm muscles are weak, every strike you attempt will do more harm to you than to him. If he tries to subdue you with a punch to your midsection—" he pounded a fist into his open palm "—you had better have a strong core."

Now Summer sat, eyes closed and head down. Was she asking herself if she could have mitigated the severity of her assault, had she been more fit?

"I'm already doing cardio," said one of the students.

"That's great," Zach said. "And we'll soon find out if you're doing *enough*."

He waited to see if anyone else would try to get out of the exercises. No one spoke up, so he continued. "In just a few minutes, you'll find out why self-defense workouts are different from other programs you've tried. Yeah, your cardiovascular system will appreciate them, and yes, they'll tone muscle and trim fat. But here, the objective isn't to make you look good. It's to make sure you can defend yourself if that—" he pointed at the frightening image on the screen "—happens to you. Our goal is to keep you safe…and *alive*."

Cardio-woman sighed.

"I think now you see why we don't accept enrollment fees on the first night." Whispers floated around the room as Zach added, "It's time for you to ask yourself the tough questions, and decide whether or not to commit to improving your self-defense skills." He crossed both arms over his chest and planted his feet shoulder-width apart. "If you believe you're physically fit enough to prevent that on your own…" Again, he gestured toward the screen. "There's the door."

Alex hit a button, and the frightening video disappeared. As he closed the laptop, Emma stood up.

"Will those of you who are staying please follow me to the workout room?" she said.

Now the only sound in the room was the quiet rustle of women rising from their chairs and moving toward the door. Zach wasn't sure if Summer would follow Emma, but at least she was on her feet.

Halfway down the hall, Emma said over her shoulder, "So who's ready to learn how to stand like a boxer?"

Normally, this was when Zach would excuse himself to sort paperwork or go through the checkbook. But when he saw Summer take a deep breath, as if summoning strength before following the others, he fell into step beside her at the back of the line.

"How you doing?" he whispered.

She looked up at him, just long enough for him to read uncertainty—and maybe a little dread—on her face.

"I'm okay."

But she wasn't, and it showed in her stance, her shaky voice and her big dark eyes. He wanted to promise her that armed with some basic skills, she'd be safe from now on. Instead, he nodded and slowed his pace, and as she caught up with the others, Zach knew it was a promise he couldn't keep. Despite protective gear and weapons, he hadn't been able to save all of his men from harm in mine-strewn Afghanistan.

He stood in the hall, hands pocketed and shoulders slumped as Emma demonstrated the fighting stance, knees bent, elbows tucked to the sides, fists at cheek level, shoulders slightly forward. Next, she went through the essential moves: the jab, cross, hook, uppercut. Then the roundhouse, and inside, front and side kicks. She concluded with a spinning leg kick that produced gasps and a smattering of admiring applause.

When Emma first came to Marshall Law, she'd been a flighty young woman, sporting a black eye and a swollen lip. "You need to teach me how to defend myself against my brothers,"

she'd said. Four brothers, to be exact, all rough
and rowdy and raised by an equally tough wid-
ower who apparently didn't have the time or mo-
tivation to teach his boys the fundamentals of
chivalry.

But look at her now. Pride swelled his chest
as Emma stood, poised and self-assured, telling
her students that in addition to the conditioning
exercises, they must maintain a balanced diet,
drink lots of water and get plenty of sleep.

"You've probably all signed up for these workshops for different reasons," she was saying. "But
me? I'm only here for *one* reason—to make sure
that when this session ends, you'll have what you
need to defend yourself if, God forbid, you get
into a bad situation."

Knowing that she had things well under control, Zach headed for the reception desk. Alex
was already there, entering student data into the
system.

"How many do you think we'll lose tonight,
boss?"

"One, maybe two. From what I could see,
Emma had their full attention."

"Yeah. Hard not to like Emma." He hopped
up on the stool behind the counter. "You think
Summer will be the one who leaves?"

The decision to make the trip into town had
taken guts. Did she have more courage to spare,

or had she exhausted the supply, showing up tonight?

"I sure hope not," Zach said, meaning every word. "For her sake."

CHAPTER NINE

ZACH'S MEETING WITH the manager of the Arrabelle at Vail Square ran longer than expected. He wasn't at all sure that he wanted to branch out, offering self-defense workshops in the resort's fitness center, especially after hearing the classes would only be offered on an as-needed basis to guests who signed up in advance. It meant being away from the studio and schlepping his gear back and forth, who knew how many times a week.

His stomach growled, a reminder that he'd skipped breakfast. He walked up to the hostess stand.

Nearby, high-pitched laughter caught his attention as a pretty young blonde said, "Just one for lunch today?"

Unless he was mistaken, the woman laughing was Susannah Lane. Today, she looked far more like the picture on Summer's foyer table. Beside her, Harrison tucked a handful of sugar packets into his shirt pocket. And across from them, Summer.

"Yeah. Just one," he said, wondering how her folks had managed to talk her into lunch in town.

"Follow me," the hostess said, grabbing a menu emblazoned with t2 for Tavern on the Square. Clever, Zach thought, glancing at the logo.

He stopped when he reached the Lanes' table.

Susannah smiled and so did Harrison. Summer...Zach couldn't describe the expression on her face.

"Sorry," her dad said, "but I'm horrible with names."

"Zach." He offered his hand, and as Harrison shook it, he focused on Summer. "Didn't mean to intrude. Just stopped by to ask how you're feeling, after a night to think about the classes."

"Don't worry, I won't quit." She opened her menu. "Yet."

Susannah pointed at the empty chair across from hers. "You aren't intruding. Please, won't you join us?"

Harrison gave a nod of approval, and the hostess placed Zach's menu on the table. He'd barely seated himself when a waiter stepped up, took their drink orders and hurried away.

"I can't thank you enough for talking Summer into signing up for your class."

"I didn't talk her into it. She came of her own volition."

Summer closed the menu and folded her hands on top of it. Without turning toward her, Zach couldn't see her face. But something told him she liked his answer.

"You'll deal with her exactly as you will the other students, right?" her father asked. "Because her ego is already fragile enough. If you single her out, give her preferential treatment, it'll reinforce her opinion that everyone thinks she's a tragic little charity case."

"Dad! I've never thought of myself as a—"

"You should know that I've never singled out a student, Mr. Lane, and see no reason to start with your daughter." He risked a quick glance, just long enough to see that he'd been correct: Summer appreciated his attitude.

"Please, none of that Mr. and Mrs. stuff. It's Susannah, and this is Harrison."

The waiter delivered iced tea and a dish of sliced lemons, then he took their orders and disappeared much too soon for Zach's taste. The Lanes pummeled him with questions about his family, his educational background, how he'd acquired his self-defense training. By the time their food arrived, he'd shared all he cared to, and decided to turn the tables.

"So tell me, Summer," he began. "How did you get into voice-over work?"

"She auditioned for a part in a play," Susannah answered for her daughter. "But the director wanted a bigger, more robust girl for the part."

"He liked her voice, though," Harrison added, "so he hired her as the narrator."

Summer had folded her napkin into an accordion shape. She smoothed it, then rolled it into a tube. "Oh, yes. And be sure to tell him all about the very important man," she said. Either Susannah didn't know sarcasm when she heard it, or chose to ignore Summer's indignant tone. Now Zach understood her comment from last night, about needing to get out of the house for a few hours.

The important man, according to her mother, owned an advertising firm that produced TV and radio commercials for the Baltimore and Washington, DC, markets. After the show, he met with Summer backstage to set up an interview. "And you know what they say," she added, laughing, "about one thing leading to another."

Harrison jumped in. "Our agent used the tapes to arrange auditions for the national market, and soon Summer was competing with some major players."

"More often than not," Susannah added, "Summer got the work."

"Because I was more affordable."

"Only in the beginning," Harrison corrected. "You should have seen her back then. Our little social butterfly!" Susannah gushed. "She dated CEOs and musicians, went to parties nearly every weekend. She was on the go so much that we barely saw her! And then..." A shaky sigh punctuated her statement.

Harrison shook his head and picked up where she'd left off. "And then that monster—"

"I'm sure Zach doesn't want to hear all the gory details." Summer daintily spread her napkin across her lap, then turned to face him. "Did you hear the latest weather report? They say it's going to snow."

"Yeah, I think I did hear something about that."

While her parents debated how many inches would fall, Zach's admiration for Summer rose another degree. She could have changed the subject with an outburst or by leaving the restaurant instead of the classy, respectful way she'd handled things. Zach made a mental note to admit it to her...when her folks weren't around.

His curiosity rose a notch, too, as he wondered what she'd meant by "all the gory details."

"So tell me, Zach, what kind of student do you think Summer will be?"

He met her father's eyes. "I haven't had a chance to evaluate her capabilities," he said, choosing his words carefully. "But I have a feeling she'll do well."

"And you say that in a strictly professional capacity?"

"Dad! You're *this* close to spoiling my appetite!"

"Sorry, honey." Eyes on Zach again, he added, "Just looking out for my daughter."

"I understand." And he did…more or less. In Harrison's shoes, Zach would probably feel protective of her, too. Heck, he wasn't even related to Summer and *he* felt protective of her!

"Oh, now look what you've done, Harry. You've made the poor man blush." Susannah patted Zach's hand. "Don't pay him any mind. He means well, even if he is a bit of a social klutz."

Zach noticed that Summer's knees were now pointed toward the exit. He felt a little like bolting, too. What would she say if he suggested they leave, together?

"So, Zach," Harrison said, "you never answered my question."

He glanced at his watch then met her father's eyes.

"*Is* your interest in Summer purely business?"

Now Summer buried her face in her hands, and he heard her whisper, "I should have said no. Should have said *no*."

He opened his mouth, fully intending to tell the truth. She was his student, and he would make sure she got her money's worth from every lesson and then some, precisely what he'd given every student since opening Marshall Law.

But Summer beat him to it. She tossed her napkin onto the table. "You know, I'm not the least bit hungry. And ditz that I am, I think I left the iron turned on." After rooting around in her purse, she placed a twenty dollar bill on the table. "That should cover the cost of a taxi to get you two back to the town house." She met Zach's eyes. "Sorry," she said, then left in such a hurry that she forgot her jacket on the back of her chair.

He considered using it as an excuse to go after her. But that would only put her in the position of apologizing again, and if that self-conscious look on her face was any indicator, she already felt embarrassed enough.

Harrison leaned both elbows on the table. "This has been an eventful couple of days for her—first getting out of the house to attend your class, then lunch with us…and running into you."

"My thoughts, exactly." Diplomacy had never been his strongest trait, but Zach decided not to tell the man what *else* he'd been thinking.

"Ah, here's our waiter," Susannah said. "Can you bring us a doggie bag for our daughter's meal? She had to leave, I'm afraid."

"Of course. Can I get you anything else?"

"No," Harrison said with a dismissive wave, "we're fine."

Fine? That isn't the way Zach would describe them. He'd sensed that Summer didn't need or want his pity, but she had it…for reasons that had nothing to do with the attack.

"Make that two doggie bags," he said, and once the young man was out of earshot, he tapped his watch. "Just noticed the time. Crazy schedule. And it's payday at the studio." He shrugged and hoped they wouldn't ask for details.

"We understand. And I wonder if we could ask you to do us a favor." A favor. Involving Summer, no doubt.

"If I can…"

"Can we rely on you to let us know if Summer's, ah, if her situation changes? I mean, she's finally getting out of the house. Meeting new people. Doing things. And while that's all well and good, I know my daughter. It's entirely possible that she'll slip back into old habits. Bad habits. So if you notice anything to indicate she's backsliding, will you tell us?"

"I'm afraid not, Mr. Lane. Summer may well have a few unresolved issues, but she's an adult. While I understand your concern, you need to know that if she ever decides to confide in me, I won't violate her trust."

A moment of uncomfortable silence passed before Harrison said, "Well, I appreciate your honesty."

Zach rose slowly. "It was good talking with you again," he said, shaking his hand, then his wife's. He tucked a twenty dollar bill under the lip of his plate, invited them to bring home his meal and wished them a safe trip.

THAT EVENING, ZACH was still mulling over lunch with the Lanes when Libby let herself into his apartment.

"Rats," she said, slamming the door. "I was hoping you'd be asleep, so I could pour cold water on your head."

It had been the last prank he'd played on her the morning she left for college. "Sorry," he said, ruffling her hair, "looks like you'll have to get your revenge another time."

She helped herself to a slice of cold pizza and flopped onto the couch. "I can't believe you still don't have any artwork on your walls. Honestly, Zach, how can you stand being surrounded by all this stark *white*?"

"Hey, I make my bed every day. What more do I need?"

Libby rolled her eyes. "How about some color, for starters. And a few personal touches." She shook her head. "I'll bet you brush your teeth with a clear toothbrush!"

"For your information, it's green." That made

him grin because—like his comb and brush—it was *see-through* green.

"Wait. You make your bed? Every day? Why? You aren't in the marines anymore. And besides, you're just gonna get right back in and mess it up again!"

"Old routines are hard to change." Zach faked a scowl. "Now eat your pizza, will you, and let me enjoy the movie."

Libby was quiet, and for a minute there, Zach thought the action on the TV screen had engaged her.

"What is it with you and cowboy flicks, any-way? Snorting horses and trail dust and toothless dudes spitting tobacco…" She grimaced. "A ra-tional person would think you got enough guns and explosions in Afghanistan to last a lifetime."

It hadn't been easy, learning to divert his thoughts from those harrowing years overseas, and Zach didn't appreciate the reminders. He cut Libby a quick glare and hoped it would be enough to put her on another track.

Thankfully, it was.

"Okay. Out with it. What's wrong with you?" she asked.

If they were twins, that might explain her un-canny knack for reading his moods—even those he tried to mask. The seven-year age difference had never stopped her from bossing him around, as if she were the older sibling. Most of the time, Zach didn't mind that a bit.

This was not one of those times. He hadn't yet figured out how he felt about his conversation with Summer and her parents, so how was he supposed to explain it to Libby?

"Your meeting at the resort fell flat, huh?"

"No, I haven't made a decision about that yet."

"I don't blame you for being apprehensive. Sounds like a lot of time and effort, with no guarantee that the classes will increase your income." She paused to sip her soda. "Then again, you could look at it as free advertising."

"Which I'd have to pay for in other ways. Might be worth it, if the folks who enrolled were local instead of tourists, but with out-of-towners, I wouldn't be able to count on return business."

"Still, word of mouth, right? When Mrs. Smith gets home from vacation, she tells her boss how much she learned from you, and when he visits Vail, he signs up then tells Mr. Green what a great teacher you are, and—" Libby bristled slightly under his impatient gaze. "You know, with a look like that, you could make pickles without so much as a flake of dill." Frowning, she added, "It isn't my fault that you're falling for her."

"Falling? What are you talking about?"

"Summer Lane." She giggled. "Summer Lane.

What a name! I'll just bet her parents lived in a commune—on Summer Lane—when she was conceived."

"You're hilarious, but dead wrong. I'm not falling for her."

"I could take that to mean you've already fallen."

"Take it any way you like. She has way too many issues, and I don't have the training or the patience to deal with them."

If he'd learned anything from the Martha fiasco, it was that getting caught up in someone else's problems could cost him. A lot.

"Uh-huh."

She had that look in her eye. He wouldn't put it past her to unscrew the shade from the overhead light and launch into a one-woman version of good-cop, bad-cop. To divert her, Zach told her about how her parents had thoroughly embarrassed her today—omitting the part about Summer leaving early. He told her that the last time he'd run into them, they told him that Summer's attacker had held her captive for hours. "I can't put it out of my mind."

"What!" Libby put down her pizza and crossed the room. "How did she get away?" she asked, sitting on the arm of his recliner.

"Don't know. Frankly, I wish her folks hadn't told me."

Libby got quiet, really quiet, no doubt reliving moments from her own nightmare. Then she sighed. "Loving someone like her won't be easy, you know, especially for someone like you."

"Someone like me?"

"With a rabid case of KISAS."

"If this isn't an example of the pot calling the kettle black, I don't know what is."

Libby must have known better than to pursue that line of thought. A good thing, because Zach had no desire to remind her that she'd left a trail of confused and disillusioned boyfriends in her wake in the past two years.

"What makes you think love has anything to do with it?" he asked instead.

Libby sang a few bars of "What's Love Got to Do with It," and when she saw that he wasn't amused, she said, "Because you're predictable. You might not be in love with her yet, but you're on the verge. You're behaving exactly the way you did with Nancy and Hillary and Gabby. And let's not forget Martha—"

"Bah," Zach cut in. "Ancient history." He didn't like being reminded that he had absolutely no talent for picking women. Women who were good for him, anyway. And since Libby had helped put him back together after each breakup, she knew that better than anyone. Still, was she *trying* to depress him?

"I've never even met the girl," she said, "but I know her type."

Sometimes, she could be such a know-it-all. But Zach was determined not to let her know she was right. "Remember when I was in that garage band in high school?"

"Yeah, I do." She smiled dreamily. "I had the biggest crush on your drummer. Barry. No, Bobby. Or was it—"

"Yeah. It's easy to see that you really had it bad for *Billy*," he teased. "But okay, remember when we performed at an assembly, and the principal made him paint over that sign on his bass drum?"

"You guys graduated years ahead of me, so I remember the after, but none of the before. What did his drum say, originally?"

"'Nobody likes a smart—'"

She held up a hand. "Message sent and received. But I'll bet you dinner and dessert at the Left Bank that I can describe this Summer person almost to a T."

"There's no way I'm risking fifty bucks per entrée just to prove a point."

"Oh, no. You're not getting off that easily." Libby stared at the ceiling and started her list. "She's smart—probably a nurse or a teacher before the, ah, *event*. Blond. Blue-eyed. Five-six or five-seven, with a figure like a model. She

doesn't talk much, but she used to until, the...
thing." Libby shrugged. "She used to love jewelry, too, only now she doesn't wear much, because she hates calling attention to herself." She
met his eyes, and looking very pleased with herself, said, "Well? How'd I do?"

Summer was intelligent, and she didn't waste
much time on idle chitchat. And except for small
gold hoop earrings and a wide silver band on
each ring finger, she wore no jewelry. It wasn't
likely Libby and Summer would ever meet—if
he had anything to say about it—so Zach saw no
point in refuting her evaluation. But if they did
cross paths, it might be fun to watch his smart
aleck sister eat a big wedge of humble pie when
she realized how wrong she'd been about everything else.

Libby sat quietly for a moment then slid an
arm across his shoulders. "She's kind of the reason I stopped by."

"Who?"

She looked at him as if he'd grown a big hairy
mole on his forehead.

"Oh. Right." He grinned. "Her."

"You're impossible," she said. "So *any*way, I
have this idea..."

Zach groaned. "Uh-oh."

"From what I've gathered, she isn't the type
who'll see me on a professional basis. So...

what if the mountain went to Mohammad, so to speak?"

He snorted.

"No, really. I could find some reason to show up at Marshall Law, maybe—"

"She's a beginner, and you have nearly two years under your belt."

"Not to take classes, you big goof. Maybe I can get her to open up, unofficially."

"How do you know she isn't already seeing a shrink?"

She groaned. "If I told you once, I told you a hundred times. People in my line of work find the term *shrink* insulting. Will you ever get that through your thick marine head?"

It was his turn to shrug. "Probably not, because it makes sense to me. People come to you with big problems, and you shrink 'em. What's insulting about that?"

Either she was too busy stuffing her face with pizza to hear him, or she chose to ignore his analogy.

"Seems to me your Summer needs a friend. Someone she can trust. Someone to confide in. And to be honest, I could use a friend, too."

"She isn't *my* Summer."

"Yet." She smirked. "But you wish she was. I can tell."

"Stop acting like my sister and start behaving like a professional. What you're proposing is worse than dumb, it's unethical."

Libby finished her soda and put on her coat. "Thanks for supper," she said, and jogged down the stairs.

When the door slammed behind her, Zach knew he'd struck a nerve. She'd been mad at him before, and he'd been mad at her, too. In a day or two, she'd cool off, and things would go back to normal.

In the meantime, he'd enjoy the nag-free peace and quiet.

And he wouldn't have to worry that she'd go prying into Summer's past.

CHAPTER TEN

OF ALL THE photos and artwork decorating her walls, Summer liked the plaque from Justin best. He'd given it to her on the day her surgeon and orthopedist released her from the rehab center. Until very recently, the meaning of Emerson's quote, floating on a watercolor painting of the unending sea, had escaped her. "Do the thing you fear," the calligraphy read, "and the death of fear is certain."

All those months, it had hung amid similar Emerson writings, some from her parents, others she'd purchased for herself. "He who is not every day conquering some fear has not learned the secret of life."

"When it is darkest, men see the stars."

"Always do what you are afraid to do." And, all those months, she'd walked past them, barely giving the words a cursory glance, even when dusting their ebony frames. Susannah stepped up behind her. "Honey, I don't believe I've seen you look this happy in months, and I have to admit, it's a sight for sore eyes."

Summer continued facing the wall and shrugged. It was sad, really, that her own mother couldn't tell when she was faking. Every moment away from the house—two Marshall Law classes, lunch with her folks, dessert delivery next door to the Petersons—had been terrifying, and with each return, she vowed never to go out again. It hadn't been easy, but she'd tamped down the fear, telling herself it would get easier with time. It had not. As a kid, she'd hated brushing and flossing, but her do-the-right-thing gene compelled her to get it done, push through the fear. Maybe in time, going out would become a habit, too.

Her grandfather loved to say things like "It is what it is" and "A leopard can't change his spots." Without realizing it, he'd prepared her for moments like these, when disappointment hurt so bad she just wanted to cry.

"I have all the fixings for made-from-scratch cocoa," Summer said, forcing cheer into her voice. "How about I fix a mug for each you and dad and me?"

"I'd love some, but your dad just left to go skiing with our agent."

"He did? For a guy his size, Dad moves like a cat, doesn't he? We'll have to put a bell around his neck," Summer said, walking beside her mom into the kitchen. She began assembling the ingredients. "I'm guessing Marty has another audition set up for you guys?"

"Just for Dad this time, but not until after the film festival. Soon as it's over, we'll drive back to the Baltimore airport and head straight for LA." She squealed quietly and gave Summer a sideways hug. "This could be his big chance, honey. It's not just some bit part, like we usually settle for. If he gets it, your father will have second billing. And who knows where he could go from there."

Acting had provided her parents with a respectable income, and Summer had never wanted for anything. But they hadn't reached the notoriety or salaries they dreamed of. She hoped her dad would get the part, and that it really would lead to bigger, better roles. She wondered which other actors would audition, but asking about the competition was sure to deflate her mother's buoyant mood. Instead, Summer listened while Susannah talked. Eventually, they fell into a familiar pattern of conversation, sipping marshmallow-topped cocoa, discussing their favorite movies and songs, giggling like teenagers about Hollywood's most handsome actors.

"I've really missed this, Mom."

"Me, too, honey."

"You're still the coolest mom ever." She spooned another dollop of marshmallow cream onto her cocoa. "I was the envy of every girl at Kennedy High, you know."

Susannah chuckled. "Only because they loved my taste in sweaters and shoes."

Suddenly, Susannah wasn't laughing anymore. "Honey, Dad and I have been talking…"

Summer tensed and topped off Susannah's mug with a generous portion of marshmallow. "Drink up, Mom. This stuff is guaranteed to sweeten even the sourest mood."

But her mom didn't even crack a smile. "We were very disappointed when Dr. Wolff told us you'd stopped seeing him. And so was he."

She didn't know which infuriated her more, that her mother had the audacity to feel disappointment in *her*, or that Wolff had breached their doctor-patient confidentiality agreement. It hadn't taken long to realize the guy was a quack, in it only for the $250 an hour she paid him twice a week. Based solely on a few vague symptoms—rapid heartbeat, trembling hands, trouble breathing at the thought of leaving the house— he had diagnosed her as agoraphobic. But rather than suggest that a trusted friend accompany her outside for extended periods of time, he wanted her to take antidepressants. When she refused Paxil and Prozac, citing the fact that she was *afraid*, not depressed, he wrote a prescription for Xanax. Summer never dropped it off at the pharmacy because she believed time, not a drug, was all she needed.

"Those sessions were a waste of time," she said. "For Dr. Wolff and for me."

"Your dad and I talked about that, too. We think you need someone younger. A woman, preferably. Maybe even one who specializes in treating people with your history. We'll be so far away, and if things go well for Dad, we could be gone awhile. We want to be sure you'll be all right."

Summer had given them their one shot at parenthood, and since her chances of finding someone to share her life with were slim, the least she could do was give them less to worry about.

"I'm sorry for all I've put you and Dad through these past two years."

Susannah wrapped her arms around Summer. "Oh, honey, there's no need to apologize! None of what happened was your fault. You've been so brave and so strong, and worked so hard. We're proud of how far you've come."

Susannah tucked Summer's hair behind her ears, a gesture that took her back to happier times.

"Maybe once you're settled in LA, I'll fly out there, see if Marty can line up a job or two for *me*," Summer said.

"That would be lovely. But in the meantime,

I might have found a therapist for you. I saw her name on the office door, just down the street from the self-defense studio. I looked her up on Google, and from everything I read, she seems very experienced. I wrote her name and number on the refrigerator board." She squeezed Summer's hand. "Why don't you call her, see if she has room in her schedule for another patient?"

Summer didn't like the sound of that. She held her breath and hoped for the best.

"I'm doing fine without therapy. Really."

Her mom continued as if Summer hadn't said a word. "Her bio says she specializes in treating victims of violent assault."

"Please don't think of me that way, Mom. It isn't how I see myself. I survived that night, all those operations, months of painful rehab, and I didn't need Dr. Wolff's help with any of it." She lowered her voice. "If I ever suspect that I need therapy, it'll have to be my decision and mine alone. Not yours. Not Dad's. Not the refrigerator board doctor. Okay?"

"Oh, dear. Now I've upset you. It's just that now that we've seen a glimpse of the Summer you were before that awful night, Dad and I want to make sure—"

"Mom. Stop. I'm nearly thirty. I know I haven't behaved like a grown-up in a while, but that's all behind me. You have my word—if I feel like I need outside help, I'll get it."

Susannah studied Summer's face then shrugged. "All right, I believe you. Besides, it isn't as though you're all alone here in Vail. You have Justin. And Alex and Rose."

And Zach?

The thought came from nowhere, and Summer didn't know what to make of it. He'd been pleasant enough. Respectful, too, in his no-nonsense, "once a marine, always a marine" kind of way, but...

"And Zach, too. He's such a nice guy. Made quite an impression on Dad, and you know how hard that is to do!"

Had her mom read her mind?

"You know, I think he might have a little crush on you."

"You wouldn't say that if you could see the way every woman in that class ogles him, as if he was the last chocolate truffle in the heart-shaped box. Why should he settle for a gimpy scar face like me when he could have his pick of any of them!" She laughed, mostly to prove she didn't really see herself that way.

"Summer..."

"I was kidding. *Kidding.*" She grabbed Susannah's mug and put it in the sink. "No more cocoa for you. It makes you way too sensitive."

She laughed again, but Susannah wasn't buying it, and frankly, Summer couldn't blame her.

Susannah yawned and stretched. "I think I'm going to take a little nap before supper."

Summer had never been one to nap, not even after the most grueling physical therapy workouts. "Maybe I'll lie down for a few minutes myself."

She wouldn't sleep, but in the privacy of her room, she could think about everything her mom had said, from seeing the refrigerator board doctor to Zach showing an interest in her…

…and why in the world she hoped it was true.

CHAPTER ELEVEN

A LIGHT SNOW had begun to fall, peppering Summer's coat and hair with crystalline flakes. She stepped into the studio, stomping her sneakers on the entry rug and brushing her shoulders. A perky young woman stood at the reception counter, whispering to Zach. He looked none too happy about whatever she'd said, and though Summer tried not to eavesdrop, she heard him say, "...I asked you not to..."

The door opened, interrupting the heated dialogue. A young mother and her little boy entered the reception area.

The child pointed. "Look, Mom, skeletons and witches and stuff! Awesome!"

"What a great idea," the mother said to Zach. "Decorating for Halloween. I bet all the kids will love it."

"It was Alex's idea. He gets all the credit."

"Well, it was very nice of you to let him." She gave her boy a gentle shove. "Better get into your classroom. You know Mr. Marshall doesn't like it when you're late."

The kid stood at attention, and smiling broadly, fired off a mock salute. "Luke McLean, reporting for duty, sir!"

Laughing, Zach tousled the boy's hair. "Get in there, funny man, and tell the rest of those jokers I'll be there in five." He held up a big hand, fingers spread wide.

As the boy darted off, his mom flashed Zach a coy smile. "I can't tell you how grateful I am for all you've done for my Luke."

Summer could have removed her shoes in the locker room, but curiosity made her choose one of the black-and-chrome chairs near the door.

"He's a different boy since you've been working with him. If his dad was half the man you are—"

"I like working with the kids," he said, interrupting her unconcealed flattery. "They haven't had time to develop preconceived notions about workouts, so I don't have to listen to a lot of 'but so-and-so said *this*,' and 'I read somewhere *that*…' Makes it a whole lot easier to teach them."

"Whatever your reasons," she said, eyelashes fluttering, "you're worth twice what you charge. It isn't easy for a single mom to find positive male role models, you know."

Summer stifled a groan as Zach tapped his watch.

"Guess I'd better get back there."

Though he'd smiled when he said it, Ms. Available bristled slightly.

That's when he noticed Summer, untying her other sneaker, and his face brightened. *I think he might have a little crush on you*, her mom had said.

Summer returned his smile. "Hey, Zach." It wasn't easy, but she broke eye contact and pretended to glance around the room. "The place looks great. Alex did a great job. The kids must think it's gr—"

"Great?" Luke's mother finished, giggling.

Zach frowned at the woman, but the sour look faded when he turned to Summer again.

"Alex is setting up your classroom—and doing a great job, I'm sure—so when you get back there, you can tell him yourself what a great job he did, hanging the ghosts and pumpkins." He paused and aimed a lopsided grin at her. "It's *great* to see you, by the way."

Luke's mom emitted a soft huff, buttoned her faux-fur jacket and turned on her high-heeled boots. "See you in an hour," she said, click-clacking across the linoleum.

Zach waited until the door closed behind her then fell into step beside Summer. "Hope she doesn't fall off those stilts and break her neck. Looks kinda slick out there."

The cute blonde stepped up on her other side

and held out a hand. "I'm Libby, this big oaf's sister. C'mon. I'll walk with you to the locker room."

Ah, Summer thought, the refrigerator doctor, in the flesh.

Halfway there, Zach called out, "It really is great to see you."

Why? Because he hadn't expected her to show up? Or because her mom's suspicions had been accurate?

"I half expected you to float in here on a cloud and ask where you could stow your harp and halo," Libby said, breaking Summer's train of thought. Laughing, she added, "It was smart, leaving your wings at home, Miss Amazing. I don't think they would have fit in that skinny locker."

"Amazing?" Summer laughed, too.

"Alex speaks very highly of you," Libby said, "and he isn't the only one."

Summer felt the heat of a blush creep into her cheeks and hoped Libby would blame it on the steamy warmth of showers and hair dryers in the locker room. She stowed her coat and valuables and set the padlock in place.

"We'd better get into the classroom," Libby said. "I have three classes to make up. Emma's not a former marine, but she doesn't go easy on grown-ups who miss sessions or come in late."

After a quick exchange of polite hellos around the room, Emma got busy. Summer had been tempted to skip the recommended exercises, telling herself she was already fit, thanks to the work she'd done for physical therapy. But with nothing but time on her hands, she'd performed every one, following Emma's instructions to the letter. Good thing, too, because the young woman seemed determined to put her students through their paces.

Afterward, Libby joined her at the long bank of sinks in the locker room and met Summer's eyes in the mirror. "I'm glad my brother wasn't there to see a newbie outperform me," she said with a playful elbow jab to Summer's ribs. "You're in pretty good shape!"

Why did she get the feeling there was more to the sentence. Like *...for somebody with a limp* or *...considering some guy ran you through a meat grinder.*

"I skipped supper, and I'm starving," Libby continued. "There's a great little pub walking distance from here, and Monday is ladies' night. One free glass of wine for any patron who wears a bra." She giggled. "They make the best Reuben sandwiches in town, but I can't eat a whole one all by myself..."

A pub, filled with guys, lured there by the women who showed up for free wine...all of them looking to pair up. What if some guy hit on Zach's gorgeous sister, struck out and made a move on *her*? Summer's heart beat faster just thinking about it.

"Don't worry," Libby said. "If some gorilla hits on you, I'll show him my business card and say 'You seem to have issues with women. Call me. I can help you with that.'"

Summer pictured the imaginary gorilla's reaction, and chuckled despite herself. "All right," she said. It wasn't like she had kids waiting for a bedtime story, or a dog to walk. Besides, she was hungry, too.

They strolled over to the pub, and Libby chose a tall table near the entrance. "I like to sit with my back to the door," she said, sliding out a stool.

"In case you need to make a quick getaway?"

"Heck, no! You can see the whole place from here. If you spot a gorilla who knows how to shave, you know what to do, right?"

Summer shrugged. "Send him a banana?"

"Hmm…that might just work!"

After the waitress took their order, Libby said, "I noticed the scar, and the limp. Accident?"

"Not exactly." If she told Libby the truth, would it raise ugly memories, or provide an opportunity to let off a little steam?

"If you'd rather not talk about it, no biggie." With that, Libby told Summer that she'd been attacked, years ago. Then she lifted her right pants leg, showed Summer the scars on her knee. "Could have been worse if witnesses hadn't interrupted the guy."

What could it hurt to share just a few of the details with someone who understood what she'd gone through—and survived.

"I was attacked, too."

It was shocking, really, how quickly the story poured out of her. No tears, no tremors.

Afterward, Libby studied Summer's face. "You *lived* that nightmare, and look at you, sitting there all calm and collected."

"Trust me, I was a mess at first." *Who are you kidding? You're still a mess...who learned to pretend.*

"No wonder Zach speaks so highly of you."

Neither Alex nor Rose could have told Zach about the incident because Summer had never shared any of the details with them. That left only her parents.

"Did my mother happen to call you?"

"Only to find out if I'm accepting new patients."

Eyes closed, Summer shook her head. "Why am I having trouble believing that's all she said?"

"Because you have trust issues?"

Summer chose to ignore the therapist-type remark. "My folks are actors. Laying things on thick comes naturally to them."

"No kidding."

"And I did some voice-over acting before the attack."

Libby looked confused. "Meaning..."

"Making mountains out of molehills is what we *do*."

Libby sat back as the waitress delivered their wine and a promise to return soon with their sandwiches.

When she was gone, Libby leaned in. "I spend my whole day looking into people's faces, listening to them talk about everything from the agony of being a middle child to surviving a suicide attempt. Vail is a good place for the rich and famous to get the help they need without the paparazzi finding out about it. So trust me when I say I know a sane, rational person when I see one."

Nodding, Summer sipped her wine. Libby hadn't been raped, probably hadn't been held captive, either, but she had some understanding—both personal and professional—of what Summer had been through. Only Detective Richards and her doctors could say that. Libby had nothing to gain from feigning friendship, and Summer had nothing to lose by trusting her.

The waitress delivered their food then left

them with another promise, this time to return with the dessert menu.

Summer lifted her wineglass. "To normal," she said, clinking it against Libby's.

"No! To *almost* normal." Libby took a sip. "I earn a living helping almost-normal people achieve normal." She picked up half of the sandwich. "You trying to deprive me of a means to buy Reubens and pinot grigio?" She lowered her voice and added, "If you tell my brother I said that, I'll deny it!"

The mere mention of him made her stomach flutter. Or maybe she was just hungry.

Lifting the other half of the sandwich, she said, "All right. To *almost* normal." *And to Zach*, she added silently, who had no idea he was the reason she'd taken that first important step into her future.

CHAPTER TWELVE

SUMMER'S DAD PADDED into the living room on white-socked feet.

"Hey, Summie, what're you doing up so late?"

She loved the nickname he'd given her as a toddler. Loved that no matter how many candles there were on her birthday cake, he continued using it.

"Guess I'm overstimulated from tonight's lesson. Or maybe it was the Reuben and fries I washed down with wine after class."

Harrison quirked an eyebrow. "Didn't realize food and drinks were part of the enrollment package," he said, sprawling on the couch.

Summer laughed. "Zach couldn't make much of a profit if it was. One of my classmates invited me out."

That sat him upright, fast.

"Male or female?"

"Female."

"Still…you said yes?"

She didn't blame him for seeming so shocked. It had been ages since she'd last ventured out on her own. "How could I say no? It was ladies' night at Pepi's."

"Man, I have to meet the gal who talked you into going to a crowded bar!"

"I thought you'd already heard all about refrigerator doctor."

He looked confused, but only for a second. "Ah, Dr. Marshall, the psychologist your mom's been going on and on about."

"Bingo."

Harrison frowned. "Wait till your mother hears that the incredible Dr. Marshall isn't so incredible after all. Therapy? In a bar? Over drinks?" He shook his head. "Doesn't sound ethical to me."

"It wasn't a therapy session. And I'm not a patient. Just two women with something in common, getting better acquainted over corned beef and free wine."

"I know that look," Harrison said. "You've already made up your mind not to see her again."

"Not in a doctor-patient capacity, no."

He picked up the remote and turned on the TV. "Your mother won't be very pleased to hear that. But I'm glad you're getting out, making friends. Frankly, I think you're doing terrific without a shrink." He rested crossed ankles on the coffee table. "So tell me, is it just a coincidence that her last name is Marshall? As in Zach?"

"Very funny, Dad. I know about the *other* lunch you shared with her brother. And before you leap to any Cupid-type conclusions, you should know that he isn't my instructor at Marshall Law...a woman named Emma is. So he's a father figure of sorts for Alex—which earns him points because you know how I feel about that kid—but that's it."

He aimed the clicker at the cable box and flicked through the channels. "Relax. I'm in no hurry to walk you down the aisle. Hey—a John Wayne movie. Watch it with me?"

"Sure, until I get sleepy."

He loved Westerns. Hopefully, a good, old-fashioned cowboy flick would keep his mind off the Marshall siblings and give her time to mull over the gossipy things Libby had told her about Zach.

The way he still felt partially responsible for Libby's attack, for starters. She called him borderline obsessive-compulsive, a term Harrison and Susannah had aimed at Summer. If only she could make them understand that locking herself in the house was the only way to regain control of her upside-down world. If Zach sometimes seemed obsessive, maybe it was because in his mind, letting things get out of control came at too high a cost, for him and those around him.

Her dad's voice broke into her thoughts. "You're awfully quiet."

"Because we're watching a movie."

"You've been quiet even during the commercials." He levered himself up on one elbow. "You okay?"

"Just a little sleepy is all. I'm not used to wine and food this late in the day."

"You know you can talk to me, about anything, right?"

"Yeah, I know," she said, even though the opposite was true. Both of her parents had run crying from her hospital room as she told the cops what had happened to her.

Summer had more or less been on her own for as long as she could remember. A good thing, if she viewed it from the right perspective, because it meant she'd never need anyone.

Her parents hadn't been there when she lost her first tooth, or skinned her knees falling from the pink two-wheeler Santa left under her grandfather's Christmas tree. And although she had no actual memory of it, there was photographic evidence proving that her grandparents, not her mom and dad, had taught her to walk.

Was it irony or coincidence that it had been Zach, not her father, who'd encouraged her to take one of the most important steps of her adult life?

Either way, Summer believed there was far more she could learn from the man who'd lived his whole life in service to others.

"LIBBY THOUGHT MAYBE you could conserve gas and ride together," Zach's mom was saying. "It's nothing fancy, just biscuits and stew for a few neighbors and friends."

"That'll warm their old bones," he said.

"I'll just ignore that *old* crack," she shot back. "But speaking of friends, Libby's looking forward to introducing us to her new one."

He didn't need to ask who *that* was.

"From everything your sister said, Summer sounds delightful." She paused. "Do me a favor?"

"Sure." Tucking the phone between chin and shoulder, he filed the bills he'd just paid to Valley Electric, Eagle River Water, Alpine Insurance and American Express, then picked up a pen to jot down whatever items she'd ask him to pick up on his way over.

"Libby means well, but don't let her push you into anything. I'd hate to see you settle, just because you're trying to prove something. After the Martha mess, I mean."

He'd thought she was going to ask him to pick up a bag of ice, a tub of butter, a carton of soft drinks on his way to the ranch. How was he supposed to put the "Martha mess" in the past if they kept bringing her up?

Zach groaned to himself. "I'm in no hurry, so don't worry—hey, that rhymes."

"Yes, it does. You always did like making up rhymes."

It was true…and the reason she used to call him Wordsworth.

"Summer is Libby's friend," he said. "I barely know her." Also true. "So what time's dinner on Sunday?"

"Get here at two, and we'll sit down at three, same as always, to give your cousins' kids time to get in a nap before we eat. Would you be a dear and pick up some ice on the way?"

"No problem."

After he hung up, Zach dialed Libby's number.

"Just wanted to thank you for locking me into a trip to the Double M," he said after the beep. "Since we're stuck going together, I'll drive. Be ready at twelve-thirty."

As an afterthought, he typed Summer's name into the Marshall Law computer files, and when her contact info popped up, he called her at home.

Zach cleared his throat, expecting to leave a message there, too. As he waited for the machine to pick up, he recalled that his mom had described her as delightful. Summer was that, all right, and then some. If he thought he had the temperament to cope with her trauma-induced issues, he might just ask her out. Something casual, like a movie or—

"Hi, Zach. What can I do for you?"

Gotta love that caller ID, he thought, grinning. *Gotta love that* voice *more.*

"Just talked with my mom. About dinner on Sunday? She said something about you and Libby and me, driving to Denver together. So how about I pick you up at around twelve-thirty?"

"Twelve-thirty," she echoed. "This Sunday? I, um… This is the first I've heard of it."

Zach chuckled. "Sorry, guess I jumped the gun. I figured Libby had already called you."

The pause that followed was so long that Zach thought maybe their call had been disconnected. But then he heard her sigh, and understood. She'd lived nearly two years as a recluse. She'd committed to the classes, ventured out a time or two for lunch with her folks, a quick bite to eat with Libby the other night, but as far as he knew, she hadn't left the house for any other reason.

"I realize the invite is kind of last minute, so no worries if you can't make it."

"Well, can I get back to you? My folks are leaving Sunday morning for a film festival in Maryland, but I'm not sure what time."

"Do you have my cell number?"

"No. Let me grab a pen."

He heard the phone clunk onto the counter, the sound of rustling paper and a whole lot of whispering.

"Why is it you can always find a pen or paper," Summer said when she came back on the line, "but never both?"

He could hear the smile in her voice and became vaguely aware of the similar expression on his own face. "Or you find both, but the ink's dried up in the pen."

She laughed. "Exactly!"

Zach rattled off his number and tried to think of a legitimate reason to keep her talking.

"So I hear you and Libs got together after class on Monday." It was a reach, but it would have to do.

"We did. She's quite a character, that sister of yours."

"That's putting it mildly."

If asked to make a short list of his flaws, small talk would make the top ten. *C'mon, Summer. Don't leave me hanging.* Say *something!*

"She said your parents keep horses?"

Thank you!

"Just a dozen or so."

"I haven't been riding in more than two years."

"If the weather cooperates, maybe we can change that, and I'll give you a tour of the Double M on horseback. If you can make it, that is."

He counted the seconds between his last comment and her next one.

"You know, I don't really have to be here when my folks leave. They always take a cab to the airport. I can make them a nice sendoff dinner tomorrow night. So count me in." A nervous giggle punctuated her statement. "It'll be a good excuse to dust off my cowboy boots."

She thanked him for calling and promised to be ready and waiting—outside on her front porch—at twelve-thirty sharp.

Zach put the receiver back into its cradle and saw her name, highlighted and blinking on the Marshall Law computer monitor. After saving the file, he shut down and decided to call it a day. There was a frozen pot pie upstairs in his freezer and a cold beer in the fridge, and unless he was mistaken, a Clint Eastwood movie on cable. Something told him even before he reached the top of the staircase that he wouldn't pay a bit of attention to the plot. He'd be too busy picturing Summer in jeans and boots, her short curls bouncing as she rode beside him on his favorite palomino, getting acquainted with his favorite place in the world…the Double M Ranch.

CHAPTER THIRTEEN

IT HAD BEEN hard enough letting Libby talk her into spending a night at the ranch, but when Zach explained that she'd decided to drive her own car, Summer nearly lost it. "Some mix-up in her patient schedule," he'd said. His tone told her he wasn't buying it, and frankly, neither was she.

Summer could blame her parents' lunchtime revelations for the like-strangers conversation between herself and Zach, but it wasn't their fault that she decided not to climb out of his truck while it was still parked in her driveway.

The Colorado landscape was more breathtaking than usual, thanks to an early morning storm. When they reached the western border of the family ranch, Zach pointed out a downed tree and a line of fencing in need of repair before cows and horses bearing the Double M brand found the gap and wandered onto the highway. Fondness and pride deepened his voice, and Summer hoped he'd been serious about asking her to go riding, because she couldn't wait to see more.

He parked out front and left their bags just inside the door. "Mom's probably in the kitchen," he said, leading the way.

Sure enough, his mother stood at the sink, wrist deep in sudsy dishwater.

"That crazy storm took out the power for a couple of hours," she said over one shoulder. "Put me way behind schedule."

Zach kissed her cheek. "Don't worry about it. Most everybody here is an adult. I think we can find ways to occupy ourselves until dinner's ready." He looked around. "Where's Libs?"

"In the living room, trying to beat your dad at chess."

"He's trying to beat her, you mean."

"Hmpf. Semantics."

He drew Summer closer. "Mom, this is Summer Lane. Summer, Ellen Marshall."

After drying her hands on a flowery apron, Ellen gave Summer a light hug. "Libby tells me you love horses. There's plenty of time for a ride, and I'm sure if you ask nicely, Mr. Semantics here will saddle one for you." She smiled up at Zach. "Won't you, son."

"Be happy to." He winked at Summer. "And she won't even have to ask me nicely." Then, one hand on the small of Summer's back, he led her to the back door. "It's pretty cold out there. You sure you're up for this?"

"Are you kidding? Just give me a second to change."

Ten minutes later, they walked side by side toward the corral, where half a dozen horses trotted toward the gate. Her heart rate accelerated, imagining how it would feel to sit horseback again. When they reached the fence, a Paint ambled up.

"This is Taffy," he said. "She's gentle and smart, so if you haven't been in the saddle in a while, she'll read your moves."

Summer held one hand palm up, and the horse nuzzled it. "Oh, Zach. She's absolutely beautiful." She took off one glove and stroked the silky mane, and the horse leaned into her hand. "Aw, you're like a great big calico cat, aren't you," she said, rubbing the mare's nose. "Did these brown blotches inspire your name?"

Taffy nickered then bobbed her head.

"You're right," Summer said over one shoulder. "She's even smart enough to answer questions!"

Zach opened the gate and took hold of the bridle's cheek piece. "C'mon, girl, let's get you saddled up. We're goin' for a ride."

He led Taffy into the barn, grabbed a saddle pad and draped it over the horse's back. After testing each cinch, he hoisted the saddle, grabbed the cantle and gently laid it atop the pad. He connected the cinches, let down the latigo strap, tightened the breast collar and dropped the stirrups into place. And repeated the process for his own horse, a massive black stallion named Chinook.

Summer took the reins and stood beside Taffy, hoping her damaged leg had healed enough to propel her into the saddle.

Only one way to find out.

She grabbed the saddle horn and slid her boot into the stirrup at the exact moment Zach gave her a helpful boost up.

His gentle touch inspired a moment of tension and she stiffened.

"I realize you could probably have gotten up there, all by yourself." He pointed to her injured thigh. "Your leg has come a long way, but why push it if you don't have to?"

"Thanks."

He climbed onto Chinook's back in one fluid movement, and *chk-chked* him into motion. They rode east, past weathered wood outbuildings and a row of powerful machines. Thanks to summers spent at her paternal grandfather's farm, she could name them all. First, a red-and-yellow haybine. A bale truck and baler. A harvester. An auger for drilling fence posts, a swather to expose grass throughout the winter. Then three ATVs. And all stood tiptop and shiny in a neat row.

"Looks like Nate's got some fencing to repair," Zach said, pointing north.

And sure enough, several posts tilted precariously, and the wire between them draped atop a bed of fresh snow.

He led Chinook along the fence line, and Taffy followed with no prodding from Summer.

"No tracks," he said. "That's good. Means everybody's where they oughta be."

She smiled, because unless she was imagining things, Zach's slight drawl intensified here at the Double M. It wouldn't bother her a bit to spend more time with him here, just so she could hear more of it.

A bright orange Cessna flew low overhead, drawing their attention to the cloudy sky above. The right wingtip dipped, then the left.

"That's Earl," he said, waving. He glanced over at Summer. "He's a card, but I'm guessin' Earl has single-handedly saved a couple dozen lost hikers." Zach shook his head. "Last winter, he flew so low it nearly cost him his life, but by gum, he found that 'gotta climb Pikes Peak' fool from Boston."

Summer laughed. "By gum? What are you, ninety?"

The lopsided grin made her heart skip a beat. "I turn thirty-five tomorrow. You can expect a big birthday cake will be part of today's dessert lineup."

"I had no idea. Happy birthday!"

Leaning forward, he patted Chinook's neck. "Thanks," he said then urged his horse forward.

They rode in companionable silence for a mile or so before Zach gently brought his horse to a halt. As Summer expected, Taffy stopped, too.

"I must've seen this a thousand times," he said, leaning an elbow on the saddle horn, "but I'll never get tired of it."

Summer followed his gaze to the striking vista before them, where snow-covered fields climbed the Rockies' Front Range, majestic mountain peaks kissing the heavens.

"I can see why," she whispered. "It's breathtaking."

Zach nodded. "You think that's good, just wait till you see what's next."

A light snow had been falling since they left the corral, and it left a layer of white dust on the brim of his black Stetson and on the shoulders of his well-worn leather coat. Did he know how noble he looked, sitting tall in the saddle that way?

The horses ascended a steep, snow-covered butte, stopping when they reached the top of a wide, flat batholith. Zach rested his hands on the saddle horn.

"Feast your eyes."

He hadn't exaggerated.

"When I was a kid, I came up here when life got crazy and confusing. One look out there," he said, forearm sweeping the panoramic view, "and all seemed right with the world." For a moment, he fell silent. Then Summer heard him sigh. "I've never brought anybody up here before."

Why me? Summer wondered.

"I still come up here when life gets crazy and confusing."

Though he was staring straight ahead, Summer could see the firm set of his jaw, the tautness of his lips. What memories, she wondered, had painted that serious, contemplative frown on his handsome face?

"After you got home from Afghanistan, you mean?"

He didn't answer for a long time. Then he thumbed the Stetson to the back of his head and said, "Yeah."

The one-syllable word did more than confirm her question. It told her he'd carried every worry and fear, every heartache and disappointment to this perfect, pristine spot. She hoped it gave him solace, however temporary, from his troubles.

"I could sit up here for days," he said, "just staring at the Front Range."

His arm moved left to right again, this time

naming the creeks and canyons, passes and peaks. His soft, smooth baritone put music to the identification of bristlecone pines and Englemann spruce. Clearly, he felt as much at home in this land as the pronghorns, moose and grizzlies, and she wondered why he'd ever left it to live elsewhere.

Summer swiped at a traitorous tear, hoping to destroy it before Zach noticed.

Then the hand that had introduced her to this magnificent place reached out. It surprised her that she so quickly put hers into it. Zach gave it a quick squeeze then turned her loose.

"Got somethin' in your eye?"

"Guess so," she choked out.

"It's nothing to be ashamed of. This place gets to me sometimes, too."

The snow was falling in earnest now. Zach removed his left glove and reached out again, this time to brush snowflakes from her eyelashes. His thumb lingered and slowly traced the length of her scar, his green eyes blazing into hers for what seemed an eternity. Summer hoped he wouldn't ask how she'd come by it, because she didn't want the memory to darken the moment.

He tapped the tip of her nose. "Silly city slicker," he said around a teasing grin. "You should have worn a hat."

When he put his Stetson on her head, it all but covered her eyes.

"Silly cowboy," she said, returning it, "you sure do have a big head."

He placed it firmly back on his head. Laughing, he wheeled Chinook around, and Taffy followed suit.

They started out slow, but Summer felt her horse's strength and power, and sensed that the Paint wanted to run, full tilt. Leaning forward, she sat deep in the saddle and let Taffy have her way. Trees and fields whizzed by on either side, and the snowy ground blurred underneath them. She loved the feel of the wind in her hair, and didn't even mind the icy sting as snow pelted her cheeks. Best of all, her leg didn't hurt.

When they reached the barn, both horses slowed automatically, no doubt anticipating a good brushing, a handful or two of flaked hay.

Zach reached up and plucked her out of the saddle as though she weighed no more than a sack of flour. This time, Summer didn't tense up, despite the fact that it put them face-to-face. Should she credit her surroundings, or the man himself?

He put her down gently, then grasped both horses' reins and led them inside.

"When you said you could ride, I never expected *that*," he admitted.

He loosened Taffy's belly cinch, removed the saddle and pad and draped both over a low wall inside the barn. He checked her hooves, and satisfied they were free of stones and debris, grabbed a towel.

"Let me finish this," Summer said, "so you can take care of Chinook."

He looked as if he might ask "Are you sure you know how?" Instead, he handed her the towel and got busy unsaddling the stallion.

"Where'd you learn how to groom a horse?"

"My grandfather taught me." She wrapped the towel around her hand and ran it along Taffy's withers. "I spent every summer and school break on his farm outside Baltimore. It wasn't anywhere near the size of the Double M. Just big enough that every time I went back home, I felt closed in."

"Baltimore, huh?" Zach nodded. "That explains the Orioles and Ravens magnets on your fridge. But...can you chuck hay bales?"

"Like a full-time ranch hand, and I earned the calluses to prove it." Summer found a clean spot on the towel, ran it along Taffy's back. "I can muck stalls, milk cows and slop hogs, too. And once," she added, "I helped deliver a breech calf."

"Admirable."

What an odd choice of words. Not marine-speak, and not cowboy jargon, either. She shrugged it off and traded the towel for a mane brush.

"How long will you wait to feed them?"

"First I need to ask Nate when he last fed 'em," he said, filling two heated water buckets.

"That was some workout," she mused, stroking Taffy's nose. "Maybe after dinner, we can sneak them some apple slices or carrot sticks."

"Maybe." He grinned. "And maybe we should get inside so you can peel off three of your four layers before dinner."

"And maybe I shouldn't."

"Why?"

"Because," she said as he backed Chinook into a stall, "something tells me your mom puts out quite a spread."

She watched him lead Taffy into the next stall. "Might be nice to blame my after-dinner bloat on the extra fabric."

Laughing, he made a move as if to drape an arm across her shoulders. She flinched, but only slightly, prompting him to step back. "I'm glad you could make it to our unofficial Thanksgiving dinner."

"Unofficial Thanksgiving? Libby didn't say a word about that! I thought we were having stew and biscuits."

"We are. Along with turkey, and everything

else that goes with a traditional Thanksgiving meal."

"Then I'm honored to be a part of it. But why celebrate it two weeks early?"

"It's the only way we can all be in one place at one time. Some family members have to work, and others are in college."

"But...Libby said it was just a casual dinner, for the neighbors."

"It is—most of whom are Marshalls." Summer had tossed and turned and paced on the night of his invitation, wondering how she'd survive the long drive from Vail to the ranch, wondering how she'd cope with a houseful of Marshalls... any number of whom would be men. But she felt strangely safe in Zach's company, and decided she could get through...if he stayed in her line of sight.

As he had in the kitchen earlier, he pressed a big palm to her back and opened the back door. Inside, when he removed it, Summer felt the disappointment all the way to the toes of her boots.

CHAPTER FOURTEEN

AT FIRST, ZACH hadn't been happy to hear that Libby would drive separately. "What am I supposed to talk to her about for an hour and a half?" he'd demanded. "Robinson Crusoe? Dickens's Miss Havisham? *Yoda?*"

"Maybe I'll start calling you the Hermit Crab, because every time you're forced out of your comfort zone, you get all mean and grumpy."

After scolding him for assuming the worst, yet again, Libby shrewdly pointed out that being alone with Summer during the drive might help him decide how he really felt about her. His sister had been right again, and he wasn't too happy about that, either. Because now, in place of comfortable ambivalence toward Summer, Zach was forced to acknowledge admiration. Instead of cowering near the passenger door, as he'd expected her to, Summer raised questions about the landscape, and shook her fist at a couple of inconsiderate drivers. When he'd popped a CD into the stereo, she'd belted out the chorus to "November Rain." She had a surprisingly good voice, and turned out to be surprisingly good company, too.

As he watched her pleasant interaction with his mom, then Taffy, Zach added *charming* to the "Things About Summer" list he'd started compiling on day one. When he witnessed her awe-struck reaction to his favorite place, he realized the pluses far outweighed the minuses.

With awareness came uncertainty, because he'd been working hard *not* to like her. At least, not as anyone more than a casual acquaintance. Why, then, were those old troublesome feelings stirring inside him?

As the turkey platter grew lighter, and steaming bowls of mashed potatoes and gravy were passed up and down his folks' long dining table, he pictured Summer, self-assured as Taffy carried her across the Double M acres. Then, half-way through the meal, her mood shifted from animated to quiet.

She'd spent nearly two years cooped up alone in her town house. Was the big family dinner too much, too soon? Did she wish her folks could be here? Or had the horseback ride taken its toll on her leg?

Zach was considering possible excuses for getting her home early, so she could call her folks and rest the leg. Then, as suddenly as she'd clammed up, Summer brightened. He followed her gaze to the swinging door between the dining room and kitchen, and saw Libby, smiling in the glow of thirty-five candles atop a two-layer chocolate cake. How was he supposed to pay equal attention to the family members who offered good wishes when he only had eyes for Summer, who, cheeks still flushed from the cold November wind, added her voice to the birthday song?

After the cake was gone, Zach gathered a stack of dirty dishes and followed the women into the kitchen.

"What are you doing in here?" his mom said as he deposited the plates in the sink.

Libby took one arm and his mother took the other, and together they ushered him into the hall.

"Go watch football with the rest of the men," his mom said, "and leave us women to our gossip!"

Unlike most Marshall males, he'd never been a fan of the game. As a small boy, he hid under the table, listening as the women shared everything from the latest cold remedies, to recipes, to stories about what happened to rude, eavesdropping children. His voice was changing before he figured out *he* was the rude, eavesdropping child. Just as well, because folding himself in two got harder with each passing year.

Now Zach knew better than to argue the point, and ducked into the parlor. Maybe a moment of quiet and solitude would help him figure out why he'd rather be in the kitchen with Summer and the other Marshall women instead of the family room with the kids and men.

The *other* Marshall women?

Eyes closed, he settled into his dad's big recliner. *Good thing Libby can't read minds*, he thought, or she'd deliver yet another of her "you're suffering from knight in shining armor syndrome" lectures. Zach shook his head at the irony, because he *did* want to help Summer, whether she needed it or not. Except for those couple of iffy moments in the dining room, it was becoming more and more clear that she did not.

Better get a grip, he told himself, *the sooner, the better*.

Hard experience taught him there was only one way to break the cycle: work. Hard work, and lots of it. Emma and Alex could run things at the studio for a few days. Once he got Summer home, he'd turn right around and come back to the ranch, give Nate a hand with that fence, maybe chop that fallen tree into firewood. If he was lucky, he'd fall into bed too tired to think about anything—or any*one*—else.

"Earth to Zach, earth to Zach…"

He blinked as Libby snapped her fingers, inches from his face.

"What planet were *you* visiting?" she teased, plopping into the chair beside his. "As if I don't know."

Zach decided to beat her at her own game. "Guess I zoned out there for a minute," he said, sitting up straighter. "I was thinking about Summer." He averted her "I knew it!" retort by adding, "We took a long, hard ride before dinner, and last time I saw her, she seemed to be favoring her leg. Guess I shouldn't have let her go full-out that way, but she was having such a good time, I didn't have the heart to tell her to slow down."

Libby's silence told him he'd succeeded in foiling whatever wisecrack she'd prepared. He found it surprisingly difficult not to gloat. "Any idea where she is?"

"Last time I saw her, she was in the kitchen with Mom and Nate."

"Nate? You women booted me out of there. Why does he get to stay?"

"Because Nate rates?" she said, smirking. He got to his feet. "Think I'll head in there, see if she's ready to hit the road."

"Leave? You mean you're not staying for the big breakfast feast?"

"Depends on what Summer wants to do."

Nodding, Libby rose, too. "Yeah, she sure has come a long way in a short time, hasn't she?"

Zach remembered the moment just before Libby had carried his cake to the dining table. Had they pushed her too far? he wondered.

"She's really sweet, Zach. I like her."

"Good. She can use a friend, and as you so astutely pointed out, so can you."

"Whatever," she said. "Just be careful, okay?"

"I'll have you know my driving record is perfect."

"That isn't what I meant. You know you're well on your way to falling Stetson over boots for her. Dumb idea on multiple levels."

He started for the door, and stopped when she said, "You're still not over Martha."

If he denied it, Libby would cite all the reasons she believed otherwise, and Zach was in no mood to delve into those murky waters again.

She took a step closer and looked around. "And anyway," she whispered, "Summer isn't emotionally strong enough for a guy like you."

"A guy like me? What does *that* mean?"

"You figure it out, smart guy."

Exasperated by her lack of confidence, Zach groaned and fixed his gaze on the rustic ceiling fixture overhead. "How'd our eagle-eyed mother miss that?" he said, mostly to himself. He stretched to his full six-two height and snagged the cobweb with a forefinger. He looked for something to wipe it on then turned back to Libby. "Give me a little credit, will you? I'm not interested in Summer." He pulled a starched white hanky from his back pocket. "She's got more baggage than an airport luggage carousel, and I don't have the time, patience or constitution for another damsel in distress."

Not the truth, but hopefully, Libby wouldn't call him on it. But just in case, Zach decided a distraction was in order. "So tell me, since you're so convinced of Summer's innate sweetness, what makes you think she'd hurt me?"

"Oh, I'm not saying she'd do it on purpose, but she's understandably vulnerable. *Exactly* the kind of woman you're attracted to. She won't be vulnerable forever. Sooner or later, she'll get her head on straight, same as Martha did, and…"

"You know what happened after that," they said simultaneously.

She gave him a playful shove. "Arrggh! You can be so exasperating!"

Ah, he got it now. This wasn't about Summer at all. It was about Libby's insistence that KISAS would dominate his life, forever inspiring stupid choices that led to disappointment and heartache.

"Never fear, Libs. I put in an order for chain mail."

"Chain mail?"

He nodded. "To top off my knight in shining armor suit."

It was all he could do to keep from laughing as surprise replaced her confused expression.

"I'm beat," Zach announced, and left the room.

He made his way to the kitchen with a plan to offer Summer a ride home. Whether they stayed or not was up to her.

"I thought Nate was in here."

"He was," Summer said, "but he wanted to make sure the corral gate was latched. Seems Chinook is something of an escape artist."

Zach puffed out his chest. "Yup. He's a smart one, all right."

Her smile seemed strained. She'd earned points, coming here and sticking it out this long. If he had to guess, he'd say she'd jump at the chance to hit the road.

"I hate to be a party pooper, but what would you say if we didn't spend the night?"

"I'd say how soon do we leave?"

His mom joined them. "What are you two doing in here? They're watching football in the family room, and *The Wizard of Oz* in the parlor."

"I was just telling Summer that I'm gonna head home tonight."

"What? And miss the annual Marshall breakfast?"

"Yeah, I'm whipped."

"Just because you're tired doesn't mean Summer has to miss out on all the fun. She can ride back with Libby."

"I really should go, too," Summer said. "I've texted my mom and dad half a dozen times today, to make sure they landed safely in LA, but so far, they haven't answered. And now my phone's battery is dead, and I forgot the charger."

Zach shot his mom a look that said, "I told you they were terrible parents."

"Maybe one of our chargers will fit your phone. Better still, you could call them on the land line," she suggested.

"I appreciate the offer. Unfortunately, I didn't bring their itinerary with me, either."

"They don't have cell phones?"

"Yes, but—"

"Well," Zach interrupted, "I'm sure they're fine, but we understand why you want check in with them."

Summer faced his mom. "Thank you so much for including me today, Mrs. Marshall. Dinner was delicious, and I had a wonderful time."

"Please. Call me Ellen." She wrapped Summer in a motherly hug. "Come back soon, okay?" Winking, she pulled Zach into their hug. "And maybe if you pretend to need a ride, this too-busy-for-his-mama son of mine will come home more often."

It felt strange, standing between these two women. Stranger still, admitting how much they both meant to him.

As though she'd read his mind, Summer stepped away and began plucking her things from the coat hooks behind the kitchen door. When the stack of extra clothes she'd brought nearly reached her chin, Zach chuckled.

"Let me root around upstairs, see if I can find something you can stow those in."

"It's okay," she said, "I managed to get it in here. I'm sure I can manage to get it out again."

"I know you can," he said, backing out of the room. "But why struggle if you don't have to?"

As he rounded the corner, he heard his mother say, "No suitcases for an overnight stay?"

"I think Zach left them in the foyer…"

He took the stairs two at a time. The quicker he found the bag, the faster he could get Summer out of there. The door to his boyhood room stood ajar, and as he stepped inside, a familiar sense of calm settled over him. His high school trophies and college awards stood shiny and still on the bookshelf, and dozens of red and blue 4-H ribbons were still tacked to the bulletin board above his desk. If years of sunlight hadn't faded the blue-and-gray plaid curtains he'd grown up with, he was sure they'd still be here, too, but his mom had replaced them a few years ago with a navy valance and white plantation shutters.

He peered through the slats. How many hours, he wondered, had he spent out there on the weathered, shake-shingled roof of the back porch, whispering to this girlfriend or that, long after the family had gone to bed? Too many, he admitted, opening the closet door.

Zach shoved aside his letterman jacket and crouched, poking through the battered footlocker that had gone with him to college. There, along-side worn cleats, his catcher's mitt and an as-sortment of scarred baseballs, he found the old duffel bag he'd carried to and from football prac-tice. *Oh, this is gonna smell good*, he thought, unzipping it. Then he said a silent thank-you to his mom, because instead of the expected stink of gym socks and workout shirts, Zach inhaled the fresh, clean scent of fabric softener sheets.

He cleared out the bag then headed back downstairs.

"Here y'go," he said, holding the duffel out to Summer. "That oughta hold all your stuff."

His mother laughed. "I should say so! Why, Summer could climb in there *with* her stuff and have room to spare. Let me get you something smaller," Ellen said. "Something that doesn't reek of high school."

"Please don't go to the bother," Summer said, clutching it to her chest. "This is fine, just fine." And then she proceeded to tuck her jacket, two sweaters, scarf and leather gloves inside Zach's bag.

Zach didn't know what to make of her peculiar smile and the odd glint in her eyes. But after spending so many months alone, he figured she had every right to look a little uncomfortable after a day as noisy and busy as this one had been.

"Don't forget your suitcases," his mom said. "I believe Zach left them in the foyer?"

They exchanged a quick, knowing glance, said their final goodbyes and made their way to his pickup.

For the first few minutes of the drive, Summer sat quietly, and he didn't think much of it. It had taken a while for her to open up on the way here, too. He was humming along with a song on the radio when she turned it off.

"What, exactly, did you tell your family about me?"

He was about to make the turn onto the interstate, and the steady *click-clack, click-clack* of the turn signal kept time with his heartbeats. "At the risk of sounding simple-minded," he said, merging with traffic on Route 285, *"huh?"*

"I'm not talking about general stuff, like the

fact that I'm enrolled in classes at Marshall Law, or I live next door to Alex," she said impatiently. "I'm talking about…about *personal* stuff."

"I didn't tell them anything. Wait. What's this all about, anyway?"

"It's about…how *nice* people were all day. How *polite.* As if they think I'm made of spun glass and might shatter if they so much as look at me cross-eyed."

Zach resisted the impulse to blurt out that they *were* nice people and of course they'd be polite.

Instead, he considered her side of things. It had riled Libby no end when anyone pitied or pampered her. Maybe that explained Summer's reaction to his family's hospitality. She'd been through a lot in the past two years. Breaking free of her self-imposed prison couldn't have been easy, but she'd done it. He told himself she was just second-guessing herself. Very normal under the circumstances. Right?

Maybe the best course of action here was *in*action.

Zach changed lanes, took the ramp onto Route 70, and turned the radio back on.

"What's your preference? Soft rock? Country? Jazz?"

"It doesn't matter. I like everything but rap."

At least she didn't sound angry anymore. If he had to, he'd put up with the silent treatment for the remainder of the drive. He'd tried to see things from her point of view. Why couldn't she do the same where his family was concerned?

Considering how close he'd come to donning his rusty suit of armor—again—she couldn't have chosen a better time to act moody and self-interested.

Zach settled on his favorite country station, where George Strait was midlyric. Summer let the song finish then reached over and turned down the volume.

"I'd just like to say one thing, and that'll be that."

He tensed. "Okay…"

"I don't confide in very many people. Not so much because I have trust issues—because to be honest, I do. I keep things to myself because it isn't fair to saddle others with my petty problems."

He'd hardly call what she survived petty, but she was on a roll, so Zach kept his opinion to himself.

"I made a mistake, sharing some of the details of that night with Libby. A *big* mistake."

"Why's that?"

"Because everyone—all day long—treated me with kid gloves. Like they knew I'd been attacked and held captive for hours."

Held captive. Zach ground his molars together.

Were the words as hard for her to say as they were for him to hear them?

He swallowed. Hard. How many more secrets was she harboring?

"Only gloves I saw were the ones we wore when we went riding."

She huffed quietly. "Look. I don't want or need pity. Not yours, not theirs." She crossed her arms over her chest. "I realize it's a natural reaction to…"

She took a deep breath. So deep that it made Zach wish he'd wiped down the dash before picking her up, because she'd probably just inhaled a million dust motes.

"I want to be in control of who knows what happened to me. And I want to be the one who decides *how much* they know. Few things make me feel more uncomfortable than seeing sympathy on people's faces."

It made sense, but he didn't understand what his family had done to make her think they felt sorry for her.

"Do you think Libby said something to my folks?" he said after a moment of edgy silence.

"If you didn't, then I don't know how else to explain the way they behaved."

"Honestly, I didn't see anything out of the ordinary. The way they were today? That's just the way they *are*."

She stared out the passenger window, where mile markers winked, and the snow covering the highway glittered in the headlights. It almost seemed that Summer was *trying* to give him reasons to distance himself from her. It was what he wanted, so why, instead of relief, did he feel regret?

Zach made a mental list of reasons to keep her at arm's length.

One: Libby was right; Summer was vulnerable.

Two: she could revert to her old hermit-like ways at any moment, and where would that leave them?

Three: What if Summer had inherited her parents' self-indulgent, nomad-like tendencies?

She had good qualities, he'd give her that. But he resented her for putting him in the position of defending his family or defending her.

Suddenly, it seemed the perfect time to stand his knight's suit in the corner, once and for all. He couldn't admit it to Libby, of course, not without also admitting he'd considered putting it *on*.

CHAPTER FIFTEEN

"SORRY FOR THE last-minute change, ladies," Zach said, "but I'm short an instructor, so we'll need to merge the beginner and intermediate classes. And it looks like you're stuck with me until the session ends. Emma is in Boulder, taking care of her ailing grandma." He held up a hand to silence their concern. "I talked with her earlier, and she said things are going as expected." He explained that for the past ten years or so, Emma's grandmother, now ninety, had been suffering from congestive heart failure.

"How long will she be gone?"

He'd almost forgotten that Luke's flirty, divorced mom, Cecile, had signed up for this class.

"I have no idea. But it's safe to assume she won't be back to finish up this session."

"Will you let us know when you hear more?"

"Sure," he said, though he didn't understand the woman's interest in a total stranger. "Of course."

Summer raised her hand, reminding him of a kid in school.

"You're planning to visit her from time to time, though, right?"

Why did the question sound like an accusation?

"If I can," he admitted.

"Then on my way to class on Wednesday, I'll pick up a card. We can all sign it, let Emma know she and her grandma are in our thoughts and prayers."

"That's a great idea, Summer," said one woman.

"Zach, if you know which hospital she's in, I'll arrange to have flowers delivered to her room," Cecile cut in.

Alex stepped forward to say, "That's really nice of you, Mrs. Murphy, but Emma told me once that her grandma is allergic to, like, *everything*." He glanced at Zach. "Kinda the way Mr. Marshall is allergic to starting class late."

The women laughed, and when Summer gave Alex a thumbs-up, he blushed.

Long before Zach met the Petersons' reclusive neighbor, Rose told him how her son felt about Summer. In typical Rose fashion, she'd shrugged it off as a teenage crush, and at the time, Zach had agreed. Now he hoped Alex's doting behavior wasn't proof that yet another male had succumbed to Knight in Shining Armor Syndrome.

Zach clapped his hands, as much to clear his head as to gain their attention. He announced that Alex would lead their warm-up exercises, then went to the office to find Emma's lesson plan. Tonight she would have taught them boxing techniques that would build self-confidence, stamina and quick reflexes.

Ten minutes later, Zach admitted that he'd procrastinated long enough. It was time to get out there and do the right thing for the class, despite his conflicted feelings about Summer.

"Remember what Emma showed you on your first night of class?" he asked when Alex finished the warm-ups. Zach got into the fight position. "Imagine there's a line on the floor, right between your legs. We'll call it the toe-heel line. First, plant your feet shoulder-width apart. Left toe touches the line, left heel angles slightly outward. Right heel is on the line, right toe angles out."

He checked to make sure everyone had planted their feet properly. "Okay, now bend your knees and crouch a little. Get that right heel up off the floor. Balancing on the ball of your foot makes it easier to move fast."

Soon, every woman was doing her best to emulate Muhammad Ali, bobbing and weaving, feinting jabs and ducking punches. After ten minutes of that, he showed them how to mix in the defensive skills they'd already learned.

"Use your head to protect your head, and

your body to protect your body." He waved Alex closer. "You're allowed to fight dirty. You're *supposed* to fight dirty when you're fighting for your life."

Zach looked at every student, and saw that Summer's assailant had succeeded in pinning her arms to her sides.

"Use combinations," he suggested. "Like elbow jabs to your attacker's eyes and ears. A knee to the groin. A foot planted hard on the knee. An elbow to the ear. The point is to inflict as much pain as possible in as little time as possible, so that the assailant will go down, and you can run for help."

He sensed, rather than saw, Summer's eyes on him. But he had to ignore her. Had to forget what had been done to her and teach *all* of these women some rudimentary skills, so that what happened to her would never happen to them. So that, in the unlikely event Summer faced a similar situation, she wouldn't be victimized again.

"Balance," Zach said, "can literally save your life. Don't kick your attacker, because it's extremely difficult to stay upright on one foot while he's doing his best to knock you down. He'll expect you to smack his face. So surprise him. Drive your elbow into that soft hollow below his sternum instead."

A few of the women held the semicrouched

position, punching at the air. Others stood, shoulders slumped and arms limp, as if they had no idea what to do. And Zach called them on it.

"What if your attacker charges while you're standing there, arms at your sides?"

He walked up to Luke's mother—one of the immobile few—and, bending at the waist, he stared her down.

"Think fast, Cecile. What would you do if, right now, an attacker approached?"

"I-I'd dig my elbow into his neck?"

"Don't tell me, show me!"

She lifted her arm, and Zach blocked it.

He stepped up to the next woman.

"Your attacker is about to punch your lights out, Anne. What do you do?"

"Stick *both* of my elbows up, to protect my face?"

"Yes! Because if you do it fast enough, he'll hurt his hand."

"You're scaring us," Cecile said.

"Good. I'm glad. That's my *job*. Whether you're attacked in a parking lot or in your own home, you'll find out real fast that you're in a fierce fight for your life. Everything is going to happen in a blur. You won't know a thing about your attacker, except that he means to hurt you… or worse. It's gonna be an ugly, noisy, dirty mess, so you have to use every ounce of aggression and power in you. If you don't win, he *will*."

Zach let his words sink in. Then he flashed his most charming smile and said, "Now go home and work on some moves. I expect to see them on Wednesday."

ON WEDNESDAY, WHEN Zach walked into the classroom, Summer was going from student to student, sharing a ballpoint so that one by one, they could sign the get-well card for Emma's grandmother. She was the first to spot him, and met him halfway between the door and the whiteboard.

"Did you have a chance to visit Emma?"

Zach steeled himself because *man*, she looked gorgeous tonight.

"No, but I've talked with her a couple of times. She says they're only allowing family into her grandmother's room."

"Oh, no. That isn't a good sign." Her eyebrows rose slightly. "How is Emma holding up?"

"Not getting enough sleep, worrying about the bills that are already stacking up. So I told her to forward them to me."

"To you? That's really n—"

"No big deal," he finished. "I invested the few dollars my grandfather left me. Between that, my penny-pinching personality and what the studio brings in, I do okay."

She smiled. "Still, it's a very nice thing to do."

He smiled, too. "I told you, nice is just the Marshall way."

Instantly, Zach regretted the joke, because it sounded cocky and self-serving, even to his own ears.

"That came out all wrong," he admitted. "What I meant to say was—"

"Your family *is* nice. Nothing wrong with admitting that."

She looked down at the greeting card she held, and Zach was tempted to tuck that mind-of-its-own curl behind her ear. He noticed a scattering of freckles peeking through her thick, dark lashes. Why hadn't he seen them before? And why did they stir a strange yearning in his heart?

She handed him the card. "Emma is lucky to have a friend like you." She tapped the card with her pen. "I know you'll probably send one of your own, but since this is from all of us at Marshall Law, I think you should sign it, too."

He laid it on his clipboard and scribbled, *We miss you around here!* and returned the card. Summer returned to the circle of women who laughed and chattered as they added their good wishes to the greeting.

Zach thought about what he'd written. He really *did* miss Emma. He'd taught her everything he could about self-defense and, when he thought she was ready, promoted her to instructor. Even before he'd made her his assistant, Zach had treated her like an equal, but he wasn't sure he'd earned the title Summer had bestowed: *friend.*

"You ready to get started, boss?"

The kid startled him so badly, Zach nearly dropped his clipboard.

"Sorry," Alex said. "Didn't mean to scare you."

"My own fault," he admitted. "Let that be a lesson to you—never let down your guard." He winked. "Now, round 'em up and tell 'em we'll get started in five."

"Should we use the big gym tonight, since you're teaching two classes at once?"

"Good idea. They'll have more elbow room that way."

While the teen ushered the women into the classroom, Zach shook his head. He didn't like feeling distracted, out of sorts. Liked the reason for it even less: Summer Lane.

He took a moment to gather his thoughts, then walked into the classroom. Later, when he was home alone, he'd figure out a way to build a wall between himself and Summer. *But where will you find a sheet of stainless steel three feet thick?*

The women were so busy talking—about

the recent snowfall, Emma's accident, Monday night's gritty and grueling class—that no one noticed him enter. No one, that is, but Summer. *Steel*, he reminded himself, and looked at anything and everything to avoid making eye contact with her.

He put his efforts into gaining the students' attention, but nothing worked—not clapping his hands or waving his arms, not even yelling.

"Ladies!" he barked, but it barely quieted the high-pitched din.

"Never thought I'd see the day," Alex said, shaking his head.

"What day?"

"When you lost control." Grinning, Alex made an *O* of his thumb and forefinger, put it between his teeth, and cut loose with an ear-piercing, two-note whistle.

Instantly, the women became silent and faced the front.

Smirking, Alex bowed. "They're all yours, boss."

Zach chuckled at his assistant's antics, then instructed his students to stand, arms parallel to the floor. "Spread out," he said, "until you're not touching your neighbor."

With the women in position, he began his lecture.

"You've learned how to apply a few moves against an assailant who approaches from the front. Tonight, I'm going to show you how to defend yourself against someone who sneaks up from behind."

Don't look at her. Do not *look at her.*

"Who practiced the moves I showed you on Monday?" He held up his right hand, and every woman facing him did, too.

"Good, because tonight, you're gonna need them."

Zach explained that being attacked from the rear was far more likely than full-on frontal assault.

"He'll catch you completely by surprise, grab the hood of your jacket, your shoulder, your hair. And once he has you, he'll bring you close, throw an arm around your neck and pull you tight against him, making it next to impossible to move…or breathe. It's a lot easier to break a hand-hold than a chokehold, so your objective is to do whatever you can to make sure you don't get into that position in the first place."

According to Libby, Summer's attacker had grabbed her ponytail, then applied the chokehold until she passed out. He didn't even want to think about what the guy did after that.

The first rule, he told the women, was to remain calm. "No matter how scared you are, take slow, deep breaths. It'll help keep your mind and body relaxed enough to think and plan your next move. Always remember—panic can be deadly."

From the corner of his eye, he saw Summer rubbing her temples. Maybe, despite her bravado, she wasn't ready for all the in-your-face reminders of what she'd gone through.

He demonstrated the chokehold, using Alex as his victim. As he demonstrated each protective, preventive move, he explained the proper way to carry them out.

"As soon as you sense someone is trying to take control of you from behind, raise your least dominant arm. Let's assume you're right-handed. You'll raise your left arm above your head and turn left, all the way around, right into the guy, and use that hand—or elbow, or fist—to deliver a strike to his head, neck, or throat. If you hit hard enough to incapacitate him, you need to run like hell, screaming at the top of your lungs.

"If he turns *with* you, raise your other arm and turn in the opposite direction. He won't expect that. The momentum generated by your turn will give you a chance to jab a knee into his groin or belly."

He stepped away from Alex and aimed his forefinger at the class.

"If you've kept up with your exercises, if your core is strong and your balance is sure, even the smallest of you can strike with enough power to dislocate an attacker's hip, crack a rib or at the very least, knock the wind out of him."

Every woman smiled at that possibility. All but Summer, that is. Was it his imagination, or did her creamy complexion look more pale than usual? How could he avoid looking at her now, knowing that she might pass out?

"I'll run through the next move," he said, watching her in his peripheral vision. "Afterward, you'll practice both tactics, first on your own then on one another, and finally," he said, emphasizing the word, "with me."

Whispers and soft gasps floated around the room, and he grinned to himself, knowing that not even the flirty Mrs. Murphy was looking forward to *that*.

"Let's assume your attacker comes at you, head-on. If you let him grab you by the throat, there's very little you can do to defend yourself. So your objective, always, is to make sure he never gets close enough to wrap his hands around your neck."

He ran down the rules they'd learned on their first night of class.

"Always be aware of your surroundings. Look at the people around you. Trust your instincts. And never ever hesitate to defend your personal space. If someone makes you feel vulnerable, or even slightly uncomfortable, get as far from the threat as you can, as fast as you can. Because more often than not, someone trying to subdue you will be bigger, stronger, might even have some experience at overpowering women. Won't he be surprised when he finds out that, although you're smaller and he outweighs you, you're anything but defenseless. You know what to look for, and you know not to let anyone get close enough to grab you by the throat."

Summer shook her head and rested her chin on her chest. But she still seemed steady on her feet, so Zach showed the class how to block an attacker's first attempt to initiate a chokehold.

"One arm across your waist, the other diagonally across your chest, chin tucked close to that hand. Remain patient—breathe in, breathe out—and don't panic. In the loudest voice you can muster, tell him to back off. He might, thinking your loud mouth attracted attention. But if he keeps coming, put your forearms on the outside of his. He's close now, off-balance, and he won't be expecting you to slam his arms together, hard. The instant he hesitates, bolt left or right and run like your life depends on it. Because it does.

"If that doesn't work, beat on his arms. Bite. Scratch. Do whatever it takes to keep that hand from wrapping around your neck. Never stop attacking. Because the instant you do, he wins."

Now it was time to step back and watch as they

practiced what he'd just preached. He and Alex leaned against the whiteboard, arms crossed and feet shoulder-width apart.

Using his chin as a pointer, the boy whispered, "What's wrong with Summer?"

Zach took one look at her, darted between his other students, and caught her just as she was about to hit the mat.

CHAPTER SIXTEEN

SUMMER HADN'T SEEN it coming.

One minute Zach was at the head of the class. The next, his big arms wrapped around her, and saved her from hitting the mat, hard.

In the tangle of arms and legs, it took a few seconds to get her bearings. When she did, Summer gazed into his blue-green eyes and searched the oh-so-serious face that hovered inches from hers. Every instinct made her want to press her palms against his rugged cheeks, finger-comb the blond hair from his worry-creased forehead to assure him that she was fine, just fine.

Then, as her classmates' voices broke through the fog, Summer remembered where she was and didn't feel so fine anymore. She wriggled free of his grasp.

"If this was some sort of demonstration, you should have asked for volunteers. I don't appreciate being your guinea pig."

His left eyebrow rose high on his forehead, and his mouth slanted in a sly grin. If she lifted her head, just a little, she could kiss those perfectly shaped lips. Would she have done it if they weren't surrounded by onlookers?

"Are you all right?" Alex asked.

"I'll be fine," she bit out, "when this big gorilla lets me up."

She waited, but he didn't move.

"Let me up," she whispered.

"Make me," he whispered back.

"*Make* you? What is this, fifth grade? Get off me before I—"

And then it hit her: this was a test, to see if she'd been paying attention, if she'd taken what Emma and Zach had said, dozens of times, to heart: "Expect the unexpected, then *do* the unexpected!"

Summer took stock. Her left arm was above her head, still pinned to the mat by Zach's strong hand.

Stay calm. Breathe. Be patient...

She threw her right leg over his back, and eyes squinted tight, put everything she had into rolling over. In less than a second, she was on top of him.

Amid her classmates' snickers and hoorays, she heard, "*That's* gonna be a nice goose egg in the morning."

She looked into Zach's face, saw him wince as he pressed meaty fingertips to his left eye. The skin around the socket had already turned bright pink. And her elbow ached. *Good thing you weren't* trying *to hurt him!*

Summer got up, and so did he.

"Better get some ice on that," Alex told Zach. "Your eyebrow is all swollen."

Zach faced his gawking students. "See, ladies, *that* is how you defend yourself against an attacker."

He gave Summer a thumbs-up. "Way to go," he said, and headed for the front of the room. With only five minutes left in the session, he dismissed the class early.

Ordinarily, she didn't shower at Marshall Law, but tonight, Summer even washed her hair. Zach couldn't lock up until everyone had left, and she intended to be the last student out the door. When she stepped out of the locker room, she saw him, back to her and feet propped on the credenza against the wall.

"Thought I was gonna have to come in there and fish you out of a drain," he said without turning around.

She hadn't made a sound, save the hard beating of her heart. So what alerted him to her presence?

"What's your plan, stand there until your eyes bore holes into the back of my skull?"

His feet hit the floor—first the right, then the left—before he swiveled to face her.

He leaned forward, elbows on the arms of his chair and hands folded on the desktop.

She didn't know what to react to first, the way his biceps strained against the fabric of his shirt, the almost sad expression on his weary face, or the golf-ball-sized lump above his eye. Why did she want to walk over there, kiss that darkening bump and apologize for hurting him?

Zach pointed at the empty chair beside his desk. "Looks like you have something to get off your chest. Might as well make yourself comfortable while you do it."

She'd gathered her things before coming out here. Against her better judgment, Summer sat down and bunched her coat atop the purse in her lap.

He slid an unopened, frosty can of soda closer to her elbow.

So he'd been *expecting* a confrontation?

After popping the tab, she took a sip. Root beer. Her favorite. But how did *he* know that?

He sat back, fingers linked behind his neck, waiting.

"I realize you're accustomed to giving orders," she began, "both as a marine and as a business owner. But I am *not* one of your soldiers, nor am I one of your employees. I paid the full price for these classes. Maybe you should take 'the customer is always right' rule a little more seriously."

"Sorry, I'm not following you."

"What was that all about in there?" she demanded, sitting up straighter.

"You were weaving and bobbing like a drunk. What did you expect me to do? Let you faint, maybe hurt yourself or the students standing near you? I don't carry enough insurance to survive a lawsuit."

"Nice to know that *money* prompted your attempt at chivalry."

"Attempt?"

In other words, his self-satisfied expression said, he'd saved her, so what else mattered?

Zach rolled his chair closer to hers. Real close. "If you think I'm gonna apologize for sparing you a sprain, or so much as a hangnail, think again."

Do not back away, she told herself. *Sit still and hold your ground*.

"Kind of arrogant, don't you think? To assume I hung around tonight just to thank you."

He shrugged, then rolled back to his original spot behind the desk and opened a file. "Weatherman is calling for six-to-eight inches of snow," he said, turning a page, "and that hill you live on gets pretty slick."

She'd been completely unprepared for how much his brusque dismissal would sting.

Forcing a smile, Summer stood and put on her coat. Through the window, she saw millions of quarter-sized snowflakes glowing against the ink-black sky. "Wow. Looks like the weatherman is right."

He didn't respond.

"If this keeps up, we might just get those six inches," she continued.

"Uh-huh."

"Guess I'd better hit the road."

"I guess," he said without looking up from his paperwork.

She paused in the open doorway. "Have a nice weekend, and…" Now he met her eyes, his expression such a blend of hope and surprise that it pained her to finish her sentence. "…and Alex is right. You should put some ice on that lump."

As the door hissed shut behind her, Summer couldn't decide if it had been hurt or disappointment that dulled his beautiful eyes.

You're giving yourself way too much credit, she thought, buckling her seat belt. *He's just glad to finally be rid of you.*

A good thing, Summer told herself. She wasn't ready for a relationship. Especially not with a guy who, according to his gossipy sister, tended to fall hard and fast. Unfortunately, that had been her tendency, too, before that crazy, life-changing night. So yes, the gap she'd opened to-night was a good thing.

For both of them.

CHAPTER SEVENTEEN

SUMMER FELT THE MAT press into her back. And felt Zach's sweet, warm breath against her cheek.

Elbows locked, he raised his upper body and studied her face. "I didn't hurt you, did I?"

"Of course not." She laughed. "I'm stronger than I look."

He buried his face in the crook of her neck, then touched his lips to hers. "Duly noted," he whispered.

In the distance, a telephone rang.

"Don't answer it." She sighed, combing fingertips through his thick, sandy-blond hair. "If it's important, they'll leave a message."

But the ringing persisted.

Summer opened one eye and squinted into the sunbeam slanting down from the skylight above her bed.

The phone really was ringing, but the rest? The rest had been a dream. A realistic, full-color, heart-pounding dream. Groaning, she threw back the covers and all but growled into the receiver.

"Hello?"

"Honey? Are you all right?"

Summer cleared her throat and peeked at the caller ID screen. "Mom. Hi. Where are you? I don't recognize that area code."

Laughing, Susannah said, "Oh, Dad and I are still in LA, of course. We forgot our cell phones back at the hotel, so I borrowed Kevin's."

Kevin? Summer waited patiently, knowing her mom would eventually get around to providing the details. *All* of the details.

Kevin O'Neill was an actor, but he also wrote, directed and produced for Olive Ranch Road Productions. His work—and the actors who'd starred in his pictures—had earned numerous awards. Summer was impressed and said so.

"The movie is *50 Hours*," Susannah said. "It's the story of a man sentenced to community service after he's found guilty of a DUI. Your dad and I are counselors at the hospice where he works off his fifty hours...and where he meets the woman who changes his life forever."

Summer laughed. "You sound like the voice-over of a movie trailer."

"I guess I do, don't I! But can you blame me?"

Her mother went on to describe the rest of the story, the cast and even the weather in LA. Her mom hadn't been expecting to land a role, so she was doubly excited.

"Sounds like the perfect job," Summer said.

"I'm happy for you. For both of you." Happy... and relieved to have something to distract her from that *dream*. "Everything about your trip to California sounds wonderful!"

"You might not think it's so wonderful in a minute."

"Don't tell me...you'll be away for Christmas?"

"How did you guess?"

Maybe because I can count on one hand the number of times you've been home for the holidays.

"We'll try to make it. You know we will."

She almost quoted Yoda: "Do...or do not. There is no try." Half a dozen times in her childhood, schoolmates had brought her home for the holidays. But try as they might, not even the warmest, most welcoming families had made her feel like one of their own. As an adult, she mostly spent those major dates alone, eating frozen pizza and watching TV. Steering clear of movies such as *Spirit of the Beehive* and *Miracle on 34th Street* made the time pass more quickly, and teaching herself not to expect too much from her parents helped Summer feel less alone. If she could survive that at eight and ten and thirteen years of age, surely she could survive it at thirty!

Summer heard whispering in the background, and hoped it was her dad, waiting his turn to talk to her. Instead, her mother said, "Sorry, honey. Gotta run."

"Okay, well, you guys take care, and call when—"

A quiet click gave way to silence.

"Love you, too, Mom," she grumbled into the phone. "Yes, of course I'll take care, and you do the same. Tell Dad I love him."

She'd no sooner put the receiver back into its cradle when the phone rang again. This time, the caller ID showed Marshall, Dr. L.

"Hey, Libby," she droned.

"Such enthusiasm. Should I be insulted?"

"Sorry." Summer forced a laugh. "I just woke up and haven't had my coffee yet."

"Haven't heard from you since Early-Thanksgiving. How goes it?"

"It goes." Summer gave her a one-sentence rundown of her mother's call, and although the tantalizing dream remained front and center in her mind, she didn't dare mention it.

"That's pretty cool. Except…does that mean they'll be away for Christmas?"

"Probably. But it's no biggie."

"What do you mean, *it's no biggie*? Of course it's a biggie. One of the biggest biggies, ever. You'll spend Christmas with us, and I won't hear another word about it."

Summer could say *thanks, but no, thanks* in any number of cliché ways. Or she could tell

Libby the truth…that she didn't trust herself under the same roof with Zach. He'd hurt her feelings that night at the studio. In time, she'd get over it. But she'd allowed herself to care about his opinion, about *him*, and dealing with that wouldn't be nearly as easy.

"Can I give you an answer later?" *After you've convinced me he won't be there…*

"You don't strike me as a 'let's see if a better offer materializes' kinda gal. So let's just assume you're coming. How do you expect me to enjoy myself, thinking about you, home all alone?"

She could almost see Libby's teasing smile. "I need to find out if my folks will be in town or not."

"What difference does that make? Bring them!"

While that would make for interesting dinner conversation, Summer didn't dare say yes. No, she needed to come up with a firm yet courteous way to decline Libby's offer.

"Okay, enough polite chitchat. The real reason I called wasn't to invite you to Christmas dinner. I need a favor."

As long as it doesn't involve your brother…

"My car is in the shop, and wouldn't you know, they have to order parts. Could take a week or more before I get it back. That's what I get for buying one of those little foreign jobs, I guess."

She sighed. "Anyway, I can walk to and from work for a few days, but I promised my mom I'd help out with a fund-raiser she's hosting on Saturday night. Which means I need to get to the ranch on Friday."

"Isn't Zach going?"

"He has meetings with some of the resort people."

Was that a yes or a no? Summer told herself that if Zach planned to attend, Libby would have hitched a ride with him, right? The Marshalls were lovely people, but even without Zach there, was she ready for two nights at someone else's house?

"What's the fund-raiser for?"

"An organization called Firefly Autism. They do some amazing stuff for kids on the spectrum, like helping parents find doctors and putting them in touch with learning programs that fit their kids' needs. My mother's best friend, Trish, has a grandson with Asperger's Syndrome, and the woman has a knack for roping friends and family into helping out every year. This time, it's a hoedown theme, and she talked Mom into volunteering our party barn."

"A hoedown."

"Yes'm, complete with cowboy hats and boots, big belt buckles and bandannas. They're expecting three or four hundred people, and rumor has it, Trish hired The Bandoliers."

Summer stifled a gasp. Three or four *dozen* people would have terrified her.

"I can't believe the pull that woman has," Libby was saying.

"I thought they were on a European tour."

"Oh. And listen to this! She rented a mechanical bull and plans to sell tickets. The rider who stays on longest wins a trip to LA."

"I'm almost tempted to try," Summer joked. "Wouldn't *that* be a Christmas surprise for my folks?"

"Sorry. No can do. You're spending the holiday with us, remember? If you buy a ticket—and last more than a few seconds on the machine— you can visit Tinsel Town some other time. Besides, Trish assigned me to the kissing booth, and I need some moral support."

"A kissing booth. You're kidding, right?"

She giggled. "Last year, I dressed up like Wonder Woman and raised five hundred bucks for Trish's very worthy cause. So can you drive me to the ranch and back to Vail? Think of it as a get-away-from-it-all weekend at the Double M."

Summer's stomach lurched, and every muscle tensed at the thought of spending two nights and three days with virtual strangers—*hundreds* of them. Before the attack, she would have jumped at the chance to attend a party of this size. Of any size. But now? What if she saw someone who resembled Samuels?

You're acting like a baby clinging to its security blanket, she thought. She'd holed up in the town house to protect herself from ugly reminders of her attack. Common sense told her that if she could survive the weekend, she'd be that much closer to the old Summer.

"What time should I pick you up?" Summer hoped Libby hadn't heard the tremor in her voice.

"I'll pack tomorrow night and bring my suitcase to the office on Friday. With any luck, we can roll into the Double M in time for movie-and-pizza night." A quiet buzz sounded in the background. "My next patient is here. Call you later to firm things up."

What were the chances that two people would hang up on her in the span of five minutes? Laughing to herself, Summer headed for her closet. She could wear jeans and boots to the hoedown, but what about Friday? And if they stayed to help clean up on Sunday morning, she'd need sneakers and sweats.

It wasn't likely there'd be time to go riding, but she'd pack boots, a hat and gloves, just in case. She'd almost forgotten how liberating and enjoyable it felt, thundering across the turf on the back of a willing horse. She'd bring her camera, too, to take pictures of the bluff…if she could find it on her own.

It still touched her that Zach had taken her to the place he'd never shared with anyone else.

There were so many things to like and admire about him. His obvious dedication to and love for his family. The strength of character required to lead men and guide boys like Alex. A willingness to share the skills he'd honed in the marines to help his students feel safer and more confident.

In retrospect, marching into his office had been a mistake. Everything about him had changed after their short set-to. Zach rarely met her eyes now, and on the few occasions he did, he looked quickly away. If getting from point A to point B meant walking near her, he didn't mind adding steps to avoid it. Each rebuff hurt her feelings all over again…and reminded her why she decided to spend the rest of her life alone. Most men were self-centered. Immature. Pushy and aggressive, with violent tendencies. Well, except for her dad, and her grandfathers. Detective O'Toole. The cops who'd been on duty that night, and the doctors who'd put her back together. In all fairness, Zach didn't belong on that list, either. But she'd come precariously close to falling for him. And if she didn't pretend he was one of them, she'd fall the rest of the way.

CHAPTER EIGHTEEN

ELLEN MARSHALL HAD invited several personal friends to help out with the fund-raiser, meaning every bedroom was spoken for. Libby was sharing hers with one of her sorority sisters, and that left only Zach's room. Coincidence? Summer didn't think so.

"I know how you feel about crowds," Libby said as they climbed the stairs. "So I found you a room all to yourself. It isn't the biggest, but it has a view of the corral."

Zach's room. It felt simultaneously weird and wonderful, being surrounded by memories of the boy he'd been...and proof of the man he'd become.

Libby must have seen her staring at the tattered US flag above the headboard. "He brought it back from Afghanistan."

The battle where he'd lost one of his men?

Libby opened the closet door and slid shirts and jackets aside. "If you have things to hang up, feel free to put them in here. I cleared a space on the floor for shoes and boots, too."

A nervous laugh escaped Summer's lips. "When did you have time? We just got here!"

Libby winked. "I did it last time you came, just in case you decided to stay the night."

"Good thing Zach won't be here, then, because I couldn't very well boot him out of his own room."

"Don't worry. He has meetings with the resort people, remember? Besides, that brother of mine is like a horse. He can sleep anywhere, even standing up." She grabbed Summer's small suitcase and tossed it onto the foot of Zach's bed. "Once a marine, always a marine, y'know?"

Yes, she knew. He'd been a lieutenant. A leader, accustomed to issuing orders and expecting they'd be obeyed. And Summer had vowed, on the night of her attack, that a man would never *ever* tell her what to do again.

"The bathroom's right across the hall," Libby added. "No one but Zach ever uses it, so you'll have it all to yourself. I think you'll find everything you need in there, but if I've overlooked something, just whistle."

"Thanks," Summer said. "That was very thoughtful of you."

"Thoughtful? Ha! You're going to work your butt off this weekend. Providing a few rudimentary niceties is the least we can do!" She linked arms with Summer and led her into the hall.

"Let's go downstairs and see what Mom is up to. I know she'll be tickled pink to see you."

They found Ellen in the kitchen, punching down a bowl of dough. "Summer!" she said. "So good of you to help out!" After wiping flour-covered hands on her apron, she welcomed Summer with a warm hug.

Hands on hips, Libby said, "Hey. What am I...chopped liver?"

Laughing, Ellen hugged her, too.

"So you're both staying the whole weekend, then?"

Side by side, they nodded.

"You put her in Zach's room?"

Libby nodded again.

"It isn't fancy," Ellen said, "but it's clean. I think you'll be comfortable there."

Surrounded by Zach's mementos? Laying her head on his pillow? Snuggling under the quilt that he'd cuddled up to as a boy? Comfortable wasn't the word Summer would choose.

"I love that the window looks into the corral," she said instead.

Ellen smiled. "That's the very reason Zach chose that room."

"That, and he had a premonition the porch roof right outside his window would someday serve as his 'whisper sweet nothings to girlfriends' perch," Libby said.

Ellen shook her head. "If I'd known about that back in the day, I would've tanned his hide. Two stories from the ground?" She shivered. "He was only six or seven when we moved out of his grandparents' house on the other side of the Double M and built this place. He ran up the steps, went straight to that window and hollered, "I want this room!""

Summer smiled at the image of him as a small, enthusiastic boy. Quite a different picture from the big, stiff-backed marine who never let his guard down. Well, that wasn't entirely true. He'd grown misty-eyed on the bluff…

"Is there anything I can do to help?" Summer asked.

"Nothing right now. But when this stuff rises again," Ellen said, pointing at four big bowls of swollen dough, "you're both more than welcome to help me pound it onto pizza pans!"

"Did you get pepperoni?" Libby asked, lifting the lid of the pot simmering on the stove.

"And mushrooms, sausage and your favorite cheese."

Libby grabbed a teaspoon from the drain board and dipped it into the pot. She sipped, then handed the spoon to Summer. "You're gonna think you died and went to heaven."

Either living on a ranch had obliterated their concerns about germs, or the Marshall women thought of Summer as family. Either way, it would have been rude to refuse the offer. Germs were the last thing on her mind as she savored the sauce.

"You two might as well find something fun to do. It'll be a couple of hours before we can start topping the pizzas."

Libby looked at Summer. "Are you up for a ride?"

"I thought you'd never ask!"

Summer rode Taffy, and Libby chose Chestnut, a black-maned roan. An hour or so into the ride, they stopped near a creek to let the horses drink. Summer photographed patches of green, peeking through snow-covered pastures, the bare and twisted branches of elms and honey locusts, and stands of pine and fir, silhouetted by white-capped peaks that kissed the azure sky.

"How can you stand living in town?" Summer asked, tucking the camera back into her jacket pocket. "I'd stay forever if I could."

Libby glanced over her shoulder, where the rambling two-story log house and outbuildings stood strong and stately against a backdrop of mountains. "It's gorgeous, I'll give you that. But it's also work, work, work from dawn till dusk. I like not having calluses, and being able to grab my skis and zoom down the slopes anytime I please." She met Summer's eyes. "Besides, a girl's gotta pay the bills, y'know? I only have one talent, and nobody up here will admit they need therapy."

The horses' ears swiveled as her laughter echoed across the valley below.

They rode until the sun began to dip down behind Mt. Evans, glowing like a golden coin sliding slowly into a slot. Once Taffy and Chestnut were cleaned up and watered, Libby and Summer walked to the back of the house, their boots crunching on the snow-covered path.

"How many people will be here tonight?" Summer asked, shoulders hunched into the wind. "For pizza and movie night, I mean."

The wooden screen door squealed in protest as Libby opened it. "Nature's burglar alarm," she said, pointing at the rusted spring. "But to answer your question, Mom never knows who'll show up. Could be just the folks and us, or Nate and a couple of the ranch hands might join us. Once in a while, a neighbor or two will show up." She studied Summer's face. "Stop looking so worried. I'm pretty sure they've all had their shots."

Summer smiled. "I was just wondering whether or not to change into clean clothes."

"I'm getting into my pj's right *now*." Libby started up the stairs, pausing on the landing. "But *mi casa es su casa*. So eat, drink and put *your* pajamas on if you want to!" And with that, she disappeared around the corner.

The warmth of the big country kitchen was matched only by the soothing scent of fresh dough. After hanging her coat and hat on the wrought-iron hooks behind the door, Summer toed off her boots and lined them up next to the others on a bentwood shoe rack.

An oversize tea kettle sat fat and squat on the six-burner gas stove. She gave it a shake and, finding it empty, carried it to the sink. As it filled with sparkling well water, she gazed through the many-paned window. Cows dotted the distant fields, where the wind caused the trees to lean west. The contented whinnying of horses filtered in through the glass.

After turning the flame under the kettle to high, Summer opened and closed cabinet doors until she found one that housed a collection of earthenware mugs. The size and heft intrigued her almost as much as the drip-paint that reminded her of mountain peaks. On the shelf above the mugs, a shallow, galvanized tray held an assortment of tea bags, and she decided to give Youthberry a try.

Steaming mug in hand, she wandered into the family room, where a roaring fire glowed in the belly of a massive stacked-stone fireplace. Above it, on a rugged mantel carved from the trunk of a tree, was a row of silver-framed photographs. Half a dozen black-and-whites of grandparents—great-grandparents, even, from the grainy look of them. A faded color snapshot of Ellen and John, kissing on their wedding day. Libby, beaming in her cap and gown. An aerial shot of the ranch. Zach, looking stern and noble in his marine dress blues. She leaned in for a closer look at the gold-braided aiguillette on his right shoulder and the collection of brass pins and colorful insignia on his chest. What had he done—or survived—she wondered, to earn them all?

She sighed and moved to the French doors, where a flagstone terrace blended into a deep expanse of snowy lawn. Matching rows of small bushel baskets lined either side of it. There were roses under them, Summer knew, because her grandmother had winterized her prized shrubs this way, too.

The soft tinkling of piano music drew her into the parlor.

"Well, hello there, Summer," Zach's dad said, lifting his fingers off the keys. "Libby told me you were coming. It's mighty good of you to pitch in for Ellen's fund-raiser."

What would he think of her if she admitted Libby's broken-down car was the only reason she'd come?

"It sounds like a very good cause," she said, "so I'm happy to help out."

For a moment, it appeared he wanted to ask her something. Had he seen through her facade?

"Well, it's good to see you, whatever the reason," he said, facing his sheet music once more.

The parlor, much more formal than the family room, reminded her of the old English libraries she'd seen in London. Beige brocade curtains hung at the wood-framed windows, and deep green wing chairs flanked the marble fireplace. Underfoot, a plush Persian rug muffled the chords of Beethoven that coursed from the mahogany baby grand.

She didn't feel uncomfortable, exactly, listening to John play. And yet...

"Can I fix you a mug of tea?"

Hands hovering over the keys, John smiled. And oh, how much he looked like Zach at that moment! There were many other similarities between this attractive older man and his handsome son—dark-lashed green eyes, a shock of hair falling over his forehead, high cheekbones and a strong jaw—that Summer smiled. She felt privileged that nature had let her in on a secret: *this is how Zach will look in twenty or thirty years!*

"It's nice of you to offer, but I'm a coffee man, myself."

"When I fixed this," she said, holding up her mug, "I noticed half a pot in the coffeemaker. Why don't I see if it's still warm and bring you some."

"You're a livin' doll. It's easy to see why my kids love you."

Kids, she thought, heading back toward the kitchen. It didn't surprise her to hear Libby had spoken highly of her, given her friend's multiple invitations to the Double M. But what had Zach said to his father to inspire a comment like that?

THE DOUBLE M LAWN looked like a mall parking lot, covered in row after row of pickup trucks, SUVs and cars.

Nate and John had strung colored lights along the roofline and gutters of the Marshalls' barn, and with the snow shimmering on the ground around it, the place looked more like a Christmas card than a party hall.

"I love the sound of banjos and bass fiddles," Libby said as they walked across the yard.

"Me, too." Summer nodded. "I only half-believed you when you said the fund-raiser would draw so many people."

"Hey, when my mom sets her cap on something, she goes all-out. I'm guessing two, maybe three hundred people when they do the final tally."

Meaning Firefly Autism would add thousands to the donor pool tonight.

"Impressive," Summer said, meaning it.

Inside, white lights winked from every overhead beam, and holly wreaths hung in all the windows. Behind the built-in stage hung an enormous poster bearing the charity's winged firefly logo.

"You'd better get into your booth," Ellen said. "There's already a line. Would you believe I need to have someone print up more tickets?"

Libby's shoulders slumped. "But the hoedown doesn't officially start for another half hour!"

Her mom winked. "It isn't my fault that you're so popular and alluring."

"Actually," Libby said, "you passed your best genes on to me, so it *is* kind of your fault."

She grabbed Summer's wrist and led her to the kissing booth.

As they approached, a big-bellied, bearded guy waved a handful of tickets. "There she is, fellers! Best li'l kisser in all of Denver County!"

Wolf whistles harmonized with hoo-has as Libby curtsied. "Be still, my adoring fans!"

She ducked into the double-wide booth, dragging Summer with her. "You have to help me out. I can't handle that mob all by myself!"

The very thought of strange men planting their lips on hers made Summer's skin crawl. How had

Libby mustered the courage to do it? Summer had overcome her fear of going outside, except for the time, a few weeks ago, when she'd felt closed in by the crowds of Black Friday shoppers at the mall. She'd taken a big leap of faith coming here. But that? Summer shuddered.

"I'm sorry, Libby, but I...I just can't. If anyone understands why, it should be you!"

Libby pulled her aside. "I know it'll be hard. I thought that's why you agreed to give it a try— to overcome another obstacle."

"What? When did I say I'd give it a try?"

"Just the other day, remember, when you said the kissing booth sounded like fun?"

"Well yes, I did say that, but—"

Libby hugged her. "Aw, Summer, *I'm* the one who's sorry. Really. I completely misunderstood. And you're right. I should have realized you didn't mean it, that you were nowhere near ready for something like this. Can you ever forgive me?"

"There's nothing to forgive." Then why had Libby's words sounded like a challenge?

Libby took hold of the cord that would open the booth's curtain.

Summer grabbed her wrist, stopping her. "There must be some other way I could help. Making change. Counting ticket stubs. *Something?*"

"Those are all my jobs," Trish said, squeezing between them. "I'll go out front, tell the men to form a second line." She put a hand on Summer's shoulder. "You're a lifesaver. A lifesaver, I tell you. Half of them would leave disappointed if you weren't here to help out."

"Oh, I'm sure that isn't true. The donations go to a good cause, after all. So if they didn't get—"

Before she could finish the sentence, the curtain went up, and she faced two lines of smiling men, all wearing Western-style shirts, Stetsons and boots. Trish leaned close and whispered, "Hundreds of dollars for kids on the Autism spectrum. How can you say no?"

"Like this," Summer said, mouthing the word. But deep down inside, far beneath the fear of coming that close to a man ever again, the outgoing, have-no-fears Summer she'd once been whispered, *If you can do this, you can do anything.*

At the front of the line stood a man who resembled Santa. He slapped four tickets on the counter, puckered up...

...and Trish shoved Summer straight into his lips.

It took all the self-control she could muster to keep from running out of the booth. There wasn't a doubt in her mind that she could be in her car and halfway down the Marshall's long, winding drive before Libby caught up.

Libby put her hands on Summer's shoulders. "I know you're scared. You'd be crazy if you weren't."

Eyes closed, Summer held her breath.

"A stranger kissed you, and it didn't kill you."

"Are you sure? I would've sworn my heart stopped beating the minute he put his ticket on the counter."

"Look at it this way," Libby continued. "When you're old and gray, rocking in your room at the old folks' home, you can tell those young whippersnapper nurses what a live wire you were in your youth."

Summer put her back to the crowd. "I'd rather tell them that the old wives tale isn't a tale, after all." In response to Libby's confused expression, she added, "You really do have to kiss a lot of frogs before you meet your prince."

Libby laughed. "Well, they don't *all* look like toads…"

Half an hour later, Trish butted to the front of the line. "Sorry, fellas, but the girls need a break. Look around you and memorize your spot in line, 'cause I'm in no mood to bust out my broom and break up any brawls when we reopen the booth."

The men laughed as she dropped the curtain.

"I thought the mechanical bull would be to-night's star attraction," Trish said, tiptoeing into the booth. She waved a thick stack of cash. "Turns out, it's you two. There must be three hundred bucks here, and the night's not half over yet!" She laughed all the way to the former tack room, which had been converted into a coat check for the night. Ellen was there, waiting to add the money to the strongbox.

Libby devoured a deep-fried Twinkie, tapping her toes while Summer checked the time. The hands of the big antlered clock above the double doors must be stuck—how could it be nine o'clock already?

"Did you get something to eat, Summer?"

She smiled up at Trish. "No. Wasn't hungry."

"You'll have time later." She pointed at the lines, which were much shorter than they had been earlier.

The way Trish chattered as they walked back to the booth made it clear she had no idea what had happened to her. Oddly, the admission made Summer smile. *You're a better actress than you thought*, she told herself.

Twenty minutes into their second shift, Summer turned to add ticket stubs and dollar bills to the cash box. Just half an hour more, and she could legitimately say she'd passed a major milestone.

Then she faced front again, and stood eye to eye with Zach. He fanned five tickets on the counter. A dozen questions flitted through her mind: What was he doing here? Had Libby known he'd show up? How long had he been at the ranch? And why did he have to look so gorgeous in his white cavalry-style shirt?

She took a deep breath. If being *near* his lips had caused a heart-hammering dream, what would the real thing do to her crazy, mixed-up mind?

"I'm surprised to see you."

"You are?"

"Libby said you had work-related meetings," she managed.

He shrugged, tapped the top ticket. "I did. But they're over."

Summer blinked. Straightened her collar. Tugged at her sleeves. Tucked her hair behind her ears as he separated one ticket from the rest.

"Don't worry," he said softly. "I don't bite."

He couldn't have known the comment would revive a repulsive memory, so she did her best to pretend he hadn't said it.

Leaning in, his lips gently grazed her right cheek. He slid a second ticket forward and bussed the left. The third ticket paid for a peck to her forehead. The fourth, a kiss to her chin. With just one left, she expected him to kiss the tip of her nose. Later, she thought as relief washed over her, she'd thank him for being so caring. And understanding. And gentlemanly.

Then Zach took her face in his hands and, using both thumbs to lift her chin, pressed such a sweet, lingering kiss to her lips that it inspired applause, hoots and hollers from the crowd.

Her knees were weak, and her pulse pounding when Libby thumped the top of his head.

"Stop that, you big ape. Didn't you read the rules?" When he straightened, she pointed at the sign behind her. "'Lips together,'" she read. "'Two-second time limit.'"

"I'd apologize," he said, never taking his eyes from Summer's, "but I'm not the least bit sorry."

CHAPTER NINETEEN

HOW HAD HE known she'd say yes when he asked
her to dance? Had he guessed that the two-step
was her favorite? The best question of all...*why*
had she said yes?

Summer blamed the sweet, caring look on his
handsome, Stetson-shaded face when she'd given
in to kiss number five.

Zach pulled her close as the band's lead singer
belted out a rousing rendition of Taylor Swift's
"Our Song." At first, Summer followed, feeling
like a cross between a rag doll and a tin soldier.
She hadn't been held by a man in more than two
years. At least, not this way.

"So was it awful?" he asked, looking down
at her.

"Was what awful?"

"All that kissing. Couldn't have been easy for
you."

"I pretended it was immersion therapy."

"Ah, Libby's idea, no doubt." He inclined his
head slightly. "So? Did it work?"

She shrugged one shoulder. "If I can get

through the next few nights without waking up to nightmares, I guess it'll be safe to assume I passed the test."

"Test." Zach shook his head. "I wonder how that sister of mine stays in business, doling out advice like that."

"It was my decision to stay."

"True, I suppose." He studied her face. "Still, I'm glad I was your last customer."

Summer was glad about that, too. How weird, she thought, that she'd mustered the courage to kiss all those guys, but couldn't make herself say, "I'm glad, too."

The music stopped, but Zach didn't turn her loose. Instead, he pulled her closer. Close enough that she felt his heart beating hard against her chest. When the band started up again, they launched into their interpretation of "Can't Live without You."

He nodded and returned the smiles of people who swayed nearby, bending slightly as an elderly couple danced past. "That's Mrs. Centrino," he said, "music teacher at my old high school."

"Well, well, well," the woman said. "Zachary Marshall, is that you under that ten-galloner?"

He tipped the hat. "Good to see you, ma'am."

She snorted good-naturedly. "Still the big flatterer, I see."

As her partner led her away, Summer heard Mrs. Centrino say, "That boy has a heart of gold…and a tin ear. Worst semester of my career was the one he decided to play the saxophone."

Laughing, Summer rested her forehead on his chest. Then, looking up at him, she said, "Do you still have the sax?"

"It's on a shelf in my closet at the folks' house." He groaned quietly. "Haven't opened the case in ten, twelve years."

"Unless Mrs. Centrino is mistaken, that's probably best for music lovers everywhere."

He threw back his head and laughed.

She did her best to look confused. "I'll have you know that wasn't a joke."

He pressed his cheek against hers. "Shh…this is one of my favorite songs."

If someone had told her six months ago that she'd help run a kissing booth at a charity function attended by hundreds, or snuggle up in a man's arms—and *enjoy* it—she would have said they were crazy.

"'You say you're happy, here in my arms,'" Zach sang, "'and I hope it's true…'" Zach began to sing along to the music.

Mrs. Centrino had been right. He *did* have a tin ear. But Summer didn't have the heart to tell him how off-key his lyrics were.

"'...'cause I'm sure am lovin' being close to you.'"

When the song ended, Zach walked her to the edge of the dance floor. "Need to talk business with that guy," he said, pointing. "Catch you later, maybe."

Maybe? Summer's upbeat mood instantly deflated, which made no sense, considering what she'd promised herself about Zach.

She joined Libby at a table near the door.

"What was all *that* about?" her friend asked. "And don't give me that 'huh?' face. I saw you and my brother on the dance floor." Giggling, she added, "You couldn't fit a sheet of typing paper between the two of you!"

"It was a waltz. People are supposed to be close."

"Not *that* close. But that's beside the point. I saw the way you were looking at each other, too." She folded her hands and tucked them into the crook of her neck. "To quote Mr. Rogers, 'Can you say moony-eyed?'"

She threw her head back and laughed, just as Zach had earlier, drawing the attention of people at nearby tables.

Libby lowered her voice and scooted her chair closer. "All kidding aside, I'm happy for you."

"Why do I sense a 'but' at the end of that sentence?"

"It's none of my business, but I have to get this off my chest. I know you're both single. But Zach's still nursing a broken heart. And you're nursing...other things."

"Don't worry. Tomorrow that waltz will be history, for both of us."

Libby sandwiched Summer's hands between her own. "You're shaking like a leaf!" She drew her into a sisterly hug then held her at arm's length. "Why are you so upset? Because of the kissing booth?" She hid behind one palm. "What kind of therapist am I, forcing you into a decision like that?"

"You didn't force me. I made a choice." In truth, Summer wasn't shaking because of the crowd, not even because of the booth. In a perfect world, she would have taken similar steps, ages ago. The problem was...she'd allowed herself to have feelings for Zach, and unless she was seriously mistaken, he cared about her, too.

She needed to tell him. *Everything*. He deserved to hear the whole ugly truth, from *her*.

"Listen, I can tell that you have reservations about starting a relationship. But I know my brother. He can be a bossy know-it-all at times, but he has a heart as big as his head. Whatever is keeping you from taking the next step..." She sighed. "Just be straight with him. If you tell him you're scared, that you want to take it slow, he'll respect that."

She spotted him in the middle of the room, laughing as he danced with a little girl who'd planted tiny pink sneakers on the toes of his boots. Her heart thumped with affection for him...and then it sank. Because if he *was* that kind of interested, he deserved to hear—before things progressed to the next level—that she might not be able to give him children of his own.

With a nod, she drew Libby's attention to the dance floor. He had scooped up the child and was now stomping across the floor, whirling and twirling as she squealed with glee.

Summer heard the fondness in Libby's voice when she said, "That big goofy idiot. He'd do just about anything to entertain a kid. I remember once, he sat cross-legged on the floor and let a pal's little girl clamp a couple dozen pink and purple plastic barrettes in his hair, then put rouge and lipstick on him!"

She laughed, and as Summer pictured the scene, tears filled her eyes. She wiped them away before Libby could see them. "You think anyone would mind if I went up to bed? I'm exhausted."

"Of course not." Libby yawned then got to her feet. "I'm tuckered out, too. I'll walk back to the house with you."

They followed the swath of moonlight that led from the barn to the corral. For a moment, they stood side by side, patting the noses of the horses that ambled up.

"If Zach said something to upset you, would you tell me?" Libby asked.

"Probably not." She grinned. "But in all honesty, he's always been a perfect gentleman. And I like him."

"Potato, poe-tah-toe," Libby said. And when Summer's brow furrowed, she quickly added, "Like, love. Just semantics." She studied Summer's face. "I hope you don't mind my saying this, but it's natural and normal to be self-focused for a while." She held up a hand. "Don't look all defensive. I'm not judging. I'm just stating facts. Walling yourself off…that's how you protected yourself from bad memories." She laid a hand on Summer's forearm. "Pardon the lack of psycho-babble, but that was then and this is now. You owe it to yourself—and Zach—to give things a chance."

With that, she said good-night, and left Summer at the corral gate.

"If only Libby knew," she told the horses, "that it's the other way around."

They nodded, almost as if they understood. Several times as a child, she'd wished she could be a horse, and run free across the green fields of her grandfather's farm.

"I hope you never waste a minute of your simple, beautiful lives, wishing you could be like us," she told them.

The horses moved left and huffed a greeting, and she turned to see who had approached.

"The lady's right," Zach said, patting each horse.

"You forgot to tell me you had a nickname," she said.

"A nickname?"

"Stealthy."

He leaned both forearms on the corral's top rail. "So what's yours?"

"My grandfather called me Pepper."

Turning to face her, he smiled. "Because of the freckles."

She nodded.

"So what are you doing out here, all alone in the dark?"

"I'm not alone."

As if to back up her story, Taffy whinnied.

"When you're right, you're right." He laughed. "Allow me to rephrase. What are you doing out here in the cold? They're about to announce the winners of the door prizes."

"Do you have to be present to win?"

"'Fraid so."

She shrugged. "I'd still rather stay out here."

"Oh?"

"I've never won anything in my life, and I'd hate to break my perfect record."

Zach nodded and faced the horses again. "So how long will your folks be gone this time?"

Was it her imagination, or had he put extra emphasis on those final words?

"I have no idea. Unfortunately, neither do they." And because it sounded self-pitying, Summer added, "They can't rush things."

"Why?"

"Because they've been waiting a long time for a chance like this."

"I see."

His tone and posture said otherwise. She watched him slide two carrot sticks out of his jacket pocket, and it surprised her how slowly and patiently the horses ate them.

"Considering how enormous they are," she said, "I've always been amazed at how gentle they can be."

Chinook sauntered off, and Taffy followed. "The equine version of 'can't judge a book by its cover.'"

"Something like that." She picked at a knothole on the fence rail. "Can I ask you a question?"

He angled his head, so that he could meet her

eyes. "Will you get mad if I can't give you the answer you're looking for?"

"Probably," she said, laughing. Leaning her backside against the gate, Summer propped a heel on the center board. "Why aren't you married? You're the right age, have the right temperament to be a good husband. And from what I've seen, you'd make a great father. So I don't get it."

"My grandmother took all of us boys aside when we went off to college. 'You're liable to meet up with someone who looks like wife material,'" he said, doing his best to imitate her voice. "Then she told us to dig deep, until we found her biggest defect, and ask ourselves if we thought we could put up with that flaw for the rest of our days."

"And if the answer was yes?"

"We'd have a fifty-fifty shot at a happy marriage."

"Just fifty-fifty…"

"The rest, according to Grandma, was good old-fashioned commitment and hard work."

Summer saw herself as a whole bunch of flaws, held together with hopes and dreams. "I see."

"Do you?"

She nodded. "I thought maybe it was PTSD or something."

"That term gets thrown around too much.

Weakens it and what it means, in my opinion. Like the word *love*. I love pizza. I love blue skies. I love my truck. And happy. When I have more money, a bigger house, that promotion, I'll be happy. If I could just lasso the moon, I'd be happy. Overuse cheapens and diminishes the words. Seems to me if people weren't just plain lazy, they'd find better ways to express themselves."

He thumbed his Stetson to the back of his head. "But to answer your question, I've never been officially diagnosed, but I don't need an MD to know I have a few symptoms. So does Libby. And you. And anyone else who has survived a major trauma."

Zach exhaled a long, hard sigh. "As for your original question, the reason I'm not married... It isn't because I'm too judgmental to tolerate a flaw or two, and it isn't PTSD, either." He faced her. "It's because I'm a big sap."

"That's the last word I'd use to describe you."

He told her about Martha, the girls who'd come before, and Libby's belief that he had a rabid case of KISAS.

His voice trailed off, but this didn't seem the time or place to press for more details.

"So how are your toes?"

"My toes?" He laughed. "What?"

"Well, I know I accidentally stepped on them

at least twice on the dance floor. And then you deliberately put that sweet little girl on them. For two or three songs!"

His expression, his posture, even his voice gentled. "My toes are fine."

For the next few minutes, neither Zach nor Summer spoke. Usually, long quiet pauses made her edgy. Not so this time, and she relished every moment of the companionable silence.

"Libby said you two went riding for a couple hours today."

"We did, and it was magnificent. My rear end is a little sore, but my leg is fine." She leaned forward, so that she could see his face. "Does it bother you? Being around someone with a limp, I mean?"

His head swiveled slowly, and when at last Zach faced her, he was frowning.

"I hardly notice it anymore, so no, I don't mind it a bit."

"What about the scar?" She tucked her hair behind her ears and took a step into a shard of moonlight. "People notice. I can see them staring at it."

He chuckled. "They're probably wondering what the *other* guy looks like."

"He didn't have a mark on him because even when I wasn't tied up, I didn't do a thing to defend myself."

Zach kept gazing straight ahead. "And?"

Summer didn't know what he meant, and said so.

"And it happened. You survived. Better than that, you're stronger than before." He met her eyes. "Does anything else matter?"

Libby was right. He *could* be arrogant and a know-it-all. But this certainly wasn't one of those times.

"When the 'why didn't I do this' or 'why did I do that' doubts get you down, ask yourself one question—'Did I have a choice?'"

Something told her it was a lesson he'd learned the hard way. Another topic for a future conversation. And she believed they'd have a future, if not in a dream-come-true way, then at least as friends. If she had to, she'd settle for that.

"Why didn't you move back to the Double M when you got home from Afghanistan?"

"Thought about it," he said. "Used to believe I'd build a house, right there." He pointed north. "I could raise a few cows, some kids, a dog or two. But then Libby got hurt."

Now Summer better understood what he'd said about being a rescuer.

"Zach! Are you out there, son?" his mom called from the party barn.

"Over here." He waved an arm over his head.

"We're about to spin the prize wheel, and Trish wants you to announce the winners."

"It's your own fault," Trish added, "for having that sexy DJ voice!"

On the heels of a heavy sigh, he shoved off the fence and pushed the Stetson lower on his forehead. "You coming inside with me?"

"Maybe. In a few minutes. I want to say goodnight to Taffy."

"Suit yourself."

Zach wasn't even halfway to the barn, and already she missed him. Maybe she needed therapy after all because she'd never felt more conflicted in her life.

CHAPTER TWENTY

ALEX TURNED THE page on the Marshall Law wall calendar from November to December.

"Well, looks like I'm not getting my license until after New Year's. Between exams and chores and work, there just isn't time for driving lessons."

Without looking up from the checkbook, Zach said, "School comes first. Always has, always will." He put the ledgers away and met Alex's eyes. "If you need some time off, we'll work it out."

"I'm okay waiting until after the first of the year. Between you and me? Mom is driving me nuts with all her 'have you done this' and 'why didn't you that.' I don't want time off. I come here to *hide*." He shrugged into his jacket. "You're sure you don't wanna marry her? Give her someone to focus on besides me?"

Zach laughed. "Yeah, I'm sure." Rose had a lot going for her, and she was nice enough. But they didn't have a thing in common. Except Alex.

"Poor Mom."

He hoped Alex wouldn't say, "She likes you, boss."

"She'll never get over my dad," he said instead. "But even if she could, I bet she'd never measure up to Summer in your book."

Zach put down his pen and looked up from the calculator. "What's Summer got to do with anything?"

"You like her. Heck. You might even love her. Not that I blame you. I kinda had a thing for her when she first moved in. Then Lexie, this girl at school, asked me to tutor her during lunch period, and, well…" Alex shook his head. "Sheesh. I sound like my mom, going on and on and never getting to the point." He started over. "What it has to do with Summer is, I've seen the way you look at her. Like the other night, when she almost fell and you caught her? Whoa. I thought for sure you were gonna plant one on her. And from what I could see? She would've let you."

Alex was smarter than most kids his age, but he didn't even have a driver's license yet. What did he know about reading people?

Then Zach swallowed, remembering the night at the Double M. The kissing booth. The dance floor. The quiet talk at the corral. That night and a dozen other times, he'd come *this close* to—as Alex put it—planting one on her. He hadn't held back because he wanted to, but because he couldn't risk that she'd associate anything he did with what that maniac had done to her.

Hypocrite. You didn't have any trouble planting one on her at the kissing booth.

"So what does your drivers' ed teacher say about you passing the test next time?"

"What does he say?" Alex echoed. "You mean out loud, or under his breath?"

"Don't let stuff like that get under your skin. I had a college professor who said a student is only as good as his teacher."

"Then maybe somebody needs to teach Mr. Somers how to teach me how to parallel park."

"Tell you what. After your exams, we'll go over to the church parking lot. I'll set up some barriers, and you can practice."

"Really? You'd do that?"

"'Course I would."

"Cool! And it's all the way on the other side of town. Nobody from school will see me smashing trash cans or mowing down lawn chairs."

"Have a little faith in yourself, kiddo." Zach used his pen as a pointer. "It's starting to snow. You want me to drive you home?"

Alex looked outside. "Nah. It's just around the corner. Besides, you're writing paychecks." Smirking, he pulled on his stocking cap. "I wouldn't want to distract you."

The studio phone rang. "Marshall Law," Zach answered.

"See ya," Alex called.

Zach waved and said into the phone, "What's up, Dave?"

"First, Adam finally got a hit on that case you were asking about."

"Good thing I didn't hold my breath. What's it been, eight, ten months?"

"Ha-ha. Always the comedian. It's only been two, give or take a week."

The time lapse wasn't as important as hearing what Noah's DA brother found out about Summer's attacker.

"Adam said to remind you this is strictly confidential."

"Got it."

"That if this gets out, he'll deny any and all involvement."

"You have my word."

"So the guy's name is Michael Samuels. Age 28. Born in Boulder, moved to Denver. They picked him up on a DDC, and—"

"DDC?"

"Drunk and disorderly conduct. He had your lady friend's wallet, plus a couple of others on him. Report says your girlfriend couldn't make a positive ID. And because the kid was wearing gloves and a ski mask, he didn't leave any DNA. She picked him out of a lineup, but only because she recognized his voice. And you can figure out what the public defender did with that." He groaned. "Anyway, with no DNA and no ID, he got two years on a Class 5 Felony Theft charge. Cleaned up his act in the Denver jail, and from everything Adam found, he hasn't stepped outta line since."

"Two years. For kidnapping, assault and battery and rape? That's ridiculous!"

"I hear ya, pal, but it's called the Justice System, not the Let's Be Fair System."

Zach stared at what he'd scribbled on the checkbook register: *Michael Samuels. Class 5 Felony. Two years.*

"So the other reason I called…"

He closed the checkbook because reading the pervert's name made him want to punch something, hard.

"While I was on my way back to the station yesterday, I saw this dog, and it seemed so miserable that I stopped to look for tags. But nothin'. So I took it to this vet I know and paid to have it checked out. No microchip, but no diseases, either. I can't keep him 'cause the wife's allergic, and so's my son. It's at Adam's for now, but his wife is about to have twins in, like, ten minutes, so it can't stay there. So I was wondering if maybe that kid who works for you might want it? It's free. Clean bill of health. Cute li'l fella—calm, quiet, good disposition, housebroken, even."

"Sounds too good to be true."

"Hey. Have I ever steered you wrong?"

No, he hadn't. But the Petersons couldn't take the dog. How often had Rose said she was allergic to life? Too many times to count.

Summer...

If she had a dog to protect and care for, to keep her company, it could bring her the rest of the way toward emotional healing. Zach ran a hand through his hair. *Watch it, dude*, he thought, *you're starting to sound like Libby.*

"I might know somebody."

"Excellent! When can you come for it? It's miserable over there. I can meet you halfway between here and Vail."

"Wait. Why's the dog miserable?"

"That clean freak sister-in-law of mine insists on keeping it in a crate. Whoever owned him before must not have used one, 'cause the poor mutt hates it. The whimpering is heartbreaking, I tell you. The sooner you can come get him, the sooner he gets outta that cage."

They worked out the drop-off details.

Now Zach just had to work out how to get the dog to Summer's house...

"YES, OF COURSE it's exciting, but it's frustrating, too," Summer's dad said. "I always feel sorry for anybody who hasn't done this before."

"Oh, honey, your dad is *so* right!"

The only time Summer used her webcam was when her parents called from their latest movie set.

"First-timers think as soon as they get word they've been booked," Susannah finished, "someone will call to tell them when and where to show up for work."

Harrison sighed. "I remember when I was a first-timer. I waited weeks for the call."

"And Chris was all 'I *told* you what your booking window was,' like we were complete amateurs!"

"We were complete amateurs!" They laughed then leaned into one another, as if Summer wasn't even there. Her parents rambled for a few minutes more, and then Susannah brought her face closer to the camera. "But we didn't call to talk about that! How are *you*, honey?"

"Still getting out—"

"To shop for your*self*?"

"And taking the self-defense classes?"

"Speaking of which," Susannah cut in. "How's that nice man, Zach?"

Summer didn't know which question to answer first. "Everything and everyone is fine."

She told them about Libby's invitation to help out with the fund-raiser. Horseback riding and pizza night, and saved the kissing booth for last.

Harrison and Susannah exchanged a wide-eyed, disbelieving glance.

"A *kissing* booth?" her dad echoed.

"Libby and I brought in $428 for the organization. Firefly Autism."

Hands folded under her chin, Susannah tilted her head. "Oh, honey, that's…that's just *won*derful! And amazing!" She looked at her husband. "Can you believe it, Harry? A kissing booth!"

Her dad pressed a palm to his chest. "I'm proud of you, sweetheart."

Summer had to admit, she was proud of herself, too.

Susannah giggled. "Did that handsome instructor of yours get in line?"

She felt a flush coming on and hoped the webcam wouldn't pick it up.

"He didn't have much choice," Summer said. "His mom was the hostess, and they held the hoedown in the Marshalls' party barn. And he couldn't very well stand in his sister's line!"

Her mom's you-can't-fool-me grin told Summer the camera was more sensitive than she'd thought.

"Look at her blushing, Harry. I think maybe our girl is in love!"

Nodding, Harrison checked his watch. "Well, our lunch break is over, and we have to be on set in five."

"I'm glad you called. Do it again, real soon, okay? I miss you guys!"

After shutting down the camera and closing her laptop, Summer did some chores. With no one leaving dessert bowls, balled-up socks and ketchup packets everywhere, it didn't take long. So she baked brownies for Alex and Rose, put a single-serving pot pie in the oven and started a grocery list.

It was so quiet. She couldn't get Zach's kiss out of her mind. Couldn't block thoughts of the way he'd held her as they danced.

She turned on the stereo, hoping the music or the lyrics of a song—any song—would give her something else to think about. It had been months since she'd used it. Evidently, during one of her cleaning frenzies, her mom had unintentionally moved the dial. Summer rolled it right, then left, nodding when the hissing stopped and a song came in, loud and clear.

What were the chances it would be *that* song? Eyes closed, she swayed in time to the music, smiling at the memory of his deep voice, singing softly off-key in her ear.

Then she came to her senses and changed the station. On the way to class the other night, she'd stopped at Traveler Books and bought a mystery novel. If the gritty story about a troubled sheriff out West didn't get her mind off Zach, what would?

Summer made herself a mug of hot chocolate,

put on her boots and coat and tucked a digital timer into her jacket pocket. That pot pie would taste even better when she came in from the cold, she thought, grabbing a fleecy throw from the sofa as she stepped onto the deck.

Whoever invented fingerless gloves should get an award, she thought, turning to the first page in the book. She looked out over her view of Vail's mountaintops. It was a sight to behold, but couldn't compare with the awe-inspiring vistas on the Double M. She closed her eyes and inhaled the crisp, heavy scent of falling snow, and used her thumb to mark her place in the novel. "Raindrops on roses," she sang softly.

"No wonder you didn't hear the doorbell."

Startled, Summer scrambled to get out of the blanket and onto her feet, and in the process, overturned the flimsy aluminum lounge chair.

"Sheesh. Didn't mean to scare you."

Zach held out a hand to help her up, and while grabbing it, her elbow bumped the cake plate he was holding, and it landed facedown on the snow-covered deck.

"Sorry about that, too," he said, pointing at the cherry-topped mess. "Rose said it's your favorite dessert, and sent me to deliver it."

"That was sweet of her," Summer said, looking at it. "But it's probably just as well."

He chuckled. "She isn't exactly Paula Deen, is she?"

Summer thought of the Christmas sugar cookies that not even birds or wandering cats would eat because Rose had doubled the baking soda and halved the sugar. And then the time she'd mistaken Italian seasoning for parsley flakes, and used it to season her baked beans.

"Well, her heart is always in the right place," Summer said. "Let me grab something to clean that up."

She hurried inside and took the whole roll of paper towels back outside with her. She tore off a couple of sheets, and so did Zach.

When they bent to scoop up the cake, their foreheads collided, knocking them off-balance. And yet again, they found themselves a twist of arms and legs, with Zach above and Summer below…at the perfect kissing distance.

"We really have to stop meeting this way," he said.

Their laughter started slow and quiet then grew in volume and intensity. Zach rolled onto his back, and they lay side by side, blotting tears of mirth from their eyes.

"Wait," Summer said between giggles. "What's that noise?"

Zach lifted his head. "Sounds like a dog to me."

CHAPTER TWENTY-ONE

THEY SAT UP at the same time and met the sad, steady gaze of the knee-high, shaggy-haired, brown-eyed mutt.

"Look at that sweet face!"

Zach chuckled. "He's probably thinking we played a nasty trick on him, luring him up here for *that*." Again, he pointed at the cheesecake.

Summer patted her thigh. "C'mere, cutie, so I can see if you have tags."

Ears perked, it moved forward, and when the dog reached her, Summer hugged him close.

"Oh, Zach! It's soaking wet. And shivering!"

Yeah, and he felt a little guilty about that, but it had only been a few minutes since he let the pup out of his truck. Besides, how else was he supposed to get the two of them together?

He watched as Summer wrapped her blanket around the dog, stroking the soft fur between his eyes and cooing reassuring words into his ears.

Zach could have kicked himself for saying *he*. Thankfully, Summer hadn't noticed, or if she had, she chose to overlook it. Because no one was that observant, that soon.

"We need to get him out of the snow and wind," she said, standing.

She opened the French doors that led into the family room and stepped inside. And much to Zach's relief, the dog followed. Instantly, it sat on the mat just inside the entry and held up its right paw.

"Aw, aren't you a considerate fellow!" Summer got down on one knee and used a paper towel to wipe the offered paw. When she finished, he held up his left paw.

"I wonder if a nice bath would warm him up?"

Without waiting for a reply, she turned off the oven and headed up the stairs. The dog followed her, and Zach followed the dog. Once they were all in the bathroom, she closed the door and pulled the stopper in the tub. And while it filled with warm water, she sat on the padded hamper and tugged off her boots and socks.

"There are towels in that cabinet behind you," she said, tossing her jacket onto the floor. "Will you grab a couple for me?"

He didn't understand why she needed bare feet to wash a dog, but did as she asked, without question. When he turned to face her again, Zach saw that she'd rolled her khakis all the way up to her knees, exposing three raised red scars that started at her shin and disappeared under the cuff.

She spread the offered towel on the floor beside the tub then climbed in and turned off the water. "C'mon, buddy," she said, clapping. "The water's great!"

Zach prepared to pick up the dog and give it a little assist, but it leaped into the water before he got the chance.

Summer lathered its multicolored fur, and seemed oblivious to how wet and soapy she got in the process. When she began a thorough massage, Zach grinned. *Lucky dog*, he thought.

"I suppose once he's good and dry, we should probably take him to a vet, see if his owners microchipped him." She kissed the top of his head. "I know if you were mine, I'd be worried sick, wondering where you are!"

During the drive between Dave's and home, Zach had called an old college pal who'd settled in Vail and worked at the Vail Valley Animal Hospital. One quick phone call and Casey would meet them at the Edwards Clinic on Village Boulevard. To secure Casey's cooperation, Zach wrote a generous check to help care for abandoned or neglected cats and dogs like this one.

"College pal of mine is a vet," he said, stepping into the hall. "I'll give him a call."

When he returned, Zach aimed his cell phone at the now-fluffy pup and snapped its picture. "I'll send that to Alex," he said, "and ask him to make up some lost dog flyers."

"That's a great idea. What do you bet by the time we get back here, he and Rose will have one tacked to every sign and lamppost in Vail?"

The dog had been found in Denver, and Dave's weeks-long search hadn't produced the dog's owners. Chances that anyone in Vail would respond were slim to none. And that was a good thing. A very good thing since, in his opinion, Summer needed the dog as much as the dog needed a loving home.

He'd give them a day, maybe two to bond, and then he'd tell Summer the truth. If finding out he'd deliberately withheld information upset her, well, he'd cross that bridge when he got to it.

As planned, the vet gave the dog a thorough exam. Summer seemed disappointed when he announced he didn't find a microchip, but brightened up when Casey said, "We'll have more information about his health when the blood work comes back, but from everything I've seen, he's perfectly normal. Clear eyes, healthy teeth and gums, no parasites, skin lesions or signs of abuse." And although he couldn't specify a breed, the vet felt the stand-up ears meant part Border Collie, part Husky. "I'm guessing three years old, but he could be a year or two older. Good combination if you're looking for a smart, sociable mutt."

She cupped the dog's chin in one hand, patted its head with the other. "Did you hear that? You got a clean bill of health from Dr. Casey!"

Copper-colored eyes moved left and zeroed in on the vet. And when he looked back at Summer, a smile turned up the corners of his black-rimmed lips.

Zach explained how they'd post flyers and put an ad in the local papers in the hope of rousting out the dog's owners. Then he opened his wallet and said, "How much, Doc?"

"No charge," Casey said, patting the dog's head. "Consider the exam my contribution to this guy's new lease on life."

Summer spent most of the short drive back to her house facing the backseat, alternately petting the dog and crooning words of comfort. And from what Zach could see in the rearview mirror, the dog was eating it up.

"I'm a terrible, selfish, coldhearted person," she said, frowning.

"Why?"

"Well, what would *you* call someone who hopes the owners never respond?"

"If Smiley back there had been chipped, he'd

be home by now. Maybe it's best he can't go back to his irresponsible pet owners."

From the corner of his eye, he saw Summer nod. "I hope they don't respond, too," he said.

She turned in the passenger seat. "Why?"

"If they really cared, wouldn't they have gone to the trouble of at least hanging a tag round his neck? What else did they neglect to do?"

Another nod. "There could have been a car accident. Maybe he got scared and ran. Or belonged to some sweet old lady who passed away without a will."

"I once knew a couple, used their cat as a weapon the way some people use their kids. The woman fought for catstody, or whatever it's called, for no reason other than to hurt her ex. A month later, her upstairs neighbors called the cops, complaining about all the meowing. Turned out she'd gone on a world cruise and left the Siamese alone in the apartment. And to make a long story short—"

"Too late for that," she teased.

"So maybe ol' Happy Face is the product of a bitter divorce."

Shoulders slumped, she said, "How sad."

"And stupid."

Summer sighed. "But if his owners don't show up, we'll never know why he's homeless, will we?"

He reached across the console, gave her hand

a gentle squeeze. "Thanks to you, he isn't homeless."

Zach didn't know how to explain her hesitation. He'd already decided that if she didn't want to keep the dog once she'd heard the whole story, he'd take it, himself.

The dog hopped off the pickup's backseat and rested his chin on the padded console. She laughed softly. "Just look at that face! You're a keeper, I tell you!"

On the heels of a quick gasp, she ruffled the inch-long fur atop his head. "I think that's what I'll call you…Keeper! What do you say to that?"

The dog's pointy ears stood straight up, and he gave a breathy, approving bark.

"Keeper," Zach echoed. "I like it, too."

"Would you mind stopping at the pet shop on Gore Creek? I'd like to pick up a few things for him."

He'd expected her to be inside ten minutes, tops. When Summer knocked on the passenger window, he realized he and Keeper had dozed for half an hour. And when saw the full cart behind her, he got out of the truck.

"Did you leave anything for any other pet owners?"

"I had to wait while they stitched his name onto his collar." She opened her hand to show him the bright silver tag. "But I made this, myself, using that cool machine at the back of the store." It said KEEPER above Summer's address and phone number.

Zach felt good, knowing his idea had made her so happy. But would she still feel this way after she found out she'd been duped?

As he loaded things into the truck's bed, she explained every purchase: stainless food and water bowls because some dogs were allergic to plastic. Four squeaky toys and two balls with bells inside them. A bite-proof stuffed dog to cuddle with. And two quilted beds. "One for beside my bed, one for the family room."

Her parents had told him she had a knack for managing money. What would they say if they saw everything their daughter had bought for a dog she wasn't sure she could keep?

"I know this arrangement might be temporary," she said, climbing into the truck. "But I want him to feel welcome. If his owners call, I'll let them take the stuff home."

He slid behind the steering wheel. "You're a big girl. You don't owe me any explanations."

Her confident smile said, "You're absolutely right!" It was all he could do to break eye contact long enough to slide the key into the ignition.

"So did you miss me?" she asked.

Zach opened his mouth to say, *Yeah, I missed you. Way too much to be healthy!* But the dog beat him to it with a quiet yip. If he didn't know better, he'd say Summer and Keeper had been together for months, if not years. It made him think of the flyers that Alex would have distributed by now. Again, he reminded himself it wasn't likely anyone would respond, but even a 1 percent possibility was too high. He considered sneaking out after dark and tearing down all the notices. But on the off chance Keeper did have a loving family out there somewhere, it would be cruel to get in the way of a reunion.

A line from his mother's favorite song pinged in his brain. *What will be will be*, he thought, pulling into Summer's driveway.

Keeper hopped down from the truck and followed her inside without a backward glance, making it tough to believe this well-behaved mutt had run off on his own. While she tended to the dog, Zach carried in the things she'd bought. He made himself a cup of coffee and watched as she introduced Keeper to each item, and considered where to put them. If she put that much effort into making a stray dog feel at home, how much more would she devote to a husband and kids?

He scrubbed a hand over his face and groaned inwardly at the thought. So much for hoping that once Summer got into a routine, caring for the dog, he wouldn't feel the pull to watch over her. Her neediness, which was pretty much nonexistent now, had little to do with his feelings of protectiveness. She'd never asked for his help, and she'd succeeded in pushing that dark night farther and farther into the past. She reminded him of a butterfly, struggling to escape its cocoon, then spreading its beautiful wings to fly, high and free. How sad was it that a small part of him wished she *did* need him, just a little bit?

Knight in Shining Armor Syndrome, four, he thought. *Zach Marshall, zip.*

CHAPTER TWENTY-TWO

"WELL, KEEPER," SUMMER SAID, "now that you've been here two whole weeks, how do you like it?"

As usual, he sat quietly, watching her. Already, she'd fallen for his thoughtful, expressive face. "Well, *I* like it enough for both of us!"

Tail wagging, Keeper sauntered into the family room, flopped down on his thick doggy bed and began gnawing on a rawhide bone. His way of saying, "It'll do."

Once a day, he brought her his leash, and they went for a walk. Keeper taught her how to recognize the signs that he needed a moment or two in her fenced backyard, and quickly made it clear that he preferred privacy. The behavior prompted a cursory search for doggy doors, but upon realizing she'd have to hire a stranger to install one, she never placed the order. Keeper also taught Summer the proper way to play fetch by dropping a toy at her feet then darting to the opposite side of the room. She'd always remember how, when she figured it out and played along, he high-fived her.

He sensed her moods, too, running in circles when she was happy, curling up beside her when a nightmare woke her or worries that she'd never work again kept her awake, as they had last night. She'd been unemployed two years now. Would she ever get another voice-over job?

Only one way to find out...

She grabbed her cell phone, scrolled to the *D*s, and dialed her agent's number.

"Well, if it isn't Summer Lane!"

She laughed. "Have you *ever* answered the phone with an ordinary hello?"

"I've been called many things, but ordinary has never been one of them," Chris Dickerson said. "So what can I do ya for, sweet cheeks?"

"You can get me some work."

"Good to hear you're ready to get back on the proverbial horse. Gimme a couple of days to see what I can scare up. So tell me...how are you?"

She could almost see him, squinting into the haze of a cigarette, reading glasses atop his bald head, the iconic Fedora within easy reach. The image made her smile.

"Better than I've been in two years."

"Well, now, that's the kinda news that warms this hard old heart. Glad to hear it. Told ya you'd bounce back, didn't I?"

"Bet you didn't think it would take this long, though."

"Listen, sweet cheeks. We all do what we gotta do to get by. Time is irrelevant. Does anything else matter?"

Almost word for word what Zach had said. She heard the squeak of his desk chair, followed by a quiet slurp, and wondered if he was sipping black coffee from the enormous mug she'd given him for Christmas a few years back. *World's Best Agent*, it said.

"So do you want to dive in headfirst with a long-term product deal, or just stick a toe in the water with a couple of onetime deals, see how things feel?"

"I suppose that'll depend on what sort of jobs you line up." Keeper rested his chin on her knee, and she stroked his silky head. "Do you have any contacts here in Colorado?"

"A*ha*!"

"Aha?"

"Okay, out with it. What's his name?"

Over the years, she'd spent almost as much time with Chris as she had her parents, so it shouldn't have surprised her when he figured out why she would prefer a local job.

"His name is Keeper."

"Is that his first name or last?"

Laughing, Summer said, "He's a dog. Literally wandered into my life, and if his owners call to claim him, I'll be a mess."

"Aha. You know what they say…you can't fool an old fool. No way I believe you sound this way because of some mutt. Now out with it, unless you'd rather I call your folks."

Summer groaned. "You wouldn't!"

He answered with a sinister snicker.

"You can't see it, but I'm waving the white flag. I've been calling him Mr. Couldn't Be More Wrong for Me."

"No way I believe that. Not if he got close enough to make you want to plant roots."

Because Zach *wasn't* wrong for her. More like the other way around…

She heard Chris's ballpoint, clicking on, clicking off. It used to drive her to distraction, but after all these months, it was music to her ears. It meant he had more to say. Hopefully, it wouldn't be Zach-related.

"So what does Mr. Wrong do for a living?"

Summer told him that she'd been taking self-defense classes at Zach's studio. That she'd met his family.

"Because," she explained, "Mom and Dad missed another Thanksgiving. And they'll miss another Christmas, too."

"Wah-wah-wah," Chris said. "Stop bein' a big whiny baby. You're what, thirty? You want to see Mommy and Daddy? Buy a ticket, pack a bag and go to LA, for cryin' out loud. Your dad is always bragging that you're a regular investment whiz, so I know you can afford it, you tightwad, you!" He punctuated the statement with a smoky laugh.

"You really need to give up those cigarettes," she said. "Smoking will stunt your growth."

"Yeah, yeah, yeah." He grew quiet for a moment then said, "How many years have we worked together now?"

"You got me my first job when I was seventeen. What's that, thirteen years?"

"Eleven, if you subtract the two you spent wallowing."

Chris had never been one to mince words. "I stand corrected."

"Most kids your age would've signed with four, maybe five agents in that much time. Tells me you learned the meaning of the word *loyal*. If Mr. Wrong doesn't realize that, kick him to the curb and find a guy who's worthy of you."

When he said things like that, Summer wished her dad could be more like him.

"Well, sweet cheeks, unlike some people who can afford to live off their investments, I have to work for a living." As if to prove it, the pen went click-clack, click-clack. "I'll make a few calls. I'm sure I can find a mom and pop store or some 'as seen on TV' manufacturers who need an honest-sounding voice to hawk their junk."

"Thanks, Chris. And I really mean that."

"I know you do. Sincerity is something else that makes you a gem. If that guy doesn't know it, walk away." Another pause, and then, "Call you soon. Love ya, sweet cheeks."

If she didn't know he ended all of his calls that way, Summer might be flattered. "Love ya right back, Dickerson."

She hung up and patted Keeper's head. "See what I did for you just now? Asked him to find jobs within driving distance of home, so I can be here to feed you and—"

The dog huffed, as if to say, "Gimme a break." And either Summer was seeing things, or he rolled his eyes, too.

"It wouldn't kill you, would it, to at least pretend to agree?"

Keeper chose a toy from his basket, walked three circles on his bed and flopped down to cuddle with his stuffed bear.

The doorbell rang, and when Summer peered through the peephole, she saw Rose holding a plate of…something.

"I hope you know how lucky you are to be a dog," she told Keeper. "Nobody would call you rude if you turned up your nose at one of her culinary misfires."

The minute the door opened, Rose handed the plate to Summer and headed straight for the dog bed. "Oh, just look at this sweet puppy!" she said, crouching to pet him.

"I thought you were allergic."

"I am. To training and dog fur and drooling."

"Rose! I'm surprised at you!"

Rising, Summer's neighbor headed for the kitchen. "These are my version of sticky buns," she said, peeling back the plastic wrap and helping herself to one. "Is there coffee?"

"I had a huge breakfast this morning, so I'll save the sticky buns for later."

Keeper repeated his skeptical huff, and Summer decided it was a very good thing he couldn't talk.

"So how's it going with this gorgeous mutt?"

"It's going great. He's funny and smart and great company." She sighed. "It'll be downright painful when his owners come for him."

"They won't."

"I hope you're right."

"Oh, I *know* I'm right. Keeper really is a keeper, 'cause Zach doesn't do things halfway."

Summer slid onto a counter stool. "What does *that* mean?"

Rose leaned forward and whispered conspiratorially, "Can you keep a secret?"

Better than you can, Summer thought.

"Surely you've figured out by now that Zach set the whole thing up. Isn't he just a living doll?"

"Wait. He…*what*?"

"Uh oh. Didn't mean to spoil the surprise." Rose bit into the bun. "I have it on good authority that one of Zach's ex-marine friends is a Denver cop. Seems he was jiggling doorknobs or whatever when he found Keeper. And since his whole family is allergic—for *real*—he called Zach to see if he knew anyone who might want to adopt a dog. You were the first person who came to mind, so he drove to Denver, and the rest, as they say, is history."

Summer remembered that day on the deck, when Keeper and Zach had appeared out of nowhere at almost the same moment. At the time, it had seemed a little weird that he'd attended one of Rose's soirees when he never had before.

Summer looked up, saw that Keeper had been watching her, his soulful, imploring eyes sending a dual message: *Please don't send me away. I had nothing to do with it.*

Her relief that no one would ever claim him was balanced by a strange blend of gratitude and resentment toward Zach.

Summer picked up a sticky bun and took a huge bite, thinking that a mouthful of the dry, flavorless cake was the perfect way to keep her tongue under control.

"What do you think?" Rose asked.

They were stone-cold, but she nodded enthusiastically. "Mmm," she said as Rose's wristwatch beeped.

"Well, I have to run. There's another batch of sticky buns in the oven for Alex to bring to the studio tonight."

She slurped the rest of her coffee. "I know that's a lot for just one person, but who knows? Somebody might drop in."

Somebody, she thought as Rose went out the door, was about to get a piece of her mind.

CHAPTER TWENTY-THREE

"WHERE'S SUMMER?" ONE of the students asked.

"I was wondering the same thing."

Cecile Murphy looked up into Zach's face. "Well, *that's* a surprise."

He decided it was safer not to ask what she was talking about.

"We all know there's something going on between you two."

The statement was a trap. No matter how he answered, he'd sound guilty.

"Class starts in five minutes," he said. "Plenty of time to finish your warm-up exercises."

"Funny. I've never heard you tell *Summer* to warm up."

Maybe that's because she does the right thing, all on her own?

"I don't know about the others," the woman continued, "but I'm not at all pleased that you consistently show her preferential treatment. We're all paying the same amount of money for these lessons, after all."

Zach inhaled deeply, summoning patience and

self-control. He'd worked hard not to show any partiality. Not an easy feat, for a host of reasons.

Alex joined them. "Phone call. In your office. Your sister, I think." He looked at Cecile then back at Zach. "Sorry if I interrupted anything."

"You didn't." Zach faced his agitated student. "Say the word, and I'll give you a full refund."

He waited for a reply. When none came, he walked toward the office.

"You don't really have a call," Alex said, closing the door. "When I heard what was going on, I figured an interruption was called for."

"Thanks, kiddo." He squeezed the boy's shoulder. "But for future reference? Don't lie on my behalf. Never lower your standards for anyone."

Alex nodded. "You think she'll want her money back?"

"I hope not, because she's the type who'll spread her crazy assumptions all over town."

"You're right. Mostly, her complaints are way off base." He hesitated, blushing as he said, "But she's right about this."

"Really."

"It isn't that you spend more *time* with Summer, it's that when you work with her…" His brow furrowed as he searched for the right word. "Let's just say your face changes when she's around. If I noticed that you're always watching her, the rest of them have, too."

This was all news to Zach.

"She has that *look*, so I get it."

"What look?"

Alex shrugged one shoulder, tucked his fingertips into his pockets. "Kinda like Keeper looked the first time I saw him. Scared, worried, lost...I dunno. Y'know?"

Yeah, he did. In fact, he was picturing *that look* as he realized she was minutes from being late. And Summer was always on time.

Cecile was his most vocal student. She'd said "we all know," or words to that effect, but he'd dismissed it as petty nonsense. But what if she'd only given voice to what the rest of them were thinking? What if she'd been their self-appointed spokeswoman? If that was the case, Summer could cost him clients now and in the future. Through no fault of her own, she'd put him in one heck of a predicament.

No, *he* was the problem. First thing tomorrow, he'd go through his files. Several former students had gone on to earn teaching certificates. Hopefully, one of them would be available, and if he could talk them into taking his place in the classroom, Zach would stay in the background from now on.

"So where *is* Summer tonight?" Alex wanted to know.

"Not sure. Her excuse last week was that she

didn't want to leave Keeper alone so soon after he moved in."

"Want me to get her on the phone?"

"Nah. If she doesn't show up, I'll check on her after class." In person. "How would you feel about running the session tonight?"

"Me?" Alex beamed. "But I'm not certified!"

"So you'll take the hands-off approach—stay up front, showing them what to do. Tonight's lesson is pretty easy. Plus, I've got a video lined up. Just run the PowerPoint and answer questions."

His excitement waned slightly. "Where will you be?"

"Right there, if you need me." He winked. "But you won't."

Alex wrapped him in a huge, clumsy hug. "Thanks, Zach! You're the *best*!"

As he ran off to teach his first class, Zach smiled at the feelings of fatherly affection that had welled up inside him.

ON HIS WAY to Summer's town house, Zach picked up a pizza, and as an afterthought, stopped at the local convenience store and grabbed a small package of dog treats.

She didn't answer the doorbell, but her car was in the driveway, so he walked around the side and peered over the fence. Sure enough, Summer was out back in the dark, flipping a Frisbee to a happy, romping Keeper.

The gate squealed as he opened it, putting a complete halt to their game.

"Oh, look," she said dully. "It's Mr. Trickster."

Zach didn't even want to think about what that might mean—especially considering the way she'd said it—so he hoisted the pizza on his palm.

"Wasn't sure what toppings you like," he said, grinning. "So I got cheese."

"How very thoughtful of you," she returned, bending to pick up the toy.

The dog followed her up the steps, and so did Zach.

"Alex and I were worried when you didn't show up for class. I tried calling," he said, thinking his surprise visit had annoyed her. "But when you didn't pick up, I took a chance that you'd be home."

Summer cleared a space on the counter, and as he opened the pizza box, she grabbed paper plates and napkins.

"Bottled water or iced tea?"

"Uh, water's good. Thanks."

He filled the uncomfortable silence with talk about Alex leading his first class alone. Summer said things like "That's nice," and "Good for him," but her lack of enthusiasm reminded him of how she'd behaved when they first met. *This is a prime example of why you need to back off,* he thought, *way off.*

After two slices of pizza, Summer leaned back and patted her flat stomach. "I'm stuffed. I skipped lunch, so that really hit the spot. Thanks."

She hadn't strung that many words together since he stepped into the backyard. Had she gotten over whatever was bugging her? he wondered, helping himself to another slice.

Zach glanced around the tidy kitchen, searching for something—anything—to focus on besides Summer. He spotted a plate of sticky buns on the counter behind her, arranged neatly on a red-and-white-checkered plate, and covered with blue plastic wrap. He'd seen both enough times to recognize the owner.

He pointed at it. "I see Rose was over here today."

She followed his line of vision. "Unfortunately for you, yes, she was."

And then it hit him: he hadn't wanted to involve Alex in his slightly dishonest plot to give the dog to Summer, but for the plan to work on delivery day, he'd needed Rose's help. She'd been so happy to help him surprise Summer that when he asked her to keep the plans to herself, she'd crossed her heart and hoped to die, held up the

Girl Scout salute and zipped her lips. He should have known better than to believe she'd keep the details under wraps forever.

"Do you play poker?"

Summer's question caught him off guard. "Played once in Afghanistan. I don't like to lose, so once was all it took."

He unscrewed the water bottle and drank like a man who'd spent too long in the desert.

"I'm not quite sure how to approach this, or even where to begin," she said, her forefinger tracing the pizza shop's logo on the box. "So bear with me if I ramble."

Zach recapped the bottle and folded his hands on the counter.

"Rose told me what you did, getting Keeper here."

The dog raised his head, ears perked at the mention of his name.

"As far as I'm concerned, he's mine, and if his former owners ever show up, it'll break my heart because I'm crazy about him."

"From that look on his face, I'd say he feels the same way."

Her expression softened, but only for a moment. "But I resent the way you went about it." She paused. Leaned forward slightly. "Why didn't you just come right out and ask me if I wanted a dog? Why did you feel the need to sneak around behind my back?"

Sneak? Zach wouldn't have put it that way... exactly.

"Because I thought you'd say no. And I wanted to surprise you." Both statements were equally true.

"It worked. I was surprised. But what made you think I'd say no?"

Because you're an emotional wreck? Because sometimes, you can be a little self-centered? That wasn't it, and he knew it. If he thought for a minute she couldn't shift the focus from herself to Keeper, Zach wouldn't have set up the whole adoption thing. He knew next to nothing about the dog's background, but the dog deserved better than that.

"I just figured with everything you'd been through, the responsibility might prove to be too much pressure." He shrugged. "And then I realized that was a bunch of hooey. You wouldn't have taken the class, or gone to the ranch or volunteered at the fund-raiser if you couldn't handle stress."

"Well, I guess I can't blame you for thinking I might be too self-absorbed to devote myself to a dog. I haven't always behaved like a sane, rational adult, and at times, even *I* wondered if I'd ever get my head together."

He was about to thank her for so graciously letting him off the hook when Summer added, "But that doesn't change the facts. What you did was manipulative and disrespectful."

"Sorry I made you feel that way." Also true. "I never meant to insult you."

Zach tossed his empty water bottle into the trash can. "Guess I'd better hit the road. Got a stack of Marshall Law bills waiting for me back at the studio."

She walked beside him to the door and stood cross-armed while he put on his coat.

"Thanks again for supper." She glanced at Keeper. "Thanks for him, too. What you did… it's one of the nicest, most thoughtful things any-one has ever done for me."

Zach had no idea where he stood with this woman. The only upside to that was, maybe this time, he could stick to his guns and *stay away*.

"Coming to class next week?"

She looked at Keeper. "I think he's adjusted well enough to be left alone for an hour and a half."

Zach took his keys from his pocket. "See you Monday, then."

As he descended the porch steps, he heard the dead bolt click into place. A few things clicked in his mind at that moment, too.

His frosty breath floated in front of him as

he climbed into the pickup. Ironic, he thought, that although the dash clock said twenty-nine degrees, he'd just survived a Summer storm.

CHAPTER TWENTY-FOUR

LIBBY SAT CROSS-LEGGED on the floor playing tug-of-war with Keeper.

"No one would ever guess you didn't get him as a puppy."

And it was true. In the weeks he'd been with Summer, the dog had settled in, roaming the house at will. His doggy smile seemed as much a part of his face as the soulful eyes that held the secrets of his former life. Trust, he had taught her, wasn't something easily or quickly won.

"I can't imagine getting rid of a sweetheart like this." Libby hugged him then kissed him right between the eyes. "Still no response to the newspaper ads and flyers, huh?"

"Not a word, and when I wonder about all the different scenarios that could have put him here, I hope his former owners never call."

"Me, too." Scrambling to her feet, Libby gave Keeper a final pat and joined Summer in the family room, helping herself to a handful of popcorn. "Did you ever meet somebody and *instantly* feel as though you've known them all your life?"

Summer nodded then met Keeper's steady gaze. "Y'know, that's a great way to describe what happened when he walked onto my deck that day."

"No, silly. I'm not talking about you and the dog. I'm talking about you and me!"

She liked Zach's sister. Who wouldn't like a smart, personable, kindhearted woman like Libby? But Summer didn't share the known-you-all-my-life thing. Then again, she'd told Libby things she'd never shared with anyone else.

"I mean, seriously?" Libby said. "I've told you things *nobody* else knows." She ran down the quick list of guys she'd dated and dumped, excuses she'd made to avoid family vacations, stupid things she'd done at psychology conventions. "If you tell anyone about what happened last year in Chicago..." Groaning, she hid behind her hands.

"Oh, I can see the headlines now—Doctors Caught Enjoying Themselves at American Psychological Association Convention.'"

"I just don't know what might happen if that story got out. The big jerk lied. I break a lot of rules, but 'don't mess with married men' is *not* one of them."

"Yeah, I suppose a rumor like that wouldn't be good for either of you."

"Oh, I'm not worried about our *peers* finding out. We'd just cite some psycho-babble excuse, and all would be forgotten. If my patients found out—or worse, my brother?" She shuddered. "Let's just say I don't have the personality to deal with the lectures I'd get every time I registered for a conference."

"Has he stayed in touch?"

"Hank?" Libby blew a raspberry. "He called soon after I got home and told a bunch of 'my wife doesn't understand me' lies. I told him never to call again, and much to my relief, he hasn't. And speaking of relief," Libby said, "I guess you feel better, getting all that 'you're not the boss of me' stuff off your chest, huh?"

The moment she'd opened the door, Summer suspected Libby hadn't just been in the neighborhood. Part of her wanted to know what, exactly, Zach had told his sister about their conversation. Mostly, she hoped her new pal hadn't been in on the scheme.

Libby sat on her feet. "Methinks thou protesteth too littleth."

That inspired a chuckle. "Careful," Summer said. "This friend knoweth things."

"Zach is right. You were doing great before the mutt showed up. But since?" She nodded knowingly. "You've really blossomed."

Libby's words, no doubt. Summer couldn't imagine Zach saying something like that.

"I'll admit that Keeper—and the Petersons and your family—helped me make some important changes in my life."

"Zach's right about something else, too. You're harder to read than Latin."

"And here I thought I was speaking English."

Libby frowned. "Sarcasm does not become you." She sipped her hot chocolate and stared into the mug. "I like you, Summer, but I *love* Zach. I can't sit idly by and watch him be hurt again."

She'd never hurt him, not intentionally, anyway. Set him straight, yes. But hurt him? Never.

"I'll admit he went about the whole 'get Summer a dog' thing in his typical jackboot way, but his heart was in the right place. Now he's worried that you've lumped him in with that monster who attacked you. He'll beat himself up for days over this."

Summer had been looking for a rationale to maintain a friends-only relationship with Zach, but letting him think she compared him to Samuels was beyond dishonest. It was downright cruel, and he deserved far better than that.

Libby glanced at her watch. "Rats. I have to run," she said, draining her mug. "Or I'll be late for my next patient." She put on her coat. "I know my brother. He's in love with you."

Summer laughed. "Don't take this the wrong

way, but that's ridiculous." But a small part of her selfishly hoped what Libby had said was true. Too bad she was the last thing Zach needed.

"Everything he says and does is proof that he cares about you."

"Yeah, but caring is in his nature. Being a father figure for Alex. Fixing stuff in Rose's house. Giving 110 percent to his students. He's paying Emma's bills while she's off helping her grandmother. Thank goodness the poor woman has insurance, or he'd probably be paying those bills, too. And I wouldn't have Keeper if it hadn't been for Zach. I agree, it's all proof that he's a big-hearted guy. But it *doesn't* prove anything more."

"And if you believe that, you need an eye doctor *and* a therapist."

Summer thought about Libby's parting comment as she loaded the dishwasher, and decided it was long past time to make some changes. Big changes.

And she'd start by calling her agent to see if he'd lined up any auditions.

CHAPTER TWENTY-FIVE

"OH, HONEY, THAT'S so exciting!" Summer's mom said. "But are you sure you're ready? This is such a big step, and you haven't traveled anywhere in two years."

Summer had to admit, her heartbeat doubled at the mere thought of crowded airports and the confines of an airplane. But if not now, when?

"I'll be fine," she fibbed. "Honest."

"Let us know when your flight gets in, and we'll meet you. Oh, and the sofa in our sitting room opens into a small bed. I'll ask housekeeping to make it up for you."

"You're sweet to offer, but I've already reserved a rental car and booked a room at your hotel."

"I can hardly wait to see you. Have a safe trip."

Summer promised to call with her itinerary, and while waiting for the taxi to take her to the Eagle County Airport, she went next door.

"As promised, a few of Keeper's things," she said when Rose answered.

Her neighbor took one look at the enormous

black trash bag and said, "You *are* coming back, aren't you?"

"It's just a few of his toys. Some kibbles. His favorite blanket and food and water bowls. The dog bed takes up a lot of room in the bag."

She crouched beside Keeper, held his face in her hands. "I know this won't be easy after all you've already been through, but don't you worry. Alex and Rose will take good care of you, and I'll be back soon." She kissed the top of his head. "Promise."

He held her gaze for a long moment then treated her to a happy, breathy bark. Wagging his tail, he got up, grabbed his leash and waited until Rose took it. Keeper-speak, she knew, for "I believe you."

Summer had barely closed the door when her taxi pulled up. She fought tears as the driver tossed her suitcase into the trunk, and as she climbed into the backseat. Fought them all the way to the airport. At the gate. As she settled into her assigned seat. A few minutes after takeoff, when the flight attendant began reciting flight safety instructions, the urge to cry finally lifted.

She stared out the window, past the wingtip and into the velvety blue sky beyond. Her mom liked to say she never felt closer to heaven than when bulleting through the sky in a jetliner. Summer felt that way now.

So she prayed that Keeper wouldn't feel abandoned…

…and that Zach would forgive her for leaving without saying goodbye.

ZACH CROUCHED AND patted Keeper's head. "What do you mean," he said, looking up at Rose. "She's gone?"

"Her agent called her, set up an audition in LA and Summer jumped at the chance to get back to work."

"But why California? Surely there are businesses in Colorado in need of a voice-over actress." What if the allure of Hollywood was so strong that she decided to stay? The image of her on the arm of some actor made him wince.

"Is your knee bothering you again?" Rose asked as he stood.

Rather than cook up some half-baked fib, he shrugged.

"So she left the day before yesterday, huh?"

Rose nodded and put on her coat.

"When will she be home?"

"She didn't say. But recording a commercial isn't like filming a movie." She clipped Keeper's leash to his collar. "I'm guessing she'll be home in a few days."

He stood up, pocketed both hands and shook his head.

"You could call her, you know."

If asked, Zach would have to describe her smile as maternal. And he didn't much like being talked to as if he was Alex's age.

He couldn't decide if he was angry or hurt or disappointed that Summer had left without so much as a passing goodbye.

Rose tucked a slip of paper into his shirt pocket, gave it a gentle pat. "Well, if you change your mind, that's her itinerary."

She tugged on her gloves and opened the door. "Hate to give you the bum's rush, but furface and I were about to go for a walk when you showed up."

Things happened in a blur after that. Zach didn't remember saying goodbye, but he must have, because there on the passenger seat lay a plate of Rose's sticky buns. Didn't remember driving home, either, but here he sat, alone in his apartment, eating one.

Summer's itinerary crackled in his pocket. Was it a coincidence that when he removed it, the paper stuck to his sugary fingertips? He'd never been the superstitious type, so he dismissed the possibility that it was a sign that he should call, make sure she'd landed safely, see if she was still planning on going to the Double M for Christmas. Because if she wasn't, didn't he owe his mom a heads-up?

Zach balled up the note and dropped it into the kitchen trash can. Disappointed. That's how he felt.

At the sink, he rinsed frosting from his fingers, wishing it could be as easy to clear his brain of Summer.

KEEPER HAD WATCHED her every move as Summer packed up homemade cookies, loaves of banana bread and brownies. Watched just as closely as she made pretty displays of each on Christmas plates, then wrapped them in red cellophane and topped the packages with big festive bows.

He'd sniffed every decorations box that she dragged up from the basement. Ears perked and eyes bright, he followed as she put up the tree, draped garlands from the banister and displayed her collection of snow globes and winter baby figurines on the mantel. Now, as she untangled a strand of lights on the porch, he stood on his rear legs, smiling out the living room window at her.

Last Christmas and the one before, she hadn't bothered to decorate. But this year, thanks in part to the tail-wagging enthusiasm of her housemate, Summer felt like celebrating.

Alex stepped onto his front porch. "Hey, Summer," he said. "Bet your house will look great… if you ever get that mess straightened out."

"If I do, I hope they'll work!"

"Plug 'em in now. No point wasting time if they don't."

She grinned. "Now, why didn't I think of that?"

He was hopping from one foot to the other, shoulders up, hugging himself.

"What are you doing out here without a coat?"

"Waiting for Zach," he said as she inserted the plug into the outlet. "He's gonna teach me how to parallel park. We'll be in his truck, and the heater on that thing is stuck on high."

Zach. If her heart counted out a few extra beats at the mention of his name, how would she react to seeing him for the first time in days? The strand lit up. *Probably just like that*, she thought.

"Haven't seen much of you since you got back. How was California?"

"Noisy and busy and smoggy, same as always," she said. "But working again made it all worthwhile."

"Will we be able to hear the commercial in Colorado? Or is it just an LA thing?"

"It's national. When it starts airing, you'll know. You eat that breakfast cereal five days out of seven."

"Cool," he said, rubbing his upper arms. "Gee, I hope Zach's okay. It isn't like him to be late."

And as if on cue, the familiar red pickup with its gray-and-gold marine insignia on it lumbered into the cul-de-sac.

Alex ran to meet him. "Wish me luck!" he called over one shoulder.

She waved. From here on the top step, she couldn't see Zach. Just as well.

Last night, Libby had called to welcome her home. "You want proof that he cares?" she'd asked. Something told Summer to say no, but she hadn't, and now she had to live with what Libby had repeated. "'She left without a word,'" Zach had apparently said. "'Without a *word*. I knew I should have told her…'"

"Told me what?" she'd wondered aloud.

"Only one way to find out," Libby had answered.

Zach jogged around the pickup, handed Alex the keys, and slid into the passenger seat. If he had looked up, she would have said hello. She couldn't hear him through the rolled-up window, but his strained expression told her he was exerting great effort to maintain calm as the clutch screeched.

If not now, she thought again, *when*?

She hurried to the truck, and Zach jumped when she pecked on the window.

"Didn't mean to startle you," she said when he rolled it down. "Just wanted to offer my car. Might be easier for Alex to handle than the stick shift?"

Alex's relief was evident in his posture. "Could we do that, Zach?"

Zach gave it a moment's consideration then faced Summer. If she stood on tiptoe, she could kiss him.

"We were going to practice in the church parking lot, but they haven't plowed it yet. So yeah, your car will make things easier."

"Excellent!" Alex said, climbing out of the truck.

Trash cans still lined the street from the morning collection, and while Zach parked his truck, Summer tossed the big brown cans into the trunk of her car. "If they can survive the garbage men, they can survive Alex," she whispered to Zach. "Have you tried the parking lot at the elementary school? Rose says it's usually one of the first to be plowed."

"I haven't, but we'll check it out."

She handed him her keys and gave Alex a thumbs-up. "Good luck...not that I think you'll need it."

"Come with us, Summer. You could stand the cans back up after I knock 'em down..." He glanced at Zach sheepishly. "While Zach explains what I did wrong."

"You won't knock the cans down." Grinning at Zach, she added, "But if you do—tall as he is—folding himself into and out of my little car will be great exercise."

To her surprise, he didn't return her smile. Summer valued his friendship. If an apology would protect it, then she'd apologize, first chance she got.

"You've missed quite a few lessons lately," was his no-nonsense comeback. "Seems to me you can use the exercise more than I can." He pulled the backseat forward and gestured for her to climb in.

She looked at Keeper, paws on the sill, still watching from the front window.

"Give me five minutes to give him a potty break," she said on her way up the steps.

Alex was raring to go when she returned. He'd already adjusted the driver's seat, rearview and side mirrors. "Hold on," he said as she buckled up. "'Cause here we go!"

Summer braced herself for a jackrabbit start. Zach's hands, planted firmly on the dash, told her he expected it, too. But the boy moved forward with all the skill and precision of a seasoned driver. If he kept that up through the lesson, she saw no reason why he wouldn't pass his test.

Zach's calm, steady voice reminded her yet again what a wonderful father he'd be. He not only anticipated what Alex might do, but also offered gentle suggestions to prevent potential mistakes. Summer didn't need to get out of the car once, and by the time they returned to the cul-de-sac, it was beginning to get dark.

As Zach returned Summer's keys, Alex nearly bowled them both over with an enthusiastic hug. "You guys are the best. I'm gonna ace that test next time around, thanks to you two." Turning them loose, he darted up to his front door. "Wait till Mom hears!"

Side by side, Summer and Zach watched him disappear inside.

"Sure would be nice if, just once in a while, he showed a little enthusiasm for life." She pocketed her keys.

Chuckling, Zach said, "It's good to have you home."

"It's good to be home." She pointed at the Christmas lights, still lying on her top step. "Guess I'd better finish up so I can enjoy the decorations for a day or two before I have to take them down again."

She'd expected him to say a curt good-night, walk to his truck and drive away. Nothing could have pleased her more than when he picked up the strand and began weaving it through the tall Leland Cyprus growing beside her porch. An hour later, they stood side by side again, this time to admire their handiwork.

"It's gorgeous," she said. "So bright and festive." Looking up at him, she added, "Thanks, Zach. Without your help, I would have been out here until midnight."

Even in the dim glow of the colored lights, she could see his slanted grin. And the tantalizing warmth beaming from his eyes reminded her of that final, soul-stirring kiss for charity.

Half a turn to the right. That's all it would take to put them face-to-face. Summer was tempted to make the first move. But first things first. "I owe you an apology."

"For what?"

"I should have called before I left for California."

"Then why didn't you?"

"I was afraid you'd talk me out of going."

"You were probably right."

Summer studied the toes of her boots.

He lifted her chin on a bent forefinger and gazed deep into her eyes. "Did you really want to go?"

"No, I *needed* to go."

His brow furrowed slightly. "Why?"

"To prove to myself that I'm beyond all that self-pitying nonsense that turned me into a hermit. Not long ago, my folks said they were worried I'd backslide. I guess I was afraid if I didn't push myself, I'd prove them right."

He was quiet for a long time. Gearing up to

say good-night? Or working up the courage to tell her to face facts: he wasn't interested in her *that way*.

"So how'd it go out there?"

"Good. Great, actually. It feels good, being productive again."

"I'm glad. I'm happy for you. And if you'd given me half a chance, I would have told you that before you left."

She didn't trust herself to ask him why.

"It's what friends do, right?" he said. "Support each other, no matter what."

Oh, but she wanted to be more than friends. So much more! Wrestling with her conscience— to determine what, exactly, was best for *Zach*— had been one of the toughest fights of her life.

"Yes, it's what friends do."

And there it was again…that smoldering yet protective gleam in his eyes. He took a step closer. Dipped his head slightly. Summer closed her eyes, waiting, hoping…held her breath when he tucked her hair behind her ears.

He pressed his lips to her forehead. "Sweet dreams, Summer Lane."

By the time she opened her eyes, he was halfway to his truck.

An odd mix of relief and regret rippled through her as she watched him slide behind the steering wheel, every plane and angle of his remarkable face illuminated by the overhead light.

She stood watching his taillights grow smaller, dimmer, as he neared the stop sign on the corner, then disappear altogether as he turned and drove away.

Sweet dreams, he'd said.

Oh, they'd be sweet, all right...if she slept at all.

CHAPTER TWENTY-SIX

"You weren't asleep, were you?"

"Gosh, no," Libby said around an exaggerated yawn. "Why would I be asleep at one in the morning?"

"I took a chance this was one of your insomnia nights."

He heard the rustle of sheets, the click of her bedside lamp turning on.

"Nope. I was out like a light. Sawing logs. Sleeping like a baby. Nix that. Babies wake up every two hours. You should've seen me, Zach, flying down Commando Run on my brand-new skis. Bet I would have slept until the alarm rang at six…if I didn't dream about crashing into a tree."

"Sorry, Libs. Maybe if I let you go, you can get back onto the mountain and pick up where you left off."

"You're kidding, right? You expect me to sleep, knowing my heartbroken big brother is pacing the floors?"

He'd done some pacing tonight, Zach would

give her that. But unless he was mistaken, a guy needed to be in the middle of a dissolving relationship to play the broken-heart card.

"Out with it, bruthah, or I'll drive over there in my nightgown and bunny slippers, eat all your Cap'n Crunch while I drag the story out of you."

"I'd tell you, if I had a clue where to start."

"Then allow me. You're falling for Summer but you don't know how she feels about you."

"Ever give any thought to becoming a shrink?"

"I'm going to ignore that term. This time."

He heard water running and the clunk of her tea kettle as she angled it under the faucet.

"Did she love LA?"

"I guess. She said it's good to be back to work. I get that."

"So why didn't she call, let one of us know her plans?"

"She was afraid we'd talk her out of going."

"Nice catch," Libby said. "And would you have talked her out of it?"

"Would've tried. But it's her life, and if it makes her happy…"

"Think she'll relocate?"

I hope not, he thought. *Oh, man, I sure hope not.*

"It was one job," he managed. "A test, she said."

"And did she pass it?"

"I have no idea. She's harder to read than Mandarin."

"So did you tell her?"

"Tell her what?"

"When you left that message on my machine, you said, 'I knew I should have told her…'"

Oh. That. The night she confronted him in the Marshall Law office, he'd come *this* close to admitting that he loved her.

Libby probably thought he'd meant to confess his part in bringing Keeper into Summer's life, and he saw no reason to tell her otherwise.

"What stopped you?"

He pictured the way Summer had looked that night, small and vulnerable as she stared out at the falling snow. He'd come *this* close to blurting it out. But memories of every bad decision, stupid mistake and character judgment he'd bungled reminded him why he shouldn't.

"Zach? You still there?"

He heaved a grating sigh. "Because being around her reminds me of those word problems Mrs. Campbell assigned in fourth grade. 'Zack needs the love of a normal woman to prove he no longer suffers from Knight in Shining Armor Syndrome,'" he began. "'He meets a beauty with big sad eyes and the voice of an angel who says one thing but does another. The price to pay for her affections is sanity and peace of mind. How many sleepless nights before Zach admits he *isn't* cured of KISAS, after all?'"

"Well, it's good to know you haven't lost your sense of humor."

He'd been dead serious, but saw no advantage in admitting it.

"Hold on," she said. "Somebody's on the other line."

She was back in less than a minute. "One of my patients is in the ER," she said. "Gotta go."

Zach told her to drive safely and hung up.

He grabbed a cold beer from the fridge, thinking he'd watch the movie he'd recorded last week. The cap bounced off the overflowing trash can, rolled across the floor and stopped at his feet. As he bent to retrieve it, Zach realized he didn't need a beer and an old Western. What he needed was to take back control of his life. What better way to distract himself from Summer's mixed messages than by putting the apartment into marine-clean order?

Plucking a trash bag from the dispenser, he went upstairs, adding old issues of *Vail Daily* and *Leatherman Magazine*, and convenience store coffee cups and napkins that reminded him how Summer's were square and printed with collaged teacups. In the bathroom, he got rid of an empty soap dispenser, the same brand Summer used. In the kitchen, paper plates and single-serve pizza boxes, like those he'd seen in Summer's trash, covered an empty pack of store-bought chocolate chip cookies.

It reminded him of the cookies she'd baked. How she'd looked on the first night of class. The way she felt, pressed up against him on the dance floor. That unforgettable, too-short kiss on the night of the fund-raiser. He dropped the overstuffed bag into the trash can out back, then queued up the movie, hoping it would blot her from his brain. But even the opening scene—two riders and their horses, silhouetted against jagged mountain peaks—brought her to mind, and he pictured her, rosy-cheeked and smiling as the wind ruffled her curls. Everything changed that day, because he'd been forced to admit that the bluff would never be his favorite place again unless she was right there beside him.

She'd turned a skittish, homeless mutt into a happy, well-adjusted pet.

Protected the feelings of the once-timid teenage boy who had a crush on her.

Met her fears head-on, enrolling in self-defense classes that no doubt roused painful and terrifying memories.

Treated her always-needy, sometimes-selfish parents with loving respect.

Pretended Rose wasn't the least bit nosy and gossipy.

Despite his excuses and protestations, Zach had a pretty good idea what life with Summer might be like. He should have kissed her tonight. Should have told her how much he admired all she'd survived…and overcome. Should have confessed that he'd fallen for her—a little bit, anyway—when their fingers touched that first day, and that he'd been falling a little more every day since.

She didn't need his protection. He got that now. But he needed her like he'd never needed anyone before.

CHAPTER TWENTY-SEVEN

"I CAN'T BELIEVE you put this off until the eleventh hour. Aren't you the gal who has everything bought and wrapped and shipped by Thanksgiving?"

Summer didn't have the heart to tell Justin that she had been 100 percent ready for Christmas before he asked her to keep him company at the mall.

"I postponed it this year so you wouldn't have to go through the last-minute craziness alone."

"Please," he said. "I wasn't born yesterday." Laughing, he added, "But thanks. I love having a friend who's always looking out for me."

"It's only fair," she said, reminding him of the countless hours he'd been there for her.

They'd each filled four huge shopping bags, and lugging them—two in each hand—had grown exhausting.

"These plastic handles are giving me blisters," she said. "Why don't we stow this stuff in my trunk, and I'll treat you to lunch?"

"I say…which way to the parking lot!"

Since Justin was in the mood for Italian, they walked to Ti Amo's. "I can't believe we lucked into a table by the window," he said, flapping a napkin across his lap. "This place is always hopping!"

"So what's your family doing this Christmas?" she asked, opening her menu.

"Same as always…dinner at Jammagramma's followed by a present-opening frenzy." He closed his menu. "I know what I want. How 'bout you?"

"I'm thinking the fettuccini con fungi. I can heat up the leftovers for supper."

"No, silly. What are you doing for Christmas?"

"Believe it or not, Mom and Dad might fly in for a couple of days."

He looked skeptical. And how could she blame him? She'd need a calculator to add up the number of times her parents reneged on their promises.

"I know, I know," she said dully. "But a girl can dream, right?"

"Well, if they do their usual no-show, you know you're welcome to join us. Mom is dying to see for herself how you're doing." He leaned forward. "When I told her how you hardly limp at all anymore, thanks to your self-defense classes, I thought she'd crack the windows, hoo-haaing." He leaned back. "How's that going, by the way?"

They'd been best friends for years. What he

was really curious about was how things were going with Zach.

"Oh, I don't know. It's all so…complicated. One minute I'm head over heels. The next I'm looking for ways to avoid him."

"Seems pretty simple to me. You like him. He likes you. Anything else can be worked out. If you're honest with one another."

"I wish it was that simple. For one thing, he loves kids. And kids love him."

Justin nodded. "So?"

"So you know my history."

"The doctor never said it was impossible or out of the question. I know, because I was there when he broke the news."

Summer didn't reply.

"Can I read this pregnant pause—if you'll pardon the pun—to mean you haven't told him?"

Summer only sighed.

"Oh, good grief," he said, drawing the attention of the couple at the next table. He lowered his voice. "Well, in *my* opinion, you need to get it all out in the open. Soon. And if the big, strong ex-marine can't handle the truth, take a hike."

"Former," she said.

"Former what?"

"It's former marine, not ex."

"Semantics."

She grinned. "Unless you're a marine."

The waitress took their order, and when she was out of earshot, Justin said, "I'll top your *unless* with an *until*. Until you tell him everything, I refuse to listen to any more of this...this speculating."

She sipped her water.

"You know I'm right, Sums."

"Yeah." She sighed. It really wasn't fair to judge Zach based on how he *might* react.

"All right, I can see you're just dying to tell me all about him."

So she told him. About the tight relationships between him and his sister, his parents, and the cousins—raised like brothers on the family ranch. About his attachment to the land his great-grandfather had purchased decades ago.

She told him about Zach's self-defense skills, and the gentle way he instructed his students. About his beautiful eyes and charming smile... and that heart-stopping, dream-inducing kiss at the fund-raiser.

"Wait," Justin said after their food was delivered, "did you just say *hoedown*? With banjos and Jew's harps and fiddles?"

"Don't be a hater," she teased. "I'll have you know they raised nearly three thousand dollars for Firefly Autism."

"Impressive." He bit off the point of a pizza

slice. "But seriously? What sort of dancing does one *do* at a hoedown, anyway?"

"Two-step, jig, reel, clog…" Summer paused, remembering the way she'd felt in Zach's arms as they waltzed across the floor.

"But enough about me," she said. "What's new at the shop? Which movie stars have you given styles to lately?"

"Please. You know I'm not a name-dropper."

But that didn't stop him from listing a dozen starlets and box-office icons who'd sat in his chair at Buzz.

"I have to tell you, Sums, I've never been happier. And it's all thanks to you."

"Me? I can barely operate a hair dryer!"

"Don't be modest. Without that loan, I could never have done it."

"Stop. You had some bank financing. In time, you would have built—"

"That's crazy talk, and you know it. In this market? I could never have competed with established salons. I'm where I am today because you had faith in me."

"Knock it off, will ya? I forgot to tuck a pack of tissues in my purse, and I hate blowing my nose on these scratchy paper napkins. Besides, you paid me back ages ago."

"Still…"

"Subject's closed."

"Okay, just one last thing, and we shall never speak of this again. You're a prize, Summer Lane, and you deserve the best. So put this ex-and-or-former marine to the test. Tell him your story. And don't leave out a single detail. If he's anything but 100 percent supportive..." He drew a finger across his throat. "Over. Done. *Gone.* Got it?"

Justin's words stayed with her as they drove home. She thought about what he'd said long into the night, too. Because he'd been right. Zach had a right to hear everything. The sooner, the better.

For his sake *and* hers.

CHAPTER TWENTY-EIGHT

ELLEN MARSHALL WAS in her element.

She wore a red gingham apron with green trim, and insisted that everyone at the long trestle table wear a belled Santa hat, just like her own.

"Your china is just beautiful," Susannah said. "It's things like this that sometimes make me wish Harrison and I weren't such nomads."

The Lanes had once owned a perfectly nice house. Zach knew because he'd seen pictures of it on Summer's mantel. He liked them, but couldn't muster any pity, because in their hopeful quest for stardom, they'd deprived their only daughter of countless childhood memories. Their regrets, in his opinion, were a consequence of their egocentric choices.

"And all this family," Susannah cooed, surveying the two rows of Marshalls, passing ham and candied yams, biscuits and butter back and forth. "Oh, what I'd give to host just one function like this!"

It was kind of amazing, Zach thought, that Susannah hadn't scored a leading part, because she was playing the I'm-so-deprived role to the hilt.

Nate, the only Marshall cousin still living on the Double M, turned to Rose. "So did I hear right? You're letting Alex go to Winter Park without you?"

"I can't believe I said yes, either. He leaves tomorrow." She punctuated the statement with a tiny whimper.

Alex pretended not to notice. "Yeah, a bunch of us on the yearbook committee are gonna spend a couple days skiing."

"What," Nate kidded, elbowing him, "Vail's slopes aren't good enough for you guys? It's where all of us learned to ski. Isn't that right, Zach?"

"It's where you and Sam learned to ski. All I learned was how to slide down the entire length of a mountain on my butt."

"Aw, don't be so hard on yourself," their cousin Sam put in. "You didn't crash into any trees, and got to the bottom *fast*. Pun intended."

Laughing, Zach decided he must have inherited his mother's love for big family gatherings, because he seldom felt more content than when surrounded by grandparents, aunts and uncles, cousins and friends like Alex and Rose.

And Summer. Seated directly across from

him, she was engaged in an animated conversation with his grandmother.

She looked especially pretty today in a red sweater dress that flattered her creamy skin and curvy figure. When he'd met her months ago, her dark waves barely covered her ears. Now, shiny chin-length curls bounced as she talked and laughed. While searching for facts about her past, he'd seen her professional head shot, taken before the assault. Long, shimmering tresses draped over one shoulder, giving her a sexy yet sophisticated look. During the impromptu lunch with her folks, Susannah had shown him a myriad of photos: Summer's high school graduation portrait; Summer in the marching band, a silver flute pressed to her lips; ten-year-old Summer on a California beach, arms raised in an exuberant *ta-da!* as the pigtails above her ears dripped with seawater.

Nate cleared his throat. Loudly. And when Zach met his cousin's eyes, he realized he'd been caught staring at Summer. He'd been on the receiving end of that mischievous expression enough times to know that if he didn't act fast, his cousin's on-your-butt jokes would seem tame by comparison.

"So, Nate, when do you leave for Nevada to pick up the new horses?"

Nate's crooked smile said, "Okay, I won't zing you…yet."

"That trip's on hold. At least until the weather's more predictable." He buttered a biscuit. "Why? You want to tag along?"

"You don't want him tagging along," Sam said. "He'd choose all the ones nobody else wants. Swaybacks, old nags, blind in one eye… If he had his way, he'd adopt them all."

His dad and uncles weighed in, recalling the feral cats, lop-eared rabbits and injured birds he'd tried to turn into pets.

"And what about that two-legged lizard he snuck into his room," Ellen said. "Went in to change his sheets and thought I'd die of fright when it wriggled out from under his pillow!"

John laughed. "And the wolf spider he taught to do tricks."

"Gimme a break," Libby said. "Only trick that arachnid could perform was eating the flies Zach caught in the barn."

From the corner of his eye, Zach saw Summer's smile fade, and he hoped it wasn't because she'd read something personal in their kidding remarks.

Ellen put the refilled biscuit basket in front of Alex. "So how many kids are you skiing with?"

He helped himself to two and reached for the butter. "Last I heard, thirteen."

"Uh-oh," Nate said. "Better talk somebody into staying home."

Alex rolled his eyes. "I don't believe in all that superstitious stuff."

"Okay, but if a giant tree falls down and blocks the slope, don't come cryin' to me."

After the table was cleared, everyone gathered in the family room. Tidy stacks of festively wrapped packages surrounded the fifteen-foot tree. As usual, Zach's dad played Santa and doled out the gifts.

"Did you tell her what to buy?" he whispered to Libby as the Marshalls unwrapped presents from Summer.

His sister shook her head. "I'm as amazed as you are."

Everybody knew Libby was into scarves. Long, short, fringed or plain, a body couldn't go wrong adding to her collection. But how had Summer known that his dad collected first edition novels, or that his mom was always on the lookout for unique, colorful teapots?

Summer *oohed* at Libby's gift of notepads that said SUMMER in fanciful letters, *ahhed* at the tin of homemade fudge from his mom, said an enthusiastic thank-you for the framed photo of Keeper Zach had given her. When the unwrapping frenzy ended, Zach held open a big plastic bag as Libby stuffed it with ribbons and bows and tissue paper. He did his best to hide his disappointment, because there hadn't been a "To

Zach, from Summer" package among the gifts she'd delivered.

"Don't look so hurt," Libby whispered. "I'm not supposed to give you your present from her until everyone else has left."

"Why?"

"I have no idea." She glanced around, a conspiratorial grin on her face. "But Summer sure was keyed up about it."

Knowing that she hadn't forgotten—or worse, deliberately overlooked him—raised his spirits. "Oh, you're a big help."

"Okay. All right. I'll give you a hint. But just *one*." Libby cupped a hand beside her mouth and said, "It's square."

Grinning, Zach wiggled his eyebrows. "So what time did you say everybody is leaving?"

CHAPTER TWENTY-NINE

"Hope I'm not calling too early."

"I've been up since six," Summer said. "I'd ask what you're doing up so early, but I'm guessing former marines always rise with the sun."

"Yeah. Old habits die hard." He traced his finger along the matte-black frame. "I meant to call yesterday to thank you for the gift, but Dad got me involved in a shelf-building project in his workshop. If I'd known it would be a two-day job, I might not have been so quick to volunteer."

"Ah, to store all those new tools your mom gave him for Christmas."

He heard the smile in her voice and found himself smiling, too. "You should see the honey-do list she tucked into his Christmas card. He'll be busy until next December, making flower boxes and matching swings for the front porch."

"The house already looks like a postcard. It'll be even prettier when he finishes."

"Speaking of pictures…" he said, gazing at the photograph. He could almost inhale the scent of Blue Spruce, and if he closed his eyes, Zach could hear the distant screech of bald eagles and the wind whistling through the scrubby Gamble Oak. She'd captured more than the sooty sky and snowy mountaintops. It was, in every way, the essence of the Double M. "I can't thank you enough. When did you take it?"

"That day when Libby and I went riding."

"I have to admit, I'm sorry she found the place."

"On my honor, I didn't tell her where it is!"

"I believe you. She thinks she got away with something, following me all those times. Even if I hadn't seen hoof prints in the snow, I would have heard her, sniffling and sneezing behind me."

"Well, I'm glad you like your gift." She paused. "It got kind of crazy on Christmas, what with the steady rain of wrapping paper and bows. I hope I remembered to tell you how much I like mine."

"You did. So…Libby tells me your agent set up another job for you in Boulder?"

"Right. Radio commercials for a home improvement company. And a used car dealership. As long as I've been out of work, I can't afford to be picky."

The call-waiting signal beeped, and he asked Summer to hold. Zach had no idea why Rose would call him, let alone at this early-morning hour.

He had a hard time understanding her hysterical rambling.

"He's lost. They're all lost. No one has heard from any of them. It's been hours."

Alex and his ski buddies? *Missing?* Zach's heart hammered.

He summoned all the calm he could muster. "Rose," he said, "where are you? At home?"

"Yes. Yes, I'm home." She whimpered. "Has anyone ever survived an avalanche?"

The word hit him like a punch to the gut. He ran the few facts he knew about avalanches through his mind. Snowpack usually kept the snow from tumbling downhill. But winter storms, like the one that passed through last week, would weaken the pack. If Rose hadn't misunderstood the phone call, any number of things might have caused the avalanche, from the echo of a human voice—or in this case, a dozen exuberant young voices—to a single skier's shifting weight. Most came and went, unnoticed by anyone. Some merely terrified winter sports enthusiasts, leaving them to escape unharmed. And others were deadly. Having witnessed a few from a safe distance, Zach hoped Alex and his friends managed to sidestep this one.

"Oh, Zach. I'm at my wits' end. I don't know what to do. The officer said… I think…"

He could ask for specifics, but in her state, it wasn't likely she'd provide lucid answers. Best-case scenario, the call woke her from a deep sleep, and she'd misunderstood the report.

"Oh, why did I let him go? I had a funny feeling about this trip. If something happens to Alex, I'll never forgive my—"

"Just sit tight, okay, Rose? I'll be there in ten minutes."

He clicked back over to Summer. "That was Rose. She says there's been an avalanche in Winter Park."

Summer gasped. "No. Oh, no. Not Alex…"

"You know Rose. She could have misinterpreted things. I'm heading to her place right now."

"I'll go right over. If nothing else, I can hold her hand and keep her calm until you get here."

When he arrived, Zach found them on the couch, Summer with an arm over Rose's shoulders, Keeper with a paw on her lap. She seemed almost catatonic, staring at the wall across the room, clenching and unclenching her fists.

He knelt at her feet, took her trembling, icy hands in his. "Hey, Rose. Let's think positive thoughts, okay?"

Nodding, she met his eyes.

"Did the guy who called leave a number?"

Another nod, and then she pointed.

He got up and went to the bar counter that separated the family room from the kitchen, and found the notepad where she'd scribbled an almost illegible message. Zach picked up the phone and punched in the digits.

"Winter Park Ski Patrol," said a gruff voice, "Harman here."

Zach identified himself and explained why he was calling.

"The kids were out on the Sunnyside lift of Mary Jane."

Mary Jane, one of eighteen new trails that had earned Colorado the right to boast about some of the steepest chutes in the country…and the run that had claimed several lives.

"We've had a high avalanche alert in place since the day before yesterday," Harman added. "But you know kids."

Zach hadn't met the rest of the boys, but Alex wasn't a risk-taker. Peer pressure being what it was, though, there was a first time for everything, he supposed.

Zach put his back to Rose and lowered his voice. "What kind of avalanche was it?" he asked Harman. With any luck, the answer would give Rose some hope that Alex had survived.

He remembered the newspaper article detailing the death of a young man from Evergreen. He'd succumbed to asphyxiation after being buried in what some experts classified as a loose-snow avalanche, the most common type, with a single point of origin that widens on the way down. Thin "slab" avalanches caused the least amount of damage, but thick ones were responsible for many fatalities. Powder avalanches had the capacity to reach speeds of more than 190 mph. And although wet-snow avalanches moved slowly at first, they had a tendency to pick up speed.

"Sorry, sir. It's just too soon to tell."

Zach sighed heavily then reined in his frustration. "So what's the plan?"

The officer explained that unless the wind died down and forecasters were wrong about the additional eight-to-ten inches likely to fall throughout the day, it would be tough going for the rescue team.

"Mrs. Peterson will want to be there. Where can we wait for more news?"

Harman gave directions, which Zach added to the notes Rose had taken.

When he returned to the family room, she looked up at him with damp, optimistic eyes, and he wished he could tell her what she wanted and needed to hear.

He held out a hand, and she let him help her to her feet as he explained the situation.

"I'll get her purse and coat," Summer said, heading for the front hall closet. "You guys head on over, and I'll meet you there just as soon as I call Libby, see if she'll stay with Keeper."

Nodding, Zach pressed the slip of paper into her palm.

"Rose," Summer said, one arm around her waist, "do you have your insurance card in your wallet?"

"No. It's…" She hid behind her hands. "I think it's on my desk. In my room. Or maybe in the bills basket."

"Don't worry. I'll find it," Zach assured her.

As he walked away, Rose fell into Summer's arms. "Oh, God," she wailed. "What will I do if—"

"Now, none of that," Summer said, her voice low and soothing. "We're going to think positive thoughts, just like Zach said. Right?"

"Thank you," he mouthed silently over Rose's head. "Couldn't do this alone."

And he meant every last syllable.

CHAPTER THIRTY

ROSE HAD SNIFFLED and cried during the entire hour-and-a-half trip from Vail to Winter Park. Second guesses, blame, guilt, shame…she covered all the bases. And since nothing Zach said offered her any comfort, he thought it best to simply drive and let her get it off her chest.

When he steered up the steep drive, she said, "This can't be the place." She grabbed his forearm. "You must have made a wrong turn, Zach."

"Sign says Winter Park Ski Patrol."

"But…it's barely more than a shed!"

"They don't need anything fancy. Just four walls and a roof so they can get out of the wind and cold, internet connection and electricity and a place to stow their gear."

She unbuckled her seat belt, and even before he came to a complete stop in front of the building, she jumped out of the truck. As he pocketed his keys, Zach saw a man in the standard-issue red-and-black cold-weather gear open the door.

"Is there any news?" she asked him. "Please

tell me you've found my son!" Rose looked around. "Where are the other parents?"

The man's face crinkled with a pitying frown. "We couldn't get hold of some of the kids' folks," he said. "But most are on their way." He placed a hand on her shoulder as they went inside the small building. "Try not to worry, okay? We're assembling a search team. In the meantime, you're welcome to wait over there." He pointed to a narrow wooden bench against the wall. "There's coffee on the warming plate and bottled water in the fridge. Help yourself."

The radio squawked and hissed as Zach led Rose to the bench and poured her a cup of coffee. "Let me see what I can find out." He helped her out of her parka then joined Harman at the long folding table.

"This," Harman said, indicating a spot on the big map, "is where the kids were supposed to be." One chaperone, he explained, had gone up with the kids, while the other teacher stayed at the bottom of the lift to keep an eye on their backpacks and other gear. "When they didn't come back at the appointed time, the teacher called 911. And the sheriff's department called us."

Zach knew that every minute could make the difference between life and death. Already, the group had been missing nearly three hours. And since it wasn't likely they'd enrolled in survival training seminars, the outlook wasn't good.

"We have a really solid unit," Harman said. "Some full-time patrollers, couple of part-timers, a few volunteers."

Every winter during his college years, Zach had been one of those volunteers. So had doctors and cops, firefighters and paramedics and an off-duty reporter or two. Days started early, usually by seven-thirty, with a rundown of anything pertinent that might have happened the day before, and a lively discussion about the weather. After a quick practice run, where one member of the unit assumed the patroller role while another played an injured skier, they would head out to check each run, making sure rope lines were firmly planted, checking the lift towers and trail signs, and surveying snow conditions. The hours passed quickly as they responded to reports of missing signs, loose ropes and skier mishaps. By the time they knocked off at three o'clock, the unit was more than happy to hand control over to the night patrol, which closed the mountain and flexed their "no skier left behind" muscles.

"Weather doesn't look pretty," Harman said. Turning, he drew Zach's attention to the computer monitor on a second long table behind him. Graphs and charts and maps detailed the jet stream forecast, wind speed, air temperature and precipitation predictions.

"Not one of those idiots was wearing a transceiver," he complained, and went back to studying his map.

Even though Alex could well be one of those idiots, Zach didn't flinch. He knew all too well what had inspired Harman's frustration. Finding the kids—if, heaven forbid, they were under the avalanche—would be a whole lot faster and easier with a signal to follow. Unfortunately, transponders were expensive. Very few skiers carried them, and even fewer took the time to properly synchronize their frequency with transceivers.

The door opened, and Summer entered, bringing with her a blast of snow-peppered wind. She jerked out of her jacket, walked straight up to Rose and wrapped her arms around her. Zach knew in an instant that she'd probably fought tears all the way here, and pulled herself together for Rose's sake.

Harman frowned. "Great. Just what I need," he said under his breath, "another hysterical female to tend to."

"Trust me. She's anything but."

"Guess I'll have to take your word for it. But let's just say for argument's sake that she's your responsibility."

"No problem," he said as Summer met his eyes.

"Any news?" Summer mouthed across the room.

Zach shook his head slowly.

Summer picked up Rose's still-full disposable cup and got to her feet. "Let me freshen this up for you. Can I get you anything else? I saw a box of energy bars over there."

"No, but thanks. Maybe later."

Harman moved to the far side of the room to answer a call, leaving the space between the tables open.

She stood so close that Zach felt the warmth of her shoulder pressed against his upper arm.

"I can't even begin to imagine what she must be going through," she whispered.

He followed her gaze to Rose, forehead resting on her drawn-up knees. Summer's shaky exhale drew his attention to her face. She looked a little rough around the edges, too. No surprise there, given her friendship with Alex.

"And poor Alex. He must be terrified." Tilting her head, she studied his face. "What about you?"

"Other than feeling like a heel and a coward, I'm fine."

Her brow furrowed, so he tried to explain. "I know Rose is waiting for me to go talk to her. But I can't. Not yet. She knows I used to volunteer with the Vail ski patrol, so she'll ask what I think Alex's chances are."

"What *do* you think his chances are?"

Zach hung his head, unable to look into her big trusting eyes. "Like you, I can't stop wondering what's going through Alex's mind," he said. "If he's conscious, that is. He's probably hungry. Scared. Colder than he's ever been. I know he's a tough, capable kid, but this?" Zach expelled a heavy sigh. "Something like this would test the mettle of a battle-trained marine."

He glanced over at Rose, still huddled against the wall. "She's probably too exhausted to even cry anymore. I don't know how she'll handle it if…" Alex was Rose's whole world, had been since he was a toddler. If he couldn't bring himself to complete the thought, Zach wondered how she would face a future without her boy.

"I don't want to get in the way," Summer said, placing her hands on his crossed forearms. "So tell me how I can help."

"You're helping more than you know, just by being here."

Tears glistened in her dark eyes. "If I ask you something, will you be honest with me?"

She'd come so far in a few short months. What if hearing the worst about her young friend sent her in the opposite direction?

"Rose needs us," she said. "*Both* of us."

"I don't know any more than you do, Summer, so—"

"Were you ever involved in an avalanche search-and-rescue mission?"

"I was. And twice," he said through clenched teeth, "we found the missing skiers alive." Zach hoped she wouldn't ask how many times they *hadn't*.

She nodded. "If they can't find Alex, who will break the news to Rose?"

Her voice cracked on the words *can't* and *Alex*.

"We will, you and I."

"Good." Another nod. "It won't be easy, but she shouldn't hear a thing like that from strangers."

Zach didn't know whether it was the strength of her words or her determined stance and expression that made him choke up. Fortunately, she couldn't see his traitorous tears because he'd given in to the impulse to wrap his arms around her.

"Sorry, folks," Harman said, looking more glum than before. "Search and rescue has pulled out all the stops—snowboards, snowmobiles, foot patrollers, dogs, helicopters, the whole nine yards. They've even gone off-piste, and still nothing."

"Piste?" Summer echoed.

"The regular ski run," Harman explained. "Meaning they've widened the search to the areas on both sides of the run."

Zach got the message, loud and clear. It was as if the mountain had thrown down the gauntlet, presenting the patrollers with a whole new set of challenges…on ungroomed, unmarked slopes. Being well-trained was more important now than ever, and the equipment—shovels, probes, ropes, first-aid kits, Recco reflectors—had better function properly. Not an easy feat with 30 mph wind gusts driving the mercury down into the single digits.

Rose joined them. "I've tried being reasonable and patient," she said, "but that hasn't worked. I have a friend who's a reporter. Maybe a little pressure from the media will light a fire under you people!"

Her sudden switch from wounded kitten to ferocious cat stunned them all. Harman got hold of himself first.

"My relief is due to arrive in a minute or two, and then I'm joining the search. We've got all our best guys out there, Mrs. Peterson, so—"

"You need all the help you can get," Zach said. "I'm going with you."

Summer led Rose back to the bench as Zach headed outside. On the way to his truck, he met Harman's replacement, who'd just jumped off a high-performance mountain snowmobile. "You one of the dads?" the man asked, tugging off his snow-crusted mittens.

There wasn't time for questions and answers, so Zach cut to the chase. "Name's Zach. I'm here for Alex Peterson."

The man never slowed. "I'm Andre," he said. Using his thumb as a pointer, he directed Zach's gaze north, and up, toward the unmistakable beam of a helicopter search light slicing through the predawn darkness.

"Pilot just radioed. Might've spotted a light up on the Cirque."

The Cirque? Zach's pulse pounded. "But Harman said they were skiing Sunnyside."

"You'd better hope they didn't, 'cause we combed it and found diddly."

Zach had braved the Cirque. Once. Accessible only by foot, the double-black diamond, back-country terrain was intimidating, even to expert skiers. He'd kissed the snow at the bottom, knowing he'd been lucky to make it down without plowing into a tree.

"Harman is going up next," Zach told Andre. He pointed at the snowmobile. "Can that thing hold two with full gear?"

"Bigfoot there can handle just about anything you throw at her." And with that, he disappeared into the shack.

If Zach was already outfitted when he joined them, maybe Harman wouldn't give him any guff. Like most volunteers, Zach had paid for his own gear. Thankfully, he'd held on to it... and stowed it under the backseat of his pickup. He donned his down-filled pants and jacket, padded hat, insulated gloves and waterproof Gators. The team would provide maps, a headlamp, radio and transceiver. Everything else was already in his prepacked lightweight backpack: bivy sack, water and power bars, even a fire-starting kit.

Harman's eyes widened when Zach marched into the shed, pack slung over one shoulder. "What's the holdup?" he asked. And meeting Andre's eyes, he added, "Did you tell him about the chopper?"

"He did," Harman answered.

Zach didn't give him a chance to object. "I volunteered six seasons in Vail. Call Paul Medford if you need confirmation."

"No time for that, and you know it," Harman growled. Shrugging into his own pack, he faced Andre. "Did you gas up Bigfoot?"

"No, sir. Not yet."

Harman looked from Rose to Summer to Zach. "Better say your goodbyes, then, while I fill the tank." He opened the door then paused. "Y'might wanna tell 'em if they aren't already praying, this would be a good time to start."

"Alex will be so glad to see a familiar face," Rose said, hugging Zach.

He nodded. "I'll be glad to see him, too."

Summer's dark, thick eyelashes had gone all spiky with tears. She held out her arms, and he stepped willingly into them.

"You'd better be careful out there," she said, and sent him on his way with a long, sweet kiss that gave him all the incentive he needed to come back whole and healthy.

CHAPTER THIRTY-ONE

ONE BY ONE, the teens piled into waiting ambulances.

Summer and Zach stood a few feet from the nearest emergency vehicle, watching as relieved and teary-eyed parents cried and hugged and gently scolded their kids.

"Poor Alex," Summer said.

"Why? He's cold and wet and scared, might have a touch of frostbite, but he's fine!" Zach said.

"After this, Rose will probably never let him out of her sight again." She looked up at Zach.

He nodded. "I see your point."

A reporter darted up, stuck a microphone near Alex's mouth.

"What was it like," she asked him, "being lost out there on the mountain?"

"What do you think it was like? It was *cold*."

"From the mouths of babes," Summer whispered.

"How did you guys get off-piste?" the newswoman wanted to know.

Alex shrugged. "Lemmings." The interviewer laughed into the mic as he added, "Somebody made a wrong turn, and like a bunch of dummies, the rest of us followed."

"One of the chaperones said you kids were supposed to ski Sunnyside. How'd you end up on the Cirque?"

"Lemmings," he said again. "After seeing it from the top, I'm kinda glad we got lost. I probably would have died of a heart attack before I got to the bottom. It's like, trees, rocks, trees and more trees."

She smiled into the camera. "Note to self," she told her audience. "Stay away from the Cirque!"

The cameraman gave her a thumbs-up and bounced the camera up and down, as if nodding his agreement.

"Mrs. Peterson," she said, turning to Rose. "What was it like, waiting for news about—?"

"Do you have children?" Rose interrupted.

"Yes, my husband and I have twins." She flashed her for-the-audience smile again. "They're seven."

"Aha," Rose said. "Have they ever wandered off, stepped out of your sight, even for a second?"

"Yes, and it was terrifying!"

"Well, multiply that terror by a million. Ten million even," Rose snarled. Eyes narrowed and fist pumping, she added, "Now get that microphone out of my face before I—"

Zach stepped up and slid an arm across Rose's shoulders. "Hey, tiger," he said, grinning, "I think this nice paramedic here would like to take Alex to the hospital now. Would you rather follow the ambulance in my truck or Summer's car?"

Right hand extended, Rose reached for Summer. "Would you be very upset if I rode with Zach?"

"No, of course not," Summer said with a smile. "I'll stop on the way over and get us all something to eat. I don't know about you, but stark-white fear gives me a ferocious appetite!"

Laughing, Zach slid his other arm over her shoulders. "Drive safely, you hear?"

She waited for them to leave before getting into her car, then she leaned her forehead on the steering wheel and let the tears come.

She remembered move-in day on the cul-de-sac, when Rose came over, Alex in tow, to deliver a welcome basket. The cookies, banana bread and fudge had all ended up in the trash can, but the hand-crocheted smiley coasters still grinned from their matching crocheted box, right beside the sandalwood-scented pillar candle on her coffee table. Summer, an only child, had always wished for a sibling, and that day, she got one. Alex couldn't wait to tell her when he'd aced— or failed—a test, taught her to play chess and Free Space, and tolerated her addiction to Tom Selleck movies.

And then there was Zach, whose patient, straightforward approach to self-defense had built up her confidence and liberated her from life as a loner. Tonight, when he and the team didn't report back for hours, she'd been forced to wrestle with the possibility that she might never see him again. Did he care for her as something more than a friend? Possibly. But she now knew without a doubt how she felt about *him*.

Life was fleeting. The mountain had proven that tonight.

Summer started the car, shifted into Drive, and made the decision.

It was time to tell Zach everything. And as soon as Alex was home, safe and sound, that was exactly what she'd do.

Until then, Summer would cling to the hope that if the truth didn't sit well with him, she'd have the strength to let him go.

"NEW YEAR'S IS the biggest bash of the year," Libby said, patting Chinook's nose. "Everybody who's anybody will be at the Double M that night. And just think of all the reasons we have to celebrate. Alex and his friends almost got buried by an avalanche—but they didn't—and Zach was part of the team that made sure they all made it off the mountain!"

She had a point. Summer couldn't deny that she had a lot to celebrate, too. Keeper had made a quick adjustment to his new life, and thanks to her agent, the next weeks would be filled with work, first in Boulder, then in Golden. She'd fought the memories of that ugly night, and won. The win gave her hope that a good and decent man like Zach might actually love her, scars and all.

"It's semiformal," Libby said. "And I don't have a thing to wear." She snapped her fingers, making Taffy's ears rotate forward. "Let's go shopping for dresses and high-heeled shoes. We'll make appointments to get manicures and pedicures. Have lunch. We'll make a day of it. What do you say?"

"There's nothing in my closet but jeans and khakis, sneakers and sweaters." Looking at her feet, Summer laughed. "And cowboy boots."

"Oh, there's a resolution if ever I heard one." She drew quotation marks in the air. "Improve Wardrobe."

When the horses finished the carrots Summer had brought them, the two women saddled them up and climbed on.

When they'd ridden half a mile or so from the house, Libby said, "Mom hired a band—sight unseen—because I recommended them. Don't tell anyone," she said, pretending to cover Chestnut's ears, "but I'm a little goofy over the lead singer. I've been following these guys for more than a year."

"Why is this the first I'm hearing about him?

But wait…you've been following him? You mean, like a…a *groupie*?" Summer teased.

"Don't laugh. That's exactly what I'm in danger of becoming." She wiggled her eyebrows. "If things go the way I hope, that midnight kiss might help him decide to work closer to home from now on."

Summer didn't like the sound of it. Musicians went on tour, and not all of them had the willpower or strength of character to stay true to their families when *real* groupies got up close and personal.

"Okay," Libby said. "Why do you look like you've just swallowed lemon juice?"

She'd heard Libby talk about dates, but never with any real interest. It wouldn't be fair to throw cold water on her enthusiasm, possibly spoil her New Year's Eve.

"I was just trying to remember where my folks will be that night," Summer said.

"If they're in town, they'll be with us, right?"

"They had a wonderful time at Christmas, so I'm sure they'd love that. I'll call them tonight." Summer had to admit, the more she heard about this semiformal party, the more exciting it sounded.

"So have you been to Zach's secret place lately?"

"Um, what secret place?"

"Oh, stop. I know he brought you there the

first time you visited the Double M. He *thinks* it's a secret, but just between you and me? I've known about it for years. And *years*. We all have. And don't look so worried. No one would ever let on. We realized he needed a place to hide once in a while. We Marshalls pester the daylights out of each other, but we can be protective, too."

How different would her life have been, Summer wondered, if she'd been born into a big, loving family like theirs?

"He acts like a tough guy, and for the most part, he is. I'm not sure why he feels duty bound to rescue people, but it has nothing to do with his military duty. He's been that way for as long as I can remember." Libby shrugged. "Least we can do is rescue *him* on the few occasions when he needs it."

Next, Libby launched into the story about the cheerleader who dumped Zach for the high school football captain. The coed who ran off with an English professor. He'd found some comfort in the arms of a female marine who, in trying to prove she was as tough as her male counterparts, nearly got herself killed. When her tour of duty was up, Zach never heard from her again.

"And then there was Martha."

The way she overpronounced the name told Summer that Martha had been the biggest heartache of all. He'd spent countless hours comforting the suicidal widow of a comrade, literally saving her life a time or two. "He finally convinced her to sign herself into Centennial Peaks. They didn't earn their 'leader in suicide prevention and treatment of depression' title for nothing. After two months of intensive therapy, Martha came out of there a new woman." Libby made a chopping motion with her right hand. "She cut Zach off like *that*, and claimed it was because she didn't want any reminders of the past."

"After all he'd done for her?"

"Tell me about it."

"How long ago did they break up?"

"Going on two years."

He'd never mentioned Martha, not that they'd had much opportunity to discuss past loves.

"I have no idea how to define whatever it is that connects you to my brother, but I know this—he's happy for the first time in ages."

The news came as a relief, and shored up Summer's decision to get things out in the open, once and for all.

CHAPTER THIRTY-TWO

HE'D PICKED SUMMER up at eight sharp, and when Libby greeted them at his parents' house at nine thirty, she'd promised, "We'll only be a minute!"

That was half an hour ago.

"Sorry we're late," Summer said when at last they appeared.

If he was a gambling man, Zach would have bet the studio it had been Libby, not Summer, who'd held them up.

"No problem," he said, stepping away from the window. "I was watching these mutts make fools of themselves."

Libby stood to his left, Summer to the right.

"Poor Keeper," Libby said. "He runs for all he's worth, but can't keep up with Olivia."

"But she's a Greyhound," Summer said, defending her dog.

Zach had to agree. Olivia towered over Keeper. If the newly rescued dog minded, it didn't show. In the months he'd been with Summer, Keeper had put on some much-needed weight, and napped with *both* eyes closed. Every now and then, he stared off into space, as if remembering his former life. But all it took was a glimpse of Summer to turn the doleful expression into a wide doggy smile.

Who would have thought the day would come when he felt kinship with a dog? Zach thought. Because Summer had turned his sour moods happy more times than he could count.

Libby giggled. "I think they're in love."

"And I think we'd better get a move on if you don't want to be late," Zach suggested.

The whole way into town, Libby dominated the conversation with lists of dress shops, shoe stores and restaurants where they might meet later for lunch.

Zach dropped them off on University Boulevard. "Text me when you choose a place to eat," he called through the open passenger window. "And let me know if you want me to meet you there or pick you up."

When the door to Pink's Boutique closed behind them, he added a silent good luck wish to Summer and the sales personnel, because his sister was more wound up than usual.

He had plenty to keep him busy while they shopped and primped, and looked forward to making his last loan payment in person. Business had been good, and the studio mats had seen better days. He'd tracked down a good price for replacements at a store in Denver. And his supply of flyers had dwindled to a dozen or two, so he'd visit his printer to order more.

Zach finished all of his errands in barely more than an hour. He hadn't visited the Air and Space museum since high school, and figured he could kill some time there. He estimated the drive to Aurora would take twenty-five minutes, each way. With his luck, he'd no sooner get there than Libby would text him to meet up, so he opted for the Museum of Nature and Science instead, an easy ten-minute drive from Pink's.

He ducked into the museum's planetarium, chose a seat in the back row and settled in to watch a film. Killing time in the dark, nearly empty theater probably wasn't the smartest idea, since he'd tossed and turned most of the night.

"NASA's Kepler spacecraft," said the narrator, "has discovered two new planets." Named for Dutch astronomer Jacobus Kapteyn, the star and its newly discovered planets were estimated to be 11.5 billion years old. That's two and a half times older than Earth. One of the planets—five times larger than Earth—orbits its star every 48 days, making it suitable for flowing water."

As expected, Zach dozed off. If not for the nonstop buzz of his cell phone, there was no telling how long he might have slept. There was a text from Libby.

I'm in the dressing room and there's a man outside, talking to Summer. Can't be sure, but I think
he's the guy who attacked her. Get here ASAP!

Zach jogged out of the planetarium and got
into his truck. It wouldn't be the first time Libby
had jumped to conclusions, but what if she was
right?

He resisted the urge to mash the gas pedal to
the floor, mostly because if a cop stopped him for
speeding, it could take half an hour to get the nasty
business of a ticket out of the way. Lady Luck must
have known the importance of time, because Zach
found a space right outside of Pink's.

"Where's the dressing room?" he asked a sales
clerk.

Smiling, she pointed. "Meeting your wife?"

"Uh, yeah," he said, and began zigzagging
between the racks.

He'd recognize Summer anywhere, even from
the back. Ramrod stiff, she faced a tall, reedy,
bearded man. A few steps more, and he'd have
the maniac in a half-nelson.

But what he heard next stopped him in his
tracks.

"I wasn't myself," the young man said, knuck-
ling tears from his eyes. "I was weak. And PCP
is a strong drug."

Don't fall for it, Summer. Don't fall for it! He

was itching to pound the guy into the carpet, but Summer had earned this chance to tell the thug exactly what she thought of him.

"Thanks to years of rehab, I realize it was the PCP that turned me into a monster. The things I did…" He focused on the toes of his high-topped sneakers. "I could live three lifetimes and never make things right. I know every ex-con says this, but I swear it's true." He raised his right hand, as if under oath. "Prison changed me. I kept my head down. Volunteered for every dirty job on the board. Went to school. I'm in school now… the Iliff School of Theology. The people at my grandmother's church took up a collection to pay for my tuition and books and…" He looked at the ceiling.

Hoping to find the rest of your lie written up there? Zach wondered.

"And I won't let them down. When I graduate, I'll have a Divinity degree, and there's a job waiting for me as associate pastor."

Summer crossed both arms over her chest. "Is that so."

"I don't blame you for not believing me. Heck, in your shoes *I* wouldn't believe me." His voice was thick with tears. "All I'm asking, I guess, is that you at least consider forgiving me."

"How did you find me?"

"I-I didn't. You found me." He gestured to

the cartons he'd been unpacking. "I work here to help earn my keep. Can't take advantage of those good people who put their faith in me." He paused, then folded his hands. "It's all my fault that you've spent the past two years under the sinful burden of hate."

Zach took a step forward, unable to listen to another word, but what Summer said next stopped him yet again.

"You give yourself far too much credit," she said. "If you think I wasted a moment or an ounce of energy hating you, then you're sadly mistaken."

The guy's eyes widened and he stood blinking, as if taken aback by Summer's proclamation.

"You're right about one thing, though. You took a lot from me. My dignity. My self-esteem." She slapped her thigh. "I'll probably always walk with a limp." Now she tucked her hair behind her ears, to expose her scar. "And I'll always have this to remind me of your...your *weakness*."

She took a step forward, a big one, and Zach readied himself to leap into action if the guy made one false move.

"Worst of all, I may never be able to have children because of you. You expect me to forgive all that?"

Never have children?

The guy repeated everything he'd already said about his addictions and rehab and promises made to those who'd helped him. And through it all, Summer stood her ground. Couldn't she see what he saw...that every word from his smirking mouth was a lie?

Through an inch-wide opening in the curtain leading to the dressing rooms, Zach saw Libby, fingers forming the Victory sign as tears spilled onto her knuckles. "Do something!" she mouthed.

He wanted to. Oh, how he wanted to! But he tried to see things from Summer's perspective. In her shoes, he'd rather handle things on his own. So he shook his head at Libby and held a hand in the air. Hopefully, she'd get the message and stay put...and silent.

"You got off easy," Summer continued. "Two years is hardly just punishment for what you did."

He gave a nonchalant shrug. "Lack of evidence, y'know?"

"Oh, believe me, I know."

Another shrug. "So-o-rry."

"What would you say if I told you I just recorded your entire confession on my cell phone?"

Way to go, Summer. Way to go!

"You did a lot of studying in prison, so I'm sure you know there is no statute of limitations on charges of rape and kidnapping."

"My lawyer never told me any of that."

"Then I suggest you call him...before you head to the college for your next *theology* class."

Summer took yet another step closer, and so did Zach.

Then she slapped the guy, *hard.* "Sorry," she said, moving toward the dressing room curtain.

"For what?"

"I'm pretty much over my encounter with you. But you? You have to live with yourself forever."

She ducked into the dressing room, and Zach watched Samuels disappear into the stock room. Something told him the guy wouldn't fulfill his promise to the congregants of his grandmother's church.

He'd known a lot of heroes in his lifetime. His great-grandfather, who turned an untamed wilderness into the Double M. His granddad and dad, who poured their lifeblood into the land to safeguard the old man's legacy. The men and women who'd voluntarily served with him overseas.

And Summer, who'd stared a demon in the eye and never flinched.

Any doubts Zach had about his feelings vanished as he admitted he'd never loved anyone more.

CHAPTER THIRTY-THREE

"YOU CAN'T SAY a word about what went on out there," Summer said, her voice a harsh whisper. "You're right...Zach needs to know. But *I* need to be the one who tells him...everything."

Libby dried her eyes then threw her arms around Summer. "From what you told me that night at the pub, I knew it was awful," she said. "But I had no idea how awful."

Summer took a step back. "Don't you dare feel sorry for me, Libby Marshall. The last thing I need from you—from *anyone*—is pity."

"Believe me, I don't feel sorry for you. I admire you. And respect you. I can think of a dozen other verbs to describe what I feel, but pity isn't one of them!" She sniffed. "When I grow up, I want to be just like you."

Summer laughed quietly as Libby added, "Guess I'd better text Zach so he can meet us for lunch. What are you in the mood for?"

"A fat, juicy steak. Baked potato with all the toppings. Some buttery rolls. And a big slice of cheesecake."

"Tiny as you are?" Libby chuckled. "Where will you put it all?"

"Putting evil-doers in their place gives me a voracious appetite. Go ahead. Text Zach and tell him to meet us at Elway's. My treat."

While Libby pecked a message into her phone, Summer went through the dresses hanging on the curtain rod. "Which did you choose?"

"The red one. What do you think of it?"

"Love it."

Summer wondered how long she could hold it together. Her insides felt like jelly, and her head was throbbing. She and Libby still had two hours of primping to get through before heading back to the Double M. Thankfully, she'd decided to give Libby's stylist a try, to save the long drive back to Vail. Because one look at her, and Justin would get the story out of her. And then? And then she'd probably lose it.

She hadn't been looking forward to spending the night at the ranch, but being all alone in the town house was the last thing she needed right now.

Things would look better tomorrow. And no doubt Ellen would keep her busy checking off items on her to-do list.

Zach was unusually quiet during the drive from town to the Double M. But then, how could he get a word in with Libby chattering like a chipmunk? Summer blamed the nervous babble on what his sister had overheard through the dressing room's flimsy velvet curtain. How much of her own story rose to the surface, hearing the brutal details of Summer's?

Zach dropped them at the front door and headed for the barn. After a day of girl talk, he'd earned a good long ride on Chinook.

Ellen inspected everything they'd bought, complimented their hairdos and nail polish, and then retreated to her room for a much-deserved rest.

Libby helped Summer stow her shopping bags in the guest room. "If you need anything— ironing board, iron, towels—just whistle."

"Thanks, Libby."

She started out the door, but never made it into the hall. "Are you sure you want to be alone? You and Keeper are more than welcome to bunk with me."

"I'm fine, but thanks."

"Sleep tight, then, and sweet dreams."

She woke at six feeling rested and refreshed after a deep, dreamless sleep. The scent of bacon and fresh-brewed coffee lured her downstairs to the kitchen, where she found Zach at the sink and his dad at the stove.

"Over easy or scrambled?" John Marshall asked.

"Over easy," she said. "What can I do to help?"

"You can just sit there looking pretty. We've got this place under control."

Evidently, Zach's long horseback ride and a night's sleep hadn't improved his mood. He'd barely cracked a smile, and hadn't made eye contact since she entered the room. Had he run into one of his exes while she and Libby shopped and preened in Denver? Hopefully not the dreadful Martha!

"Where are Ellen and Libby?" she asked.

"Libby's still asleep, Ellen's in the barn, doing…" John chuckled. "Who knows what she's up to."

"Soon as I help you two with the dishes, I'll run down there, see what I can do to pitch in."

When father and son joined her at the table, Summer wished she knew what to say or do to help cheer Zach up.

The day passed quickly, what with covering the entire ceiling in crystal ornaments and placing silver wind-up clocks in the center of each table…all set to ring simultaneously at the stroke of twelve. It would look so beautiful after dark, when bright white mini-lights glinted from the beautifully appointed place settings. Last time the guests entered this space, it had been decked out for a good, old-fashioned hoedown. Wouldn't they be surprised when they passed through the entrance and saw how Ellen had transformed the barn into a dazzling ballroom. Most of all, though, Summer couldn't wait to see Zach in a suit and tie.

Now and then, the encounter with Samuels came to mind, but she was determined not to dwell on it. A good thing, she decided, because tonight, for the first time in two years, she had reason to celebrate the coming year.

When the caterer and band arrived and began setting up, the Marshalls headed back to the house to change into their evening attire.

"Weatherman says we'll have a good night," John said, linking arms with his wife.

"But of course," she said. "I had a long talk with Mother Nature today, and laid down the law."

Libby and Summer, walking a few steps behind them, laughed. "I wouldn't want to be Mother Nature," Libby said, "if it snows or rains!"

"It's going to be a perfect night," Ellen said.

"I sure hope so," Libby whispered to Summer, winking and wiggling her eyebrows.

They'd been in the shoe store, trying on high heels, when Libby told Summer that at the stroke of midnight, she intended to drag her musician into a dark corner...and pop the question.

Summer whispered back, "You're still going through with it, then?"

"Absolutely."

Inside, Ellen hung up her sweater and poured

herself some coffee. "Who'll join me?" She held up her mug.

"I'm good," John said. "I'll check on the dogs and then head upstairs. That way," he explained, kissing Ellen's cheek, "you'll have the bathroom all to yourself."

"I'm going up, too," Libby chimed in.

It was just Ellen and Summer now, alone in the kitchen.

"Won't you join me?"

"Actually, coffee sounds great." She helped herself to a mug and sat across from Zach's mom. "You did a beautiful job out there. If I ever have a grand party, I know who I'll ask to arrange it!"

"From what Libby told me, it sounds like you two had a grand time in Denver yesterday."

"Only Libby could make shopping an enjoyable experience."

"You don't like to shop? Goodness. Don't let John hear you say that, or my son, for that matter!"

"I haven't seen him all afternoon." She didn't want to tell Ellen that Zach had seemed out of sorts since their excursion. The poor woman had enough to worry about this close to the party's start.

"I sent him riding. Said my horse needed vigorous exercise and told him not to come back until he got rid of his Gloomy Gus attitude."

So. His mom had noticed it, too. "I thought maybe he ran into Martha in Denver."

"You know, I'm not sure she's even in Colorado anymore. But whatever is bugging him, he'll come back a whole new man. A little time in the saddle never fails to put a smile on his face."

It hadn't earlier, but Summer kept it to herself.

"I can understand that. The Double M is a magical place."

"Can I ask you a question? Feel free to tell me to butt out. I promise not to be offended." When Summer didn't respond, Ellen continued. "You're in love with him, right?"

It was a very good thing she'd already swallowed that last sip of coffee, because she might have choked on a question like that.

"I only ask because I've never seen him like this before. He's had girlfriends, of course, and once I thought he might actually pop the question."

Ellen paused when her wristwatch beeped. *Saved by the bell*, Summer thought.

Ellen pushed a button to silence it. "It was supposed to alert me fifteen minutes from now, or so I thought." She shook her head. "Every time I put in a new battery, I have to learn how to set the silly thing all over again."

Fifteen minutes would seem like an eternity if

Ellen continued with her interrogation. Sitting in the beautiful kitchen of a bona fide ranch, it made perfect sense to head the woman off at the pass.

"If you're worried that I might hurt him the way Martha did, please don't be. I respect him far too much to put him through anything like that. I'd much rather be the one who shows him what it's like to be on the receiving end of some caring and protection for a change."

Ellen smiled. A genuine, maternal smile that warmed the space between them. When her watch beeped again, she took it off and tossed it into the sink, where it landed in the sudsy water with a quiet *plop*. Then she got up and headed for the hallway.

"Next time you see me," she said, "I'll look like a whole new woman!"

Summer carried their coffee mugs to the sink and fished out the still-beeping watch. It made her laugh a little as she hunted for the button that turned it off.

"Starting tonight," she said, towel-drying it, "I'm going to be a little more like you." She placed the watch on the table, right where Ellen's mug had been moments ago. "Unstoppable."

CHAPTER THIRTY-FOUR

"THE PLACE LOOKS GREAT, Mom." Zach kissed her cheek. "You're something else, you know that?"

"Doesn't everyone just look wonderful," Ellen said.

He had to agree. Every man had worn a starched shirt, bow tie and polished black shoes. And the women had unboxed all their fanciest jewelry, including his mother and sister.

"I take it Chinook worked the kinks out of that foul mood you were in?"

"Wasn't in a foul mood."

"Have you seen Summer?"

He glanced around the room. "Not yet."

"I can't wait to see her in that new dress. But the poor thing is probably stuck upstairs, helping Libby with her hair or makeup, or zipping that slinky gown your sister bought yesterday."

The sparkly red number she'd been wearing in the dressing room as she eavesdropped on Summer chitchatting with that animal? Zach hoped not, because contrary to popular fashion theories, not every man liked red.

"Oh, look, Rose and Alex are here." She squeezed his hand. "Let me just go over there and say hello."

"I'll catch up later. Right now, I need something to wet my whistle."

He walked up to the bar and surveyed the shelf. Soft drinks, wine, beer...his mother had thought of everything. "I'll have a beer," he told the bartender, and after stuffing a dollar bill into the man's tip jar, he turned, pressed the bottle to his lips...

...and he saw her.

She'd tied her dark curls back with a wide black satin ribbon that exactly matched her dress. She'd made no attempt to hide the scar tonight, and it touched something deep inside him. Other women had worn spangles and sparkles, bright colors and gauzy materials. Summer's dress was elegant in its simplicity. In place of the heavy chains and big gems her counterparts had worn, she'd opted for tiny earrings that winked from her lobes.

Zach watched her scan the crowd, smiling, waving, saying hello to those she knew. When those enormous eyes locked on his and she aimed an *I'm happy to see you!* smile his way, he felt a little weak in the knees.

She walked toward him, only the slightest trace of a limp despite high-heeled black shoes that exposed red-painted toenails.

Zach put his beer on the bar. "You're… gorgeous," said a deep, gravelly voice. He almost laughed when it dawned on him that the voice was his.

"So are you." She reached up and tapped the right side of his bow tie. "Quite a change from denim and flannel. I can't decide which I like best."

For the moment, he'd all but forgotten how confused he'd felt when she let that scumbag off so easily. Right now, all he could think about was holding her close and kissing those full, red lips.

"Oh, listen," she said, forefinger in the air, "the band's playing our song."

Our song. Oh, how he liked the sound of that.

Zach took her hand and led her to the middle of the dance floor. They were alone out there. Completely alone. Ordinarily, he would have felt conspicuous and uncomfortable. Not tonight.

She melted into him, like liquid gold, right there in his hands. He liked the analogy, because he'd come to think of her as a precious treasure.

"'You say you're happy,'" she sang softly, "'Here in my arms, and I hope it's true, 'cause I sure am lovin', being close to you.'"

"You know," he said, resting his chin atop her head, "if this voice-over thing doesn't work out, you could probably make a buck or two in tips, doing karaoke at the pizza parlor."

Summer stepped back slightly to gaze up into his face, and he instantly regretted the joke because now he couldn't feel her heart beating soft and steady against his chest.

"They have karaoke at the pizza parlor? This I have to see. Or hear."

"Or both," they said together. Much to his disappointment, the waltz ended. They stood for a moment, fingers linked and palms pressed to one another's, waiting to see what the band would play next. *Not a fast song*, he hoped. *Anything but a fast song*.

Someone up there must like him, Zach thought, because the male singer broke into the first few lines of "Tennessee Waltz."

"Oh, I've always loved this one," she said.

There was something distinctly different about her tonight, like she knew a secret that he wasn't in on.

"Did you hear that my agent called?"

"Again?" He looked into her sweet face.

When she nodded, her curls bounced, tickling his chin.

"He found me a couple more jobs."

His heart thudded with dread. "Where?"

"One in Denver, one in Vail. Seems the TV stations need someone to do a few 'why ours is the station to watch' commercials. And they change every month or so, meaning more voice-overs."

Relief surged through him. If she'd said her agent had lined up jobs in New York or LA—even temporary ones—he'd hate it. He'd pretend it was a good thing, for her sake, but he'd *hate* it.

"It's gonna seem weird, hearing your voice when I'm watching the news."

"No weirder than it'll be for *me*, hearing myself during the news!"

He laughed and pulled her closer. It felt good, felt right, holding her this way. During this afternoon's ride, he'd thought long and hard about what she'd said to the creep: "Worst of all, I may never be able to have children because of you."

"I guess we should give your mom a break, making the rounds."

Keeper, her parents, Justin, Rose and Alex, and now his mom. Summer had the heart and mind of a natural-born mother. It seemed beyond unfair that because of that pig, she may never get the chance to shower her own kids with her unique brand of love.

Where was the justice in Samuels serving a few measly months, while Summer had to pay for the rest of her life, just for being in the wrong place at the wrong time? Even if she hadn't recorded Samuels's cocky confession, he and Libby had witnessed the entire exchange. If Summer wanted to make him pay for what he'd done, they'd both testify on her behalf.

Why did he get the feeling that that would never happen? Reopening the case would mean reopening old wounds.

"Are you okay?"

Zach blinked himself back to the here and now, and met her eyes.

"Sure. I'm fine. Why?"

"The dance ended, and the band's on a break."

Sure enough, they were alone on the floor, just as they'd been when he first took her hand.

Zach laughed, a little too loudly, a little too long, and when it drew the attention of a few guests, he felt the heat of an embarrassed blush coloring his cheeks.

Difficult as it was to let her go, Zach did just that. "Guess we should mix and mingle, shouldn't we?"

She went left, and he went right. A couple of times, they crossed paths. No matter, he told himself, because at midnight, he intended to make sure she was in his arms. Zach made his way to the bar and pretended to be engrossed in a rebroadcast of the Ohio vs. Perdue game.

When the bandleader tapped his microphone, guests scrambled to don sparkly hats and grab noisemakers.

"According to German folklore," the musician said, "your first encounter of the new year, good or bad, sets the tone for every day that follows until *next* New Year's Eve. You have just two minutes to hunt down the lady or gentleman you most want to spend the new year with, and make sure he or she is close by, so you can seal the deal with a kiss!"

Zach didn't need to hunt. He knew exactly where Summer was, because he'd been watching her out of the corner of his eye ever since they'd left the dance floor.

The emcee counted down to seven before Zach began making his way to her. He was close enough to touch her when the man said "Three…"

Gently, he turned her to face him, and Summer smiled. That same *I'm so happy to see you!* smile that had made his heart pound like a parade drum hours earlier.

He didn't hear the emcee finish the countdown, because his lips had already found hers. Colorful confetti and black-and-white balloons rained down all around them, but he barely noticed.

The band struck up a rousing rendition of "Auld Lang Syne," but he hardly heard the old Scottish tune or the hundred and two guests who'd gathered round the stage to sing along.

Horns tooted. Laughter erupted. People shouted,

"Happy New Year!" and the sound of fireworks drew everyone outside.

Everyone but Zach and Summer, and the band—minus its leader—playing their song.

CHAPTER THIRTY-FIVE

LIBBY DECIDED TO stay at the Double M an extra few days, helping her mom put the house and barn back in order. She linked arms with Zach and Summer and walked them to his truck.

"I'm making supper at my place, either tomorrow or the next day. Depends on Dad's schedule. I want you both to come, too."

"Dad is retired," Zach pointed out. "He has no schedule."

"That isn't what Mom says. She claims he's busier now than when he put in all those hours on the ranch."

He slid in behind the wheel. "And now he *putters* on the ranch."

"Speaking of parents," Libby said as Summer climbed into the truck, "have you heard from yours?"

"Not since the other day, when they called to apologize for missing your mom's party."

"Well, when you talk to them, say hi for me."

"You bet. Thanks for everything. And you'd

better call me soon, to tell me all about your, ah, you-know-what with you-know-who."

Blushing, Libby stepped back as Zach revved the engine. "You guys drive safe, hear?"

He steered onto the highway and asked, "What was that all about?"

"Libby's secret meeting, you mean?" She grinned. "Seems she has a mad crush on the band's lead singer."

"What! That old geek?"

"He's the same age as you are!" She let that sink in for a moment.

"Really?" He stroked his jaw. "Man. A musician's life must be tough. Accent on *musician*. On the road all the time, fighting off beautiful wo…" He snickered. "Okay, so that part of my argument falls flat." He glanced over at her. "What do you suppose she sees in him?"

Summer shrugged. "I think it's just that he's completely different from everyone else she's dated. Or that he's talented. He brought her a dozen red roses, one for every month of the new year. So he's thoughtful and romantic, too. And I'm guessing she's thinking of all those nights when he'll sing sweet nothings into her ear."

"Sweet nothings."

"You know," she said, and sang a bar of their song, ending with the word *happy*.

"Another one of those 'means different things to different people' words."

Summer remembered their "people overuse the word *love*" conversation. And since she had no intention of finding other ways to express her appreciation for pizza and chocolate and daisies, she decided to change the subject. Besides, she had much more important things to tell him on the drive home.

"I have something to tell you," she began.

"And I have a confession to make."

"You first."

"I overheard you talking to that...to that *guy* at Pink's."

But how was that possible, when Libby hadn't texted him until after Samuels left the dressing room area?

"Libby figured out pretty quick who he was and sent me a message to get over there, in case you needed backup."

"I didn't see you."

"I was behind a post. Next to the sports coats. Or whatever it is you call those suit-type jackets."

"Blazers. Not that it matters. How much did you hear?"

"Enough to wonder if you're going to take that tape to the cops."

"I didn't tape anything. I just wanted him to think I did."

"Doesn't matter. Libby heard everything. So did I. We'd testify. In a heartbeat."

"Testify?"

"You could reopen the case. And with the new proof, he'd get more than a couple months behind bars. *This* time, he'd go away for a long, long time."

She thought of those long, exhausting days in the courtroom, and sitting in the hallway while witnesses who could influence her testimony were on the stand. She'd hated the pitying looks of the jurors, and the long-suffering attitude of the defense attorneys, the bailiff, the judge. If she had to go through that again, she might end up right back at square one.

"I don't want to reopen the case."

"Why *not*? He caused you nothing but grief. Altered your life a hundred and eighty degrees. You've suffered, physically, mentally and emotionally since that night. Help me understand why you don't want him to pay for what he did to you!"

If Zach had heard her say she was recording Samuels's admission of guilt, he'd also heard what she said right on the heels of it: *Worst of all, I may never be able to have children because of you.*

"Each day of the trial was almost as torturous

as that night." Summer stared straight ahead. "I can't… I don't *want* to relive it."

"Not even if he gets what he deserves?"

"There's no guarantee he'll get what he deserves. I won't go through it on a big fat *if*."

From the corner of her eye, Summer could see him working his jaw. She'd been around him enough to recognize the signs of impatience.

"Okay. All right. We'll just agree to disagree on that one. But I still don't understand why you forgave that no-good, lousy—"

"You were there. So you know very well that what I said was blatant sarcasm."

"But he's an arrogant idiot. You shouldn't have given him the satisfaction of thinking you might have meant it."

"I'm going on the assumption here that you're reacting this way because you feel like it's your duty as my…as my friend to defend me. Let me remind you what I said that night in your office. I am *not* a marine under your command. Much as I appreciate your somewhat clumsy attempt to protect me, I don't need it. But if I *do* ever need your help, I promise to ask for it."

He fell silent for what seemed like ten minutes. And then he said, "You're right. I'm sorry."

"Did you hear that, Keeper?"

The dog woofed quietly from the backseat, inspiring soft laughter from Zach.

He could be the sweetest, most thoughtful man, Summer admitted to herself. But sometimes, he could be equally exasperating…

Zach had overheard the entire conversation with Samuels, so why hadn't he addressed the "might not be able to have kids" part of it?

She considered asking him, right now, how he felt about that, but decided against it. Better to practice a nonchalant reaction, because if his reaction *wasn't* sweet and thoughtful, it would break her heart.

CHAPTER THIRTY-SIX

FOR TWO DAYS and two nights, Zach racked his brain, trying to come up with a legitimate excuse to get Summer back to the Double M so he could put his plan into action.

It had rankled him at first, holding his tongue when she'd stood up to him. Again. That didn't last long, though, and by the end of that first sleepless night, he'd applauded her boldness. Gradually, over the past four months, he'd come to realize how darned near perfect his life was. The only thing missing, really, was a woman to share it with. Not just any woman, but Summer Lane, whose bravery and kindheartedness outshone her beauty. Which was saying something.

He picked up the phone and dialed Libby's number.

"Libs," he said when she picked up, "I need a favor."

"I dunno," she said. "Last time you said that, I ended up storing five years' worth of marine gear in my spare room."

"You have my word, this won't take up one

square inch of your precious real estate. I just need you to help me come up with a way to get Summer to the Double M."

"Why?"

"I want to take her riding."

"Have you forgotten about that cold front that just blew through here? The temps haven't hit thirty degrees in days, and there are two feet of snow on the ground. Tiny as she is, she'll freeze to the saddle!"

"No, she won't. I'll make sure of it."

"Hmm...why do I smell a proposal coming on?"

"Because you're an incurable romantic. Now concentrate. I need you to get her to the ranch."

"When?"

"The sooner, the better."

"Well, I suppose *I* could invite her to go riding. And then at the last minute, you can show up, you know, like a knight in shining armor!"

Zach groaned. "You're hilarious. Just let me know when you've set things up so I can have the horses saddled and ready to ride."

"Y'know, this might just be fun."

"I'm only too happy to add enjoyment to your life, little sister."

"Hang up, already, so I can call her."

"SORRY FOR THE SUBTERFUGE," Zach said when they stopped at the bluff. "But I didn't know how else to get you up here."

Summer rested gloved hands on Taffy's saddle horn. "You could have just asked."

"How much fun would that have been?" he asked, climbing down from his horse. He tethered Taffy and Chinook to the branches of a wild buckthorn shrub, then gently helped Summer to the ground.

"So here's the deal. I've been giving this a lot of thought. A *lot* of thought, and I think I love you, Summer. From the minute that cookie crumbled between us," he said, linking his gloved fingers with hers, "to this one. But more important than that, I like you. Respect you. Admire you. The better I get to know you, the *more* I like and respect and admire you."

"I can't have kids, Zach."

"Be quiet, will ya, and let me finish my speech? Besides, it doesn't make a lick of difference to me if our kids inherit our DNA, or we adopt a few. As I was saying, I want you to help me design a house for them to run around in. One with a big wraparound porch, where we can sit in matching rockers and watch the sun come up every morning."

"I've always been partial to sunsets."

Oh, how he loved this woman! Grinning, he continued. "Where we can sit in matching rockers and watch the sun set every night."

He turned one of her hands loose, leaving his

free to touch her cheek and trace the scar that told the world she'd fought a hard fight, and won.

"Remember when you called me a white knight, and you said you didn't need a hero?" Zach bracketed her face with his hands, his thumbs raising her chin so that she had to meet his eyes. "Well, you were right. You don't need a hero. You *are* a hero."

He kissed her forehead, the tip of her nose, each wind-chilled, freckled cheek, then reached into his saddlebag. "I made this last night."

She held the dinner-plate-sized construction paper heart in trembling hands. "I'm Zach's heart," she read aloud, "and I'm yours for the taking."

Summer pressed it to her chest and blinked back tears. "Is this your roundabout way of asking me to marry you?"

"Funny," he said, pulling her close. "I didn't think it was the least bit roundabout."

"I love being in your arms. And I'm not just saying that because it's ten degrees, and you're warmer than my electric blanket." She snuggled closer, rested her cheek on his chest. "This feels good. Feels *right*."

He'd had a similar thought not so very long ago. A good sign, Zach told himself. A very good sign.

"Is that your roundabout way of saying yes?"

Summer stood on tiptoe, linked her fingers behind his neck and answered with a long, meaningful kiss.

EPILOGUE

Valentine's Day

MUCH TO ELLEN'S DISAPPOINTMENT, Zach and Summer decided on a small, close friends-and-family-only wedding at the Double M. Still, with all the Marshalls assembled, the party barn was just about filled to maximum capacity.

They'd opted for the hoedown theme from Ellen's fund-raiser. Same decorations, same food, same band playing the same songs, including the waltz—their first dance as man and wife—that had become their song.

"You say you're happy, here in my arms, and I hope it's true," Zach sang, "'cause I sure am lovin', being close to you."

Summer remembered Mrs. Centrino whispering to her husband that Zach had a tin ear. The retired music teacher's assessment still rang true, but from Summer's point of view, he was making the most beautiful music she'd ever heard.

When the first dance ended, Ellen pinged a

butter knife against a half-filled goblet. "It's time to cut the cake!"

Theirs was not an ordinary wedding cake, three tiers tall with a bride and groom on top. Instead, pointy-toed boots—the left, big and chocolate frosted; the right, smaller, with white icing—perched on a double-layered horse shoe. At one end of the shoe, a dark-haired bride held one end of a rope. At the other, her lasso had captured a Stetson-wearing cowboy.

Gentleman that he was, Zach didn't smear icing all over Summer's face. But Summer wasn't a gentleman. He was still wearing a chocolate mustache when his mom said, "Gather round, all you unmarried ladies…Summer is going to throw the bouquet!"

Summer's spray of flowers was no more typical than the wedding cake. Daisies and Colorado blue columbines poked out of an old, hollowed-out saddle horn.

"Wouldn't want to knock anybody unconscious, so I'll lose the horn," she announced, fringed skirt twirling around her white cowboy boots as she put her back to the single women.

Libby stood front and center, waving at the Buddy Holly lookalike who stood on the bandstand. Summer gave the flowers a toss, and after flying through the air, stem over bloom, they landed right in Libby's outstretched hands.

Libby and her beau were nowhere in sight when Zach knelt to remove Summer's garter.

"That's odd," she whispered. "I thought surely your sister would be here, fingers crossed and hoping her musician would catch it."

"She's probably off somewhere putting the bouquet into water," he said, "to make doubly sure the luck will hold."

He got to his feet and put his back to the bachelors, and just as he turned it loose, Libby reappeared.

"Paybacks!" she hollered, and tossed a big cup of cold water at Zach.

The garter had landed on Nate's shoulder. "That doesn't count," he said, stretching it around his biceps. "And that's a good thing, because no way, no how am *I* getting married, ever!"

The Marshall clan laughed at their self-proclaimed bachelor.

"We'll just see about that," Sam said.

"You got into the line," Zach's dad said. "So it counts. You're next, and we're all witnesses!"

Summer wiggled a finger, inviting Zach to bend down. He puckered up, but instead of the kiss he expected, she blotted water from his face with her grandmother's lacy handkerchief—the "something old" she'd tucked into her tiny drawstring purse.

"You know," he whispered, "nobody would

blame you if you changed your mind about becoming part of this wacky family."

"Are you kidding? I love these people." Summer stood on tiptoe and grabbed his lapels. "And
I love *you*." Pulling him closer, she added, "Like
it or not, you *are* my hero."

"Sorry, sweetheart, but I'm all through with
that knight in shining armor stuff."

"I might let you off the hook…after you carry
me over the threshold."

"It's a deal." He scooped her up as the band
started playing an upbeat tune.

"Are you happy?" she asked, laying her head
on his shoulder.

"Well, it's one of those words that—"

Laughing, she silenced him with a kiss.

* * * * *

LARGER-PRINT BOOKS!

GET 2 FREE LARGER-PRINT NOVELS PLUS 2 FREE MYSTERY GIFTS

Love Inspired

Larger-print novels are now available...

YES! Please send me 2 FREE LARGER-PRINT Love-Inspired® novels and my 2 FREE mystery gifts (gifts are worth about $10). After receiving them, if I don't wish to receive any more books, I can return the shipping statement marked "cancel." If I don't cancel, I will receive 6 brand-new novels every month and be billed just $5.24 per book in the U.S. or $5.74 per book in Canada. That's a savings of at least 23% off the cover price. It's quite a bargain! Shipping and handling is just 50¢ per book in the U.S. and 75¢ per book in Canada.* I understand that accepting the 2 free books and gifts places me under no obligation to buy anything. I can always return a shipment and cancel at any time. Even if I never buy another book, the two free books and gifts are mine to keep forever.

122/322 IDN F49Y

Name _____ (PLEASE PRINT)

Address _____ Apt. # _____

City _____ State/Prov. _____ Zip/Postal Code _____

Signature (if under 18, a parent or guardian must sign)

Mail to the Harlequin® Reader Service:
IN U.S.A.: P.O. Box 1867, Buffalo, NY 14240-1867
IN CANADA: P.O. Box 609, Fort Erie, Ontario L2A 5X3

**Are you a current subscriber to Love Inspired books and want to receive the larger-print edition?
Call 1-800-873-8635 or visit www.ReaderService.com.**

* Terms and prices subject to change without notice. Prices do not include applicable taxes. Sales tax applicable in N.Y. Canadian residents will be charged applicable taxes. Offer not valid in Quebec. This offer is limited to one order per household. Not valid for current subscribers to Love Inspired Larger-Print books. All orders subject to credit approval. Credit or debit balances in a customer's account(s) may be offset by any other outstanding balance owed by or to the customer. Please allow 4 to 6 weeks for delivery. Offer available while quantities last.

Your Privacy—The Harlequin® Reader Service is committed to protecting your privacy. Our Privacy Policy is available online at www.ReaderService.com or upon request from the Harlequin Reader Service.

We make a portion of our mailing list available to reputable third parties that offer products we believe may interest you. If you prefer that we not exchange your name with third parties, or if you wish to clarify or modify your communication preferences, please visit us at www.ReaderService.com/consumerchoice or write to us at Harlequin Reader Service Preference Service, P.O. Box 9062, Buffalo, NY 14269. Include your complete name and address.

LILPDIRI3R

LARGER-PRINT BOOKS!

GET 2 FREE
LARGER-PRINT NOVELS
PLUS 2 FREE
MYSTERY GIFTS

Love Inspired®
SUSPENSE
RIVETING INSPIRATIONAL ROMANCE

Larger-print novels are now available...

YES! Please send me 2 FREE LARGER-PRINT Love Inspired® Suspense novels and my 2 FREE mystery gifts (gifts are worth about $10). After receiving them, if I don't wish to receive any more books, I can return the shipping statement marked "cancel." If I don't cancel, I will receive 4 brand-new novels every month and be billed just $5.24 per book in the U.S. or $5.74 per book in Canada. That's a savings of at least 23% off the cover price. It's quite a bargain! Shipping and handling is just 50¢ per book in the U.S. and 75¢ per book in Canada.* I understand that accepting the 2 free books and gifts places me under no obligation to buy anything. I can always return a shipment and cancel at any time. Even if I never buy another book, the two free books and gifts are mine to keep forever.

110/310 IDN F5CC

Name	(PLEASE PRINT)	
Address		Apt. #
City	State/Prov.	Zip/Postal Code

Signature (if under 18, a parent or guardian must sign)

Mail to the Harlequin® Reader Service:
IN U.S.A.: P.O. Box 1867, Buffalo, NY 14240-1867
IN CANADA: P.O. Box 609, Fort Erie, Ontario L2A 5X3

Are you a current subscriber to Love Inspired Suspense books and want to receive the larger-print edition?
Call 1-800-873-8635 or visit www.ReaderService.com.

* Terms and prices subject to change without notice. Prices do not include applicable taxes. Sales tax applicable in N.Y. Canadian residents will be charged applicable taxes. Offer not valid in Quebec. This offer is limited to one order per household. Not valid for current subscribers to Love Inspired Suspense larger-print books. All orders subject to credit approval. Credit or debit balances in a customer's account(s) may be offset by any other outstanding balance owed by or to the customer. Please allow 4 to 6 weeks for delivery. Offer available while quantities last.

Your Privacy—The Harlequin® Reader Service is committed to protecting your privacy. Our Privacy Policy is available online at www.ReaderService.com or upon request from the Harlequin Reader Service.

We make a portion of our mailing list available to reputable third parties that offer products we believe may interest you. If you prefer that we not exchange your name with third parties, or if you wish to clarify or modify your communication preferences, please visit us at www.ReaderService.com/consumerchoice or write to us at Harlequin Reader Service Preference Service, P.O. Box 9062, Buffalo, NY 14269. Include your complete name and address.

LISLPDIR13R

ReaderService.com

Manage your account online!

- Review your order history
- Manage your payments
- Update your address

*We've designed
the Harlequin® Reader Service
website just for you.*

Enjoy all the features!

- Reader excerpts from any series
- Respond to mailings and
  special monthly offers
- Discover new series available to you
- Browse the Bonus Bucks catalog
- Share your feedback

Visit us at:

ReaderService.com